SPIRIT OF THE CENTURY™
PRESENTS

DINOCALYPSE NOW

BY
CHUCK
WENDIG

EVIL HAT
PRODUCTIONS

An Evil Hat Productions Publication
www.evilhat.com
feedback@evilhat.com

First published in 2012 by Evil Hat Productions

Editor: John Adamus
Proofreading: Amanda Valentine
Art: Christian N. St. Pierre
Design: Fred Hicks
Branding: Chris Hanrahan

Hardcover ISBN: 978-1-61317-004-5
Softcover ISBN: 978-1-61317-003-8
Kindle ISBN: 978-1-61317-005-2
ePub ISBN: 978-1-61317-006-9
iBooks ISBN: 978-1-61317-007-6

Printed in the USA

THIS BOOK WAS MADE POSSIBLE WITH THE SUPPORT OF...

Michael Bowman *and a cast of hundreds, including*
"The Cap'n" Wayne Coburn, "The Professor" Eric Smailys, @aroberts72, @syntheticbrain, A. David Pinilla, Aaron Jones, Aaron Jurkis, Adam & Jayce Roberts, Adam B. Ross, Adam Rajski, Adan Tejada, AJ Medder, AJT, Alan Bellingham, Alan Hyde, Alan Winterrowd, Alex, Alien Zookeeper, Alisha "hostilecrayon" Miller, Alosia Sellers, Amy Collins, Amy Lambzilla Hamilton, Andrew Beirne, Andrew Byers, Andrew Guerr, Andrew Jensen, Andrew M. Kelly, Andrew Nicolle, Andrew Watson, Andy Blanchard, Andy Eaton, Angela Korra'ti, Anonymous Fan, Anthony Laffan, Anthony R. Cardno, April Fowler, Arck Perra, Ariel Pereira, Arnaud Walraevens, Arthur Santos Jr, Ashkai Sinclair, Autumn and Sean Stickney, Axisor, Bailey Shoemaker Richards, Barac Wiley, Barbara Hasebe, Barrett Bishop, Bartimeus, Beena Gohil, Ben Ames, Ben Barnett, Ben Bement, Ben Bryan, Bill Dodds, Bill Harting, Bill Segulin, Blackcoat, Bo Saxon, Bo Williams, Bob Bretz, Brandon H. Mila, Bret S. Moore, Esq., Brian Allred, Brian E. Williams, Brian Engard, Brian Isikoff, Brian Kelsay @ripcrd, Brian Nisbet, Brian Scott Walker, Brian Waite, Brian White, Bryan Sims, Bryce Perry, C.K. "Velocitycurve" Lee, Calum Watterson, Cameron Harris, Candlemark & Gleam, Carl Rigney, Carol Darnell, Carolyn Butler, Carolyn White, Casey & Adam Moeller, Catherine Mooney, CE Murphy, Centurion Eric Brenders, Charles Paradis, Chase Bolen, Cheers, Chip & Katie, Chris Bekofske, Chris Callahan, Chris Ellison, Chris Hatty, Chris Heilman, Chris Matosky, Chris Newton, Chris Norwood, Chris Perrin, Christian Lindke, Christina Lee, Christine Lorang, Christine Swendseid, Christopher Gronlund, Chrystin, Clark & Amanda Valentine, Clay Robeson, Corey Davidson, Corinne Erwin, Craig Maloney, Crazy J, Cyrano Jones, Dan Conley, Dan N, Dan Yarrington, Daniel C. Hutchison, Daniel Laloggia, Danielle Ingber, Darcy Casselman, Darren Davis, Darrin Shimer, Daryl Weir, Dave BW, Dave Steiger, David & Nyk, David Hines, David M., David Patri, Declan Feeney, Deepone, Demelza Beckly, Derrick Eaves, Dimitrios Lakoumentas, DJ Williams, DL Thurston, Doug Cornelius, Dover Whitecliff, Drew, drgnldy71, DU8, Dusty Swede, Dylan McIntosh, Ed Kowalczewski, edchuk, Edouard "Francesco", Edward J Smola III, Eleanor-Rose Begg, Eli "Ace" Katz, Ellie Reese, Elly & Andres, Emily Poole, Eric Asher, Eric Duncan, Eric Henson, Eric Lytle, Eric Paquette, Eric Smith, Eric Tilton, Eric B Vogel, Ernie Sawyer, Eva, Evan Denbaum, Evan Grummell, Ewen Albright, Explody, Eyal Teler, Fabrice Breau, Fade Manley, Fidel Jiron Jr., Frank "Grayhawk" Huminski, Frank Jarome, Frank Wuerbach, Frazer Porritt, Galen, Gareth-Michael Skarka, Garry Jenkins, Gary Hoggatt, Gary McBride, Gavran, Gemma Tapscott, Glenn, Greg Matyola, Greg Roy, Gregory Frank, Gregory G. Gieger, Gus Golden, Herefox, HPLustcraft, Hugh J. O'Donnell, Ian Llywelyn Brown, Ian Loo, Inder Rottger, Itamar Friedman, J. Layne Nelson, J.B. Mannon, J.C. Hutchins, Jack Gulick, Jake Reid, James "discord_inc" Fletcher, James Alley, James Ballard, James Champlin, James Husum, James Melzer, Jami Nord, Jared Leisner, Jarrod Coad, Jason Brezinski, Jason Kirk Butkans, Jason Kramer, Jason Leinbach, Jason Maltzen, Jayna Pavlin, Jayson VanBeusichem, Jean Acheson, Jeff Eaton, Jeff Macfee, Jeff Xilon, Jeff Zahnen, Jeffrey Allen Arnett, Jen Watkins, Jenevieve DeFer, Jenica Rogers, jennielf, Jennifer Steen, Jeremiah Robert Craig Shepersky, Jeremy Kostiew, Jeremy Tidwell, Jesse Pudewell, Jessica and Andrew Qualls, JF Paradis, Jill Hughes, Jill Valuet, Jim "Citizen Simian" Henley, Jim & Paula Kirk, Jim Burke in VT, Jim Waters, JLR, Joanne B, Jody Kline, Joe "Gasoline" Czyz, Joe Kavanagh, John Beattie, John Bogart, John Cmar, John D. Burnham, John Geyer/Wulfenbahr Arts, John Idlor, John Lambert, John Rogers, John Sureck, John Tanzer, John-Paul Holubek, Jon Nadeau, Jon Rosebaugh, Jonathan Howard, Jonathan Perrine, Jonathan S. Chance, José Luis Nunes Porfírio, Jose Ramon Vidal,

Joseph Blomquist, Josh Nolan, Josh Thomson, Joshua K. Martin, Joshua Little, JouleLee Perl Ruby Jade, Joy Jakubaitis, JP Sugarbroad, Jukka Koivisto, Justin Yeo, K. Malycha, Kai Nikulainen, Kairam Ahmed Hamdan, Kal Powell, Karen J. Grant, Kat & Jason Romero, Kate Kirby, Kate Malloy, Kathy Rogers, Katrina Lehto, Kaz, Keaton Bauman, Keith West, Kelly (rissatoo) Barnes, Kelly E, Ken Finlayson, Ken Wallo, Keri Orstad, Kevin Chauncey, Kevin Mayz, Kierabot, Kris Deters, Kristin (My Bookish Ways Reviews), Kristina VanHeeswijk, Kurt Ellison, Lady Kayla, Larry Garetto, Laura Kramarsky, Lily Katherine Underwood, Lisa & M3 Sweatt, Lisa Padol, litabeetle, Lord Max Moraes, Lorri-Lynne Brown, Lucas MFZB White, Lutz Ohl, Lyndon Riggall, M. Sean Molley, Maggie G., Manda Collis & Nick Peterson, Marcia Dougherty, Marcus McBolton (Salsa), Marguerite Kenner and Alasdair Stuart, Mark "Buzz" Delsing, Mark Cook, Mark Dwerlkotte, Mark MedievaMonkey, Mark O'Shea, Mark Truman of Magpie Games, Mark Widner, Marshall Vaughan, Martin Joyce, Mary Spila, Matt Barker, Matt Troedson, Matt Zitron & Family, Matthew Scoppetta, Max Temkin, Maxwell A Giesecke, May Claxton, MCpl Doug Hall, Meri and Allan Samuelson, Michael Erb, Michael Godesky, Michael Hill, Michael M. Jones, Michael May, michael orr, Michael Richards, Michael Thompson, Michael Tousignant, Michael Wolfe, Miguel Reyes, Mike "Mortagole" Gorgone, Mike Grace (The Root Of All Evil), Mike Kowalski, Mike Sherwood, Mike 'txMaddog' Jacobs, Mike Wickliff, Mikhail McMahon, Miranda "Giggles" Horner, Mitch A. Williams, Mitchell Young, Morgan Ellis, Mur Lafferty, Nancy Feldman, Nathan Alexander, Nathan Blumenfeld, Nestor D. Rodriguez, Nick Bate, Odysseas "Arxonti" Votsis, Owen "Sanguinist" Thompson, Pam Blome, Pamela Shaw, Paolo Carnevali, Pat Knuth, Patricia Bullington-McGuire, Paul A. Tayloe, Paul MacAlpine, Paul Weimer, Peggy Carpenter, Pete Baginski, Pete Sellers, Peter Oberley, Peter Sturdee, Phil Adler, Philip Reed, Philippe "Sanctaphrax" Saner, Poppy Arakelian, Priscilla Spencer, ProducerPaul, Quentin "Q" Hudspeth, Quinn Murphy, Rachel Coleman Finch, Rachel Narow, Ranger Dave Ross, Raymond Terada, Rebecca Woolford, Rhel ná DecVandé, Rich "Safari Jack Tallon" Thomas, Rich Panek, Richard "Cap'n Redshanks" McLean, Richard Monson-Haefel, Rick Jones, Rick Neal, Rick Smith, Rob and Rachel, Robert "Gundato" Pavel, Robert M. Everson, Robert Towell (Ndreare), Ross C. Hardy!, Rowan Cota, Ryan & Beth Perrin, Ryan Del Savio Riley, Ryan E. Mitchell, Ryan Hyland, Ryan Jassil, Ryan Patrick Dull, Ryan Worrell, S. L. Gray, Sabrina Ogden, Sal Manzo, Sally Qwill Janin, Sam Heymans, Sandro Tomasetti, Sarah Brooks, Saxony, Scott Acker, Scott E., Scott Russell Griffith, Sean Fadden, Sean Nittner, Sean O'Brien, Sean R. Jensen, Sean T. DeLap, Sean W, Sean Zimmermann, Sebastian Grey, Seth Swanson, Shai Norton, Shaun D. Burton, Shaun Dignan, Shawna Hogan, Shel Kennon, Sherry Menton, Shervyn, Shoshana Kessock, Simon "Tech Support" Strauss, Simone G. Abigail C. GameRageLive, Stacey Chancellor, Stephen Cheney, Stephen Figgins, Sterling Brucks, Steve Holder, Steve Sturm, Steven K. Watkins, Steven McGowan, Steven Rattelsdorfer, Steven Vest, T I Hely, Tantris Hernandez, Taylor "The Snarky Avenger" Kent, Team Milian, Teesa, Temoore Baber, Tess Snider, Tevel Drinkwater, The Amazing Enigma, The Axelrods, The fastest man wearing a jetpack, thank you, The Gollub Family, The Hayworths, The NY Coopers, The Sotos, The Vockerys, Theron "Tyrone" Teter, Tim "Buzz" Isakson, Tim Pettigrew, Tim Rodriguez of Dice + Food + Lodging, TimTheTree, TJ Robotham, TK Read, Toby Rodgers, Todd Furler, Tom Cadorette, Tom J Allen Jr, Tony Pierson, Tracy Hall, Travis Casey, Travis Lindquist, Vernatia, Victor V., Vidal Bairos, W. Adam Rinehart, W. Schaeffer Tolliver, Warren Nelson, Wil Jordan, Will Ashworth, Will H., William Clucus Woods...yes, "Clucus", William Hammock, William Huggins, William Pepper, Willow "Dinosaurs and apocalypse? How could I NOT back it?" Wood, wufl, wwwisata, Wythe Marschall, Yurath, Zakharov "Zaksquatch" Sawyer, Zalabar, Zalen Moore, and Zuki.

PART ONE:
INVASION!

CHAPTER ONE
NEW YORK CITY

Jet Black fell.

The wind whistled around him, the cold breath of the city a cutting edge. Windows whipped by as he plummeted, his jet pack sparking and hissing, crumpled like a soup can in a lion's mouth—the illusion completed by the series of very real bite marks perforating the metal.

He felt dizzy. No, it was worse than that. He felt *empty*—like a hollowed out pumpkin.

Beneath him, the crowd gathered, now looking like little more than colored pins stuck in corkboard—but as he tumbled end over end through the air, jet pack boosters bursting with loud ragged coughs of worthless flame, the little people got bigger and bigger.

Soon, he would crash amongst them. Into them. On them.

Thoughts escaped him like slippery snakes and what the assassin did to him—did to his *mind*—left him lost and confused.

But one word—a name—continued to rise up out of the fog:

Sally.

He was going to crash in the middle of all those people, into all those supporters and dissenters of Franklin Delano Roosevelt, but worst of all, he was going to fall in front of Sally Slick. That was the heck of it.

Sally!

He wanted to impress her.

The heroes of the Century Club caught wind of the assassination attempt on FDR's life just this morning, but that's how these things always went: life did not afford the hero easy answers or comfortable timelines. Everything was always by the scrape of the teeth, by one's chinniest of chin hairs—most heroes not only expected it, but learned to thrive on it.

The campaign scheduled Roosevelt to speak outside the brand spanking new Empire State Building, a shining spire of metal and glass and human ingenuity that was like an extension of man's own reach, reaching for the stars and the heavens beyond. There, Roosevelt planned to outline the tenets of his Second New Deal, bolstered as he was by a supportive Congress.

The message came in scrawled on a ratty slip of fabric—

The President is going to die.

They mobilized fast. Jet, Sally Slick, Mack Silver, and the Grey Ghost— more than enough of a team to take down any cold-blooded assassin.

Little time remained, affording them no chance to scope out the place beforehand. The President had already arrived, had already wheeled himself onto the dais flanked as he was by Eleanor and all his supporters in their dark suits and broad-brimmed hats, shuffling papers in his lap as he was wont to do.

Sally said she'd stick to the stage. Mack would canvass the crowd. Ghost planned to check the tunnels beneath.

Jet's job? To go up. Observation deck of the Empire State. Mack said it would afford him a powerful vantage point over the crowd—somehow, Mack appointed himself de facto leader of their little squad, even though Jet had been there longer and Mack was always in and out, sometimes disappearing in his plane for *months*.

To Jet, it felt like—well, it felt like dismissal. Up top, he wasn't going to be able to see squat. Just people like ants and cars like little bricks and once again he'd be out of the action and set aside like a child, a child who might accidentally knock over somebody's coffee cup or spill a saucer of milk. Great. Wonderful.

Aces.

But hey, he was a team player. He did what he had to do.

So he took to the skies as FDR began to speak and he did a steady orbit around the circumference of the building, rising in slow spirals as he ascended. The building was a marvelous feat of architecture—6500 windows, each a glimpse into another world. Or would be, if most of the building were occupied. Way Jet heard it, the building couldn't fill its offices. Lingering effects of the busted economy. Not a lot of desire and so the building sat mostly empty.

So there Jet was, flying circles around the building, gazing into empty office after empty office and—

Movement.

A dark shape, just a shadow, behind one of the windows.

Time to get a closer look.

Jet pivoted his hips, cocked the wings of his jet pack just so, and hovered there in front of the window, peering past the bright gray reflection of the city and sun.

Nothing.

He planted his hands against the glass and eased his way alongside the building, the way a swimmer might pull himself along the edge of a pool.

There!

In another window, a tall shape—black suit, broad-brim hat.

Jet's heart leapt in his chest like a snake-bit stallion. Could this be the assassin?

He pulled his wrist radio to his mouth, prepared to tune to Sally's frequency and—yelling over the din of his portable jet engine, an engine that should burn his legs to crispy cinder-black matchsticks but didn't thanks to Sally's own ingenious suit design—tell her about what he's seeing. But a little voice inside him gave him pause.

You don't know what you're looking at, pal, Jet thought. *Could be anything or anyone. Janitor. Sales agent. One of the Secret Service men keeping an eye on the place.*

A trickier voice chimed in, too:

And if this is the assassin, then you can handle it. It's just one killer. Finally you can show them why you belong on this team. You can show Sally why you matter.

Mack would just kick in the window. That's how he was: act now, think—and often apologize—later. Damn the consequences. Jet was a good boy. Not the type to break windows (well, there was that one time with the first jet booster prototype, blew out all the barn and farmhouse windows in a five mile radius, but he still says that was Sally's fault).

He'd go in from the top down. Hit the observation deck. Use a door.

Jet pushed away from the building—and gunned it straight up.

To the 86th floor!

Jet's boots—padded with shock absorbers so, according to Sally, he didn't shatter his spine every time he came in for a hard landing—thudded against the observation deck, the city splayed out around him.

He found the door, and shouldered it open.

And came face to face with the man in black.

Pale flesh. Dark-lensed glasses in the shadow of a broad-brimmed hat.

But it was his grin that was the most troubling. A wide, shark's grin with yellowed needle teeth—teeth plainly not human! —stitched from corner to corner.

Those teeth opened. A slow, gassy hiss emitted.

Then they snapped shut.

Jet moved fast: backpedaling as two .45 pistols descended from spring-loaded arm-holsters and leapt into his grip fast as firesparks.

But where Jet moved fast, his opponent did not—the assassin took a slow and measured step forward, that needle-mouthed grin never wavering.

Guns up. Jet bracing for anything.

"Stop right there, assassin," Jet commanded.

But the man took another step.

Hissing. Pink tongue playing against razor teeth.

"Fine," Jet said. "You want to play it that way? I can play it that way."

Thumbs cocked dual pistols.

But before he could do anything to subdue the malefactor, a sharp pain shot through his forehead like a railroad tie blasting clean through his cerebral cortex—

Ghostly waves, like ripples from a pond after a pebble struck the surface, radiated from the man in the black suit, dissipating as they reached Jet.

A pulsing, booming voice erupted suddenly inside Jet's head.

YOU ARE WEAK, the voice said.

"No," Jet said, struggling against the voice. He tried to squeeze the triggers—

DROP YOUR WEAPONS, FOR THEY ARE AS INEFFECTIVE AS YOU.

He tried to say something, but his word came out a strangled squawk.

GIVE UP. GIVE IN. SAY GOODBYE.

A warm flare, soft and comfortable, lit bright inside Jet's mind—the light and heat became a doorway and he saw a way out, saw a way to leave this place and to shed his weakness the way a snake sheds his skin, and for a moment he smelled heady rains and the lush greenhouse odor of a sodden jungle and it all became so clear, so easy.

Give up. Give in. Say goodbye?

Yes.

No.

Sally.

Sally wouldn't want him to give up. That wasn't the Centurion way. He'd never earn her respect if he just curled up like a kicked dog.

Fight back. Break free.

Jet staggered backward, one shuffling step at a time. The razor-grinned man continued to match Jet's every movement, approaching in perfect tandem.

His muscles burned. Every effort set his body and mind on fire. He managed to raise one of the guns but then it felt like a puppet string tugged hard on his hand and his fingers shot open—the weapon clattered to the deck, with his second gun following seconds later.

Backward, backward, ever backward.

His heel struck something. His jetpack clanged against the fence of the deck.

Fight back. Break free.

For Sally.

It was like moving a boulder with just a pinky finger.

Like crawling up a mountain on your belly.

Like pulling the moon to earth with naught but a ratty fraying rope.

But somehow, he exerted the will.

Jet grabbed the fence behind him and spun around with a grunt, then braced himself and triggered the jet engine's boosters—two hot plumes of flame shot out like fire from a dragon's nose. The man shrieked, flailing. *Yes. Yes!*

That voice, again. Thunder in his mind, rumbling:

YOU HAVE MADE A TERRIBLE MISTAKE.

Jet looked over his shoulder.

Turns out, 'cold-blooded assassin' was more accurate than he ever imagined.

The man's face—his *human* face—was gone, dissipated like the illusion it was. Left in his place was a reptilian thing, a smashed saurian rictus with leathery red flesh and foul green eyes—two knife-slash nose-slits sniffed the air above that same horrible needle-tooth maw.

The monster shrieked.

Jet clambered up the fence—

But jaws closed hard around his jetpack. The saurian shriek gave way to the crunch of metal and the snapping of sparks. Jet hit the boosters one more time, again bathing the beast in the flames of his jetpack. This time, the pack was pointed to the floor—

The momentum lifted Jet above the fence and over the edge of the building.

And then the engines died with a sputtering cough and a rattle-clang.

Jet Black fell.

"What was our hope in 1932?" FDR asked the gathered crowd, his hands gripping hard the sides of his shortened podium. He leaned forward in the chair and told them: "Above all things, the American people wanted peace. Peace of mind instead of a gnawing fear."

The crowd applauded. Sally stayed off to the side but couldn't help feeling taken in by the President's words: she looked forward to a world that didn't need the likes of her and the other Centurions, a world that had not forgotten the Great War and its cousin, the Great Depression, but instead had moved past them and instead found greatness in better things.

"Americans sought to escape personal terror. They looked for the peace one feels when they have security in their home, safety in their savings, permanence in their jobs."

Feeling the power of his words drawing her in, Sally steeled herself: *Eyes peeled, remember why you're here! You can agree with him later, but for now he needs our protection.* She spied a glimpse of a leather aviator's cap moving through the crowd:

Mack Silver, refusing to take the damn thing off even though they stood firmly on the ground and were nowhere near the sky. *Admit it,* she thought, *you like it.*

You like him.

She quieted that voice with a mental kick.

FDR continued: "...Americans sought peace with other nations and peoples in this time of upheaval, this time of dread unrest. This nation will not fall again toward..."

He continued speaking, but for Sally, the voice was lost.

Because there, in the sky, she saw something. A glint, a tiny dark figure against the endless windows of the Empire State Building, the body turning end over end—

She spied the wings. The suit. The goggles.

Oh, no.

Jet was in trouble.

Falling. Fast.

Good thing Sally knew things about Jet Black's jetpack that Jet himself didn't even know. This wasn't the first time he'd fallen from the sky like a meteor rocketing to earth—last time she did an upgrade on his equipment, she tucked away a parachute in a secret compartment. A parachute that would release with the hit of a single button, a button on a small radio box that Sally happened to carry for times just like this.

She reached for her leather belt, around which hung an array of critical Sally Slick tools—spanner, ball peen hammer, sonic emitter, net gun—and found the box. She moved to quickly unclip it and extend the two pairs of antenna—

Behind her, a footstep.

And a terrible, terrible hiss.

She wheeled in time to see one of the men in dark suits emerge from the line of FDR's on-stage supporters.

Sally caught a flash of sharp teeth.

Then her mind seized and she found inside her a warm light and the smell of verdant rainforest. *Jet...*

GO TOWARD THE LIGHT.

The box dropped from her hand.

Vile thing, the ground. Mack hated it. Hated stomping around on the— well, which was it? The fundament? The firmament? Whatever you called it, he despised it. On the ground he always felt as good as a boat anchor stuck in the sucking mud. Nothing like soaring up there in the skies in Lucy, his heavily-modified Boeing 314 clipper, with the always-escaping horizon providing proof that adventure waited in the distance—

Jet had the right idea. At least, about that.

It was worse here in the crowd. Shoulders and elbows and feet. Mack wasn't claustrophobic, but he felt like he might soon be if he didn't get out of this throng.

Sally: so wide-eyed to hear the President speak. Blah blah blah, leaders of nations, proud men, blah blah blah. Just figureheads yapping. Give Mack the tribal chief of a Micronesian cargo cult any day of the week.

She was—well, she was pretty enough. Eyes had that certain twinkle, that *go-get-'em* gleam, that sparkle of *sticktoitiveness*. Sally Slick was the strongest and cleverest woman Mack knew. Hell, she was stronger and smarter than just about *anybody* he knew, man or woman.

Why didn't he go after her, then? That was it exactly. Too strong. Too smart. Mack liked them... softer, sweeter, and more apt to put up with his nonsense. Just easier that way. A woman should feel more comfortable in an evening gown than a pair of dusty overalls.

On the stage, his and Sally's eyes met—

Still, those eyes *did* twinkle, sparkle, gleam...

She looked up, suddenly. A panicked tilt of the head like a spooked animal.

He moved to follow her gaze, but someone bumped into him. Hard.

"Hey, watch it, Pally!"

Another body shouldered against him from the other direction.

Mack turned, fingers curling into rock-hard fists.

"Push me again and you're gonna get a taste of—"

Wide eyes. Razor teeth.

BREATHE DEEP AND SURRENDER.

Mack's breath caught in his chest—he smelled something like tilled earth and heard the rustle of leaves inside the cavern of his mind.

His jaw went slack, his eyes rolled toward the back of his head.

Sally felt the tidal pull on her own consciousness, drawing her mind deeper and deeper toward that rainforest smell, toward the warm radiating light.

But the crowd knew something was going on, now—they started to murmur and yell, to wake up to the fracas, and it was just enough to pull her back.

Sally dropped to one knee. Her hand darted to the stage, feeling around until it found the box—

Jet!

But again her body seized! Rigid against the psychic assault, her muscles frozen in place.

The assassin stood above her. Grin stretching too wide, teeth like knitting needles. A terrible thought struck her: *they're not going after Roosevelt, they're coming after us.*

But as that struck her, something *else* struck her assailant:

A mic stand. The stand and microphone—a Volu-Tone mic, square as a brick and just as heavy—cracked the attacker in the side of the head. As the assassin stumbled sideways, Sally caught a deep breath and saw Roosevelt himself sitting there in his chair, wielding the microphone stand as if it were a baseball bat and this was Yankee Stadium.

"Sometimes," FDR said, "on the road to peace you have to break a few heads."

Sally smiled, swooned, but then realized—

Jet was falling.

Only a few more seconds and that'd be it for him *and* the crowd.

Sally grabbed the box, stabbed the button and—

Jet heard a *pang* of metal behind him; his body jerked hard as a silken parachute blasted out from its secret back panel and caught air with the heads of the crowd staring up at him from less than a hundred feet beneath him.

He waved his hands wildly about—"Clear the way! I'm coming in hard!"

The crowd parted, opening a circle, and Jet's boots pounded the asphalt. He tucked into a low roll and was already up again, popping the buckles on his pack and letting it *thunk* against the street. Already the crowd had come alive, not yet caught in the full grip of panic but still hovering about, curiosity still holding them fast.

There!

Jet caught sight of Mack Silver, with his eyes unfocused and mouth hanging agape, caught in the grip of two more assassins—they dragged him through the crowd, heels scraping against pavement.

"Oh, no you don't," Jet said, sliding through the agitated crowd and coming up behind the two interlopers—just as they turned to hiss at him he grabbed the side of each of their heads and slammed them together. As he did, their costumes—costumes that weren't real, masks that were just illusions, projections putting forth a false human face—fell away like running water...

Revealing their snarling saurian features.

The one opened its toothy maw and screeched at Jet—

A screech cut short as Mack's fist fired up from underneath like a breaching whale.

The second of the pair lunged—not with a pair of human hands but rather, a trio of gleaming, black claws—and Jet narrowly ducked out of the way and used the creature's momentum to further fling the beast into the crowd.

Mack grabbed Jet in a headlock, kissed him on the top of his helmet. "Thanks, kid."

"We're the same *age*," Jet said, squirming from his grip.

"Sure, sure, I'm just more mature," Mack said with a wink. "C'mon, Flyboy. Time to regroup. Let's find Sally and Ghost."

She could barely find her voice long enough to say *thank you* before the Secret Service men were already whisking Roosevelt away, wheeling him to the street and into a car and peeling rubber before disappearing.

At Sally's feet, her attacker curled up on his side.

But his face was gone. Replaced by a foul reptilian visage. A clear membranous lid slid open and closed over the creature's eyes, jaw working like the mouth of an oxygen-starved fish. A slow wheeze like the leak in a tire whispered from his puckered scale lips.

He was coming to.

Then: a shadow fell over her.

Sally whipped around, threw a hard fist—

Which Mack caught like a fastball. Even he seemed surprised by its speed and power.

"Whoa, Slick, pull back the reins," he said. "You're gonna work up a froth."

"This wasn't an attack on the President," she said.

"What?" Jet asked.

"Nah," Mack added. "She's right. It was an attack on us."

Jet seemed to consider this. "A trap."

The other two nodded, and in unison said: "A trap."

Beneath them, the saurian stirred.

"We need to find Ghost and get to Lucy," Mack said. "And fast."

CHAPTER TWO
OXFORD UNIVERSITY

The drums, the drums, the jungle drums. Screaming monkeys, a cacophony in the canopy above. River waters churned. Birds screeched overhead. The drums thumped and pounded faster and faster, a thunderous hoof-rumble of blood pulsing through the ape's heart and rattling the brain inside his primate cranium—

"Professor Khan?"

The churning river sounds faded. The screeches of monkeys and the hammering drum-beat were suddenly cut short.

The ape blinked.

He was standing at the lectern.

A class of college-age women in gray sweaters and collared shirts stared at him from a half-moon of seats. One of the students—Maggie Gilroy—had her hand to her mouth.

It was she that spoke.

"Are you all right, Professor?"

Maggie. One of the few women comfortable speaking to him. The rest sat timid, as if he might one day pound the lectern to splinters, vault over the rail, and come at them.

"I'm... fine," he said in crisp accented English. Each word short, but contained within the guttural growl like rocks tumbling in the deep of his throat. "What was I saying?"

"You were saying how dinosaurs could not have gone extinct and left no descendents in the world. You were noting the research of a Doctor Rudolph Ostarhyde—"

"Yes, yes. I remember now." He adjusted his houndstooth jacket, and continued the lecture. But all the while, he felt the lectern vibrating with the heart-thudding drums.

"You're troubled," Edwin said.

The boy—that's how the Professor thought of him, even though he was 19 years old, old enough to fight in wars and have a pint and sire children—tended to hover.

And right now, he was hovering. Like a skittish dragonfly over a pond's surface.

"I'm troubled by the way you perch on my shoulder like a bird," Khan said.

"Sorry! Sorry." Edwin took a step to the side, quickly shuffling around to the other side of the table. All around them were shelves upon shelves of books, dusty and bound in tattered leather, some off shelves and in display beneath glass. This was Khan's space—not an office, not really. Some derisively referred to it as his "lair." He let that slide, though he felt the term more than a bit crass. "But something else seems to, ahh, be bothering you."

"It isn't. Everything is perfectly normal." A lie.

"One of the girls, ahh, Maggie, she came to me after class and said—"

"That I stopped speaking."

"You had another episode."

"I was just collecting my thoughts, Master Edwin. The university and the women's college has been good enough to let me push past the classical teachings and begin to instruct the students with a proper, more modern education. This is unfamiliar territory and so sometimes I choose to..." *Choose to fugue out and become lost in the drums and the jungle sounds, sounds that appear out of nowhere and draw you in the way a honey cup draws flies.* "...

sometimes I choose to take time to consider my words. Your human language presents occasional difficulty."

Another lie. Human language was all he knew. He could not communicate as an ape. He'd met gorillas before. Their chuffs and chest thumps, their grunts and snorts—it was to him just mammalian posturing, animalistic gobbledygook.

Thing was, he and Edwin shared a problem. Not that he'd ever tell the gawky tow-headed boy that, ogling at him from behind that pair of prodigious spectacles.

But Edwin was a child of privilege and shelter. He'd come from a cloistered academic family and was expected to remain in Oxford's vaunted halls. They assigned Edwin as his assistant. The world to the boy was a place not experienced but rather read about in books.

That, too, was Professor Khan's problem.

He was a highly intelligent ape. Not just the most intelligent ape in the world, but frankly more intelligent and better read than the majority of humans.

But all of it was theoretical. Learned, not experienced.

It was a problem Chaucer struggled with—the *Canterbury Tales* author reportedly warred with himself. Was it better to live a sheltered life and write of greater things, or was it wiser instead to experience things yourself?

Khan had little choice in the matter. The world didn't trust him. They saw what he was and imagined him a beast and a brute: yes, yes, he cleaned up quite nice and was very polite and as erudite as any man, but all the same they suspected it to be a ruse.

Once in a while, heroes from the Century Club would come to him. They would consult. It was them, after all, who brought him here, who gave him a place—and in repayment, he helped plan their missions, helped offer academic support whenever called upon.

But then they always left, didn't they? Armed with the knowledge he'd given them, they'd go back out into the world to battle whatever threat presented itself: time-traveling pirates or the spiderlings from the recently-discovered Pluto or the clanking robot-men of the Steam-Kaiser. Every time, Khan wished he were out there. Throwing fists. Roaring at the enemy.

Grunting. Chuffing. Screaming the ape language rather than the human one.

That, he felt, was what the drumbeat was trying to tell him.

And he feared what happened when he opened his heart to it.

Soon, he imagined, he might not have much choice.

"I'm glad you're all right," Edwin said. Smiling nervously, as he was wont to do.

"I'm excellent."

"Truly."

"Yes. Truly."

Again: screeching. Inside the hollow of his mind.

Professor Khan stirred, lifting his massive head from its pillow—which was, in fact, not a pillow at all but rather a book on Tibetan cryptozoology.

But the dream—and with it, the sound of screeching—did not fade.

Distant, yes. But it did not soften.

Stranger still: it did not seem to be inside his head this time.

He cleared his throat, stood up at his desk, brushed the scone crumbs from his tartan kilt (it was much easier wearing a kilt than trying to shove his gorilla body into a pair of human trousers), and took off his reading glasses.

Then: footsteps. Plodding, clumsy footsteps racing down steps to here, his "lair"—even before the door flung open and he came tumbling in like an open closet of loose broomsticks, Khan already knew the sound belonged to Edwin.

Edwin. Wearing a long gray nightshirt and sleeping cap. Carrying a small oil lamp; Khan wished the university allowed him to experiment with the "free energy" discovered by Nikola Tesla only just last year. Carrying a lamp with a proper bulb that lit up without any connection to the power source was, to some, like magic: but to Khan, it was proper science.

"Professor," Edwin said, gulping great heaves of breath. "Professor!"

"Spit it out, lad. It's late."

"You must come... you must see."

The boy's face wore a mask of horror.

Fine. He seemed shaken—probably found a rat under his bed or a bat above it. Khan urged the boy to lead the way, and the massive gorilla trundled after.

It was a surprise then when Edwin took to the stairs but at the top did not head right toward the dormitory. Instead, he turned left.

To the exit. To the courtyard.

Curious.

Outside, the springtime air of Oxford had teeth, but it didn't bother the Professor, what with his body being covered in a heavy coat of ape-fur.

Above: a screech.

Khan tilted his head skyward, saw a shadow pass over the moon. A shadow shaped like a bird but much, much larger. Narrow head with backward skull crest. Wings more like that of a bat stretched wide.

"Oh my," Khan said, breathless.

It was a pterosaur. But much bigger than any of the fossils that had since been discovered. Bigger than pterodactylus, to be sure.

And it was not alone. As one shadow passed, so did another, and another.

Then a dirigible drifted into view, hazy running lamps diffuse in the night.

As Khan's eyes adjusted, he saw the shadows: dozens of them, some were pterosaurs flying, others great dirigibles drifting.

An invasion force.

Heading toward London.

"Inside boy," Khan chuffed, grabbing the boy's bony matchstick arm in his epic primate's grip. "We must discover the truth of this thing. And quickly."

In his mind, he heard the drums begin anew.

CHAPTER THREE
NEW YORK CITY

Mack tuned into the radio on his wrist, dialed to Grey Ghost's frequency—

And heard only static whispering back: the pops and crackles of dead air.

They thought to follow him, to descend into the sewers to track his radio, but then more of those assassins turned onto the street, all dark suits and black glasses and wide razor mouths. A half-dozen here, another half-dozen marching around the other corner.

The fake-faced killers hadn't yet spied the Centurions.

Sally pulled them into the lobby of the Empire State Building. Above their heads, the art deco gold leaf relief of the stars and planets in a long line. Beneath them, the cold terrazzo floor.

"They're coming," she said.

"They got Ghost?" Jet asked.

"They got Ghost," Mack said. "What in the name of Snow White and the Seven Dwarfs is going on? Anybody else feel like those things got in their head?"

"They told me—" Jet began but then decided not to share the whole story. "They told me to go toward the light. I heard it but I didn't hear it."

Sally chimed in: "Like they were inside your head."

Jet nodded. He felt his palms go slick.

"If Flyboy here hadn't bonked their heads like a pair of island coconuts, those freaks would've had me for sure," Mack said. "Ghost didn't have a shot."

"We have to get him back," Jet said.

"Not yet, kid. We gotta regroup. Get our bearings. See what we're up against. If they can get in our heads easy as apple pie, then we don't stand a chance. If this attack really was on us and not on Roosevelt, then it's time to be extra-cautious."

Jet felt his face growing red. "Cautious? *You*? Selfish. That's what you mean."

"Hey now! Where's this coming from, Flyboy?"

"You're protecting your own hind end, not ours."

Mack grabbed Jet by his suit. "You're damn right I am. Somebody has to watch out for A-Number-One. You picking up what I'm laying down?"

"Oh, I'm picking it up," Jet seethed.

A loud whistle cut through the lobby, echoing. Sally stood there, fingers between her lips. "Everybody listening? Good. Mack's right, though maybe for the wrong reasons."

"Hey—" Mack protested, but Sally cut him off with a look.

"We have no defense here. Our only hope is to get to the plane and find our way to another chapter house. Philadelphia, maybe. Regroup. Learn about—"

Outside came screams. Screams of people, yes. But something else, too.

The three of them crept toward the door. Peered out the glass.

Just as a massive winged dinosaur crashed down on a black Buick 41. Denting the car's hood like it was made of tinfoil.

"That's a dinosaur," Mack said.

"It's not the only one," Sally said, pointing up. They tilted their heads and glimpsed what little vantage they could—across the sky drifted other winged lizards, darting between massive black dirigibles, blimps lined with strange tribal markings.

"This situation is *all wet*," Jet said.

"Not only do we have a bunch of lizard-faced mooks with the ability to get in our heads standing in our way," Mack said, "but now we got real dinosaurs in our way?"

"And dirigibles of unknown origin," Jet added.

"Follow me," Sally said, grabbing the both of them by the crook of their arms and pulling them toward the elevator. She stabbed a button with her wrench.

The elevator dinged.

"My jetpack is long gone," Jet said, thumbing toward the street. "It's still out *there*. We can't go up. We go up, there's nowhere else to go."

"Who said we're going up?" Sally asked.

She pushed them both inside.

Once in after them, she stabbed the *down* button.

Sally explained as she ushered them through the darkened Empire State Building subbasement and toward a locked door marked with a plaque: NO ENTRY.

The Federal government, in all its wisdom and autocracy, decided that it needed a rat's warren of secret tunnels laced throughout the city's underground. Hidden evacuation tunnels for government officials, clandestine offices, fake "steam" tunnels and the like.

Using these tunnels, she said, would take them across Manhattan and dump them out at the Hudson—where Lucy sat docked.

The tunnels were twice as dark as night. The air sat still and cold.

"Got it," Sally said, voice echoing. She fumbled around at the back of her belt, and hanging there she pulled a micro-torch she invented for on-the-go jobs.

Or, of course, to light pitch-black tunnels.

Blue flame erupted in a crackling cone, and as a result, they once again could see.

Mack checked his compass. "We just need to head east."

Ahead of them, the tunnel was only big enough for one of them—each elbow rubbing along a cement wall. But as they crept along, the space widened and the floor dropped while the ceiling remained the same. It went from being a bog-standard utility tunnel to looking instead like a cathedral that had been buried beneath the earth—the sudden vault of the ceiling and the deco pillars in the wall only helped to complete the illusion.

"How'd you know about these tunnels?" Jet asked.

"Remember the giant rats?" About five years ago, Sally was called to investigate a warren of super-sized rodents beneath the city. She didn't expect they'd also be *super-intelligent*. But, so it went—the rats, harmless and actually quite friendly, now kept to a small island off the coast of Norway. "I had a sandhog show me the way down."

Mack laughed. "Sandhog."

"That's what they're called."

"No, no, I know. It's just—c'mon, doll, that's funny. Sandhog."

"I'm not your doll."

He stiffened. "I know you're not."

"The hogs *built* this city," Sally asserts through clenched teeth. "Sewers? Subway tunnels? Ever hear of something called the Brooklyn Bridge, smart guy?"

Mack chuffed. "All right, okay, everybody settle down—"

A wretched screech echoed through the tunnels. Stopping the three of them in their tracks. Mack whispered: "Don't suppose that's one of your rat pals?"

Sally didn't answer. She didn't have to.

Suddenly, the ground began to shake. Streamers of dust fell from the ceiling as the ground rumbled.

Another screech. Closer this time.

And the floor shook harder.

"Do we need to run?" Mack asked.

"We need to run," Sally confirmed.

Jet was about to throw his own two cents into the cup—but behind them, a massive beast with pale, scaled flesh crashed through the wall. In the uncertain light of Sally's torch they saw milky eyes, a head shaped like an iron forge, a lashing tail thick as an elephant's leg.

Nobody needed to say it, this time:

They ran, the beast in swift pursuit.

CHAPTER FOUR
OXFORD UNIVERSITY

Professor Khan threw open the bottom drawer of his desk, lifted the false bottom (with a finger hole cut out for one of his massive ape digits) and withdrew the Televisor Talk Box, a bulging bubble screen with a fat black dial underneath and a series of aluminum conduits forming a metal labyrinth (as if for a very tiny mouse) behind it.

Khan drew the box, extended the antenna, and spun the hand-crank.

The screen flared to life.

A blurry black-and-white image showed a library not unlike his own—but upon further inspection one would see this looked equal parts "war room." The table in the back lined with a single map and a series of tiny flags gave it away, as did the many weapons—sabers and scimitars and blunderbusses— hanging on the visible walls.

The Century Club. Chapter house, London.

And it was empty.

It was never empty. Not once, not ever. Someone always manned the Televisor—necessary to monitor communications, to keep track of emergencies, to send messages between the chapter houses across the world, from Philadelphia to Mumbai to Paris and back again.

"Sir?" Edwin squeaked.

"What is it, boy?"

"What's that I'm looking at, Professor?"

But Khan didn't have time to explain. He turned the dial to one of the 12 tic-mark positions—the image warped like melting candle wax and was, for a moment, supplanted by a series of horizontal lines chasing each other.

Then a new image resolved:

The Philadelphia chapter house.

This one, different: less a library and more a Colonial workshop space, which was apt given that it once belonged to Benjamin Franklin. Franklin's second secret illegitimate son, Barnard, served the Century Club as a hero known only as "The Key."

What wasn't different was that it, too, was empty.

Khan turned the dial again.

Shanghai, with its giant fish tank walls and foo dog statues: empty.

Paris, with its mirrors and the back window view of the Eiffel Tower: empty.

So too with Mumbai, Havana, Moscow, Sao Paolo.

And then he turned to Los Angeles.

The Los Angeles chapter house—austere with a Spanish mission vibe—was not empty, and for just a moment, Khan's massive ape heart leapt light and free in his chest.

But then a hard knot formed in his throat.

"That's the Projector," Khan said. Mouth dry.

"Who, Professor?"

On screen, a small man with a massive helmet on his head, a helmet that to Khan looked a little like a kitchen colander with a series of wires sprouting from the top like worms or weeds, backed into the back corner of the room. Hand to the helmet. Projecting his psychic waves as he was wont to do.

Three other men advanced on him. Three eerily similar men—same build, same dark suit, same black glasses. Reaching. Smiling.

Their faces flickered. As if they were themselves projections—images inside images, a screen within a screen where the horizontal hold went kablooey. In the skipping stuttering facial flickers, Khan saw their heads replaced with monstrous reptilian ones—soulless eyes, gnashing knife-like teeth, the flesh forming ridges and scales.

"Projector!" Khan barked into the device—and with that, the small man with the big helmet turned toward the screen.

"Khan!" the Projector struggled to say. "The Century Club..."

The trio of saurian malefactors advanced upon the Projector.

Hissing. Tongues licking the air.

"...is under attack!"

"Run!" Khan said. "Run!"

The Projector suddenly tensed his whole body, shrinking even smaller, elbows tucked to his side, knees bent, as if he were ready to spring forward like a tensed-up jackrabbit. But it was not a physical release he sought—

A psychic blast radiated out from his helmet, an opaque ripple that knocked the three men back and, soon as it struck the Televisor on that end—

It destroyed the signal.

A loud squelch of noise drove deep into Khan's head like a pin puncturing his eardrum and then the visual was lost, replaced with static.

Edwin staggered back, holding his ears.

"Professor, what's going on?"

Khan pinched the bridge of his simian nose.

The jungle drums—subtle, quiet, but there just the same—thumped in between his heartbeats. *Boom ba ba boom ba ba boom ba ba boom.*

He pinched hard enough so that they stopped short.

"The Century Club is under attack," Khan said, repeating the Projector's dire warning.

"The Century Club? Those people. The ones you—you sometimes help." Again Edwin hovered. A bundle of nervous energy in a knee-length sleep-shirt.

"I'm just a Professor," Khan said, rebuffing a statement that was never made.

"I don't understand."

"This isn't me. This isn't my place. I'm just—I work *behind the scenes.* Don't you see that?" Khan stood up suddenly, the chair beneath him rocketing backwards. "I'm just an intellectual. A thinker. That's my job, you understand: *to think.*"

Boom ba ba boom ba ba boom.

"Professor, you seem to be rambling—"

Khan paced, and Edwin trailed after like a frittering terrier.

"So *think*," Khan exhorted himself, rapping his ape knuckles against his brow. "Think! What did we see? We saw men who were not men. Whose faces were masks—but no! Not masks. Not in the traditional sense. Projections."

"They looked like lizards—"

"Lizards. Indeed. Reptilian. Saurian. And what was it we saw outside? Pterosaurs. Flying reptiles. Dinosaurs—ancient, extinct—"

"They didn't look extinct."

"No, they did not. But the connection is clear just the same—saurian agents and flying dinosaurs. And all the chapter houses, empty save one. Why the Projector?"

"He has a rather spiffy helmet?"

"No." Khan snapped his fingers—*crack*. "But also: yes. It's not the helmet, it's what the helmet does—it amplifies. It *projects*. And what does it project?"

"His voice? Nightlights? Talking pictures?"

"His mind powers. His psychic mind powers. That's why he was the last Centurion left. Because he was battling them on their own turf."

"Psychic dinosaurs?"

"*Psychosaurs*," Khan corrected, as if that had always been the term.

"Ohhh. That's really quite clever!" Edwin smiled a smile of teeth so crooked it looked like a picket fence blown down in a bad wind. "You are a clever man."

"Man." Khan tasted that word. He felt the call of the jungle inside, but quickly tamped it down. "I am a man. Aren't I, Edwin?"

"That's what I said, Professor."

"I am not a beast. It is not the body that makes us but rather the mind—is it not?"

"It... is?"

"It is."

Khan took a deep breath. He knew his words sounded confident but he only wished what he felt inside radiated that same measure of authority.

No matter.

Khan moved back to the desk, pulled out another item from within the drawer's secret space. This time: a tube. Opened and unrolled: a map. "We are being invaded, Edwin. First the Centurions are sidelined why? Because they're the only ones who can stop this cataclysmic intrusion. Take out the guardians and the door becomes unguarded, does it not?"

Khan tapped the map. His finger thumped a location in the Pacific, crinkling against the time-worn blue of a cartographed ocean.

His finger revealed a series of small islands. A chain of them. Midway between the California coast and Asia. Edwin leaned over and squinted at it through the thick lenses of his glasses.

"The... Hawaiian islands?"

"Indeed, indeed. Location of the Century Club's most secret chapter house. A fallback position of last resort."

"How do you know about it?"

Then came a twinkle in Khan's eye, a gleam of lion's pride. "Because I helped them choose the location *and* design it."

Edwin blinked in apparent awe.

Professor Khan continued: "I've never been there, you know? But I think it's time to change that. Edwin Jasher, do you care to accompany me on an adventure?"

"Me, sir?"

"You heard me, boy."

Edwin's face melted into a beacon of unrestrained joy. He said nothing: the look in his eyes was all the answer the erudite ape required.

Khan, meanwhile, felt his own flurry of joy, his own giddy rush—the call to adventure was sounded. But not with a horn, no.

Jungle drums. This call came from the thumping of jungle drums.

CHAPTER FIVE
NEW YORK CITY

It was bad enough being in the crowd above. It was bad enough having to set foot on the streets of the city and feel anchored to the earth in unspectacular fashion. It was *bad enough* to have to climb down into the city's secret bowels through a series of doorways and boltholes.

All of that paled in comparison to being chased through those aforementioned bowels by a shrieking albino hell-a-saur bent on ripping them to shreds.

Mack was not happy.

As his footfalls echoed through the tunnel, he couldn't help but think of flying over some tropical isle, gazing down at waterfalls and crashing surf—in his mind's eye he imagined the soft leather of Lucy's controls in his hand, all her buttons and gauges splayed out before him. It's why he named his plane with a woman's name—beyond it being the convention, of course; it was nice to have a woman in his hands who did everything he asked. Predictable as the tickity-tock of a Swiss clock.

Unlike, say, Sally Slick.

The three of them were running together, the beast snapping at their heels—when suddenly she *and* the light she carried were gone, snuffed out in the darkness. As Mack and Jet barely managed to squeeze into a side tunnel, they found themselves without their third.

No Sally.

And, stranger still, no monster.

"Sally," Jet said, breathless. Then he called out: "Sally!"

"Shhh!" Mack said, clamping a hand over Jet's fool mouth. He hissed: "You want to draw that thing's attention?"

Jet wriggled free. "It's probably chasing her, you dolt."

"You don't know that."

"I'm sure they each just went their separate ways."

Mack felt sure the kid was rolling his eyes. He couldn't see him in the dark, but a gesture like that, you could *hear* in a person's words. "Don't you roll your eyes at me."

"I don't know what she sees in you."

"Wait. What? Sally sees something in me?"

"No. What? Nothing!"

"No, hold on one second, you just said—"

Their conversation was quickly cut short.

Just behind the two of them, the beast roared. With it came the scent of rotten food in its maw, the belching breath of blood and meat and fur. Its tongue slapping against teeth.

Mack did the only thing Mack knew to do in a situation like this:

He winced and cocked a fist.

A fist he never had to throw.

There came a sound of groaning metal, and a shadow moving to the right of the beast—suddenly, a great gout of white steam bloomed in the air, blasting the creature's head.

The beast screamed—a horrible sound that cut clean to Mack's marrow. But then it reared its head and wriggled swiftly backward, twisting its body in such a way so that it managed to turn itself around and flee.

As it did, Mack saw something.

At the back of the creature's head, Mack caught sight of a tiny glowing spot—soft, diffuse, an eerie icy blue something pulsing against the creature's leathery flesh. And then Mack could no longer see it, for the beast was fast escaping. He tucked that information away, not sure what it was that clung to the creature...

Or what it meant.

Flame erupted—the light from a hand-held torch illuminating Sally's face. In her hand she held a wrench, and dangling beside her was the pipe breathing great gouts of steam.

"Boys," she said over the steam-hiss.

In this light, Mack suddenly found her—

—with her brow slick from the steam and almost glowing, really—

No, no, couldn't be. This wasn't—

No.

He liked women like Lucy. Soft, comfortable, putty in his hands.

Jet laughed. "Nice moves, Sally."

"Don't I know it." She gave Mack's shoulder a little punch and the touch sent a thrill grappling up his arms. A thrill that quickly got the kibosh. "What's wrong, Silver? You look like you saw a ghost."

"I almost just lost my *arm* in a dinosaur's mouth. Pardon me for being rattled."

"Maybe you shouldn't try to punch angry dinosaurs," Jet said.

Sally waved them both ahead. "Hush up and come on. That monster is gone now, but it won't be for long. That blast of steam wasn't much more than a whack of a rolled-up newspaper on the nose for a monster like that."

Mack found himself seeing Sally in a new light as he wrestled with new feelings and...

Well. Mack would've rather been wrestling with the *monster*, instead.

The door rattled on its hinges against Sally's boot. Rust whispered from old hinges, hinges made that way from their proximity to the water. A second kick, and a third, and finally the door swung open.

The gray light of a day moving from afternoon into evening hit them like a blinding tide, but it wasn't long before their eyes adjusted...

And they saw just how much trouble they were really in.

The door opened out of a small marine shed and overlooked the Hudson River. The sinking sun was caught in pools of liquid light, plainly and perfectly highlighting Mack's heavily-modified Boeing-314 clipper—a "boat plane" that needed no runway as long as it had a good stretch of water. One problem, though:

The boat was guarded by the enemy. A dozen saurian agents—once again projecting their smiling human faces—clustered together like an arrangement of humanoid bowling pins by the end of the floating dock, blocking anybody hoping to get close to Lucy.

They didn't move. They didn't even stare at one another.

They just... stood there.

Stock still. Staring forward. Fake reptile smile.

"They got Lucy," Mack growled.

Jet sighed. "We're going to need to find another way."

"They got *Lucy*."

"We heard you—"

"Nobody stands in the way of me and my plane."

Mack started taking off his boots.

"You think that water's cold?" he asked.

"Frigid," Sally said.

"Good. I could use a little wake-me-up. I hope you two can swim."

And with that, Mack ducked low and bolted toward the water.

CHAPTER SIX
OUTSIDE NEW YORK CITY

The dinosaur roared, and the Conqueror Ape roared with it.

The dinosaur in question: a Giganotosaurus, its head lifted high, its wretched scream ululating from its rippling throat.

The Conqueror Ape in question: Gorilla Khan, warlord ape and all-around megalomaniac.

Gorilla Khan wore his best outfit today. This day of true conquest, this day the world was made finally to kneel and see its weakness splayed out before all eyes. Armor made of bones and teeth and painted red-and-gold—red for blood, gold for the color of kings—adorned his broad primate's chest. And upon his head, a helmet made from the skull of a long-dead saber-toothed cat, the colorful plumage of the similarly long-dead archaeopteryx thrust up from a ring mounted in the top of the hand-made helmet.

Both creatures, the cat and the bird, were ones Gorilla Khan hunted and killed himself.

One should wear his conquests, he said. You do not conceal your gifts.

That was why he sat astride this massive reptilian carnivore. Bit in the beast's mouth, braided leather reins gathered up in one of Khan's crushing fists.

Let the world see him upon this most glorious of creatures. A creature that died out millions of years ago. Before mankind and the trappings of so-called "civilization." Before time itself. Before the meteors came and changed everything.

Ahead of them: the Brooklyn Bridge. Beyond it, the rising spires of Manhattan.

In the sky above, the setting sun highlit the circling pterodactyls and the first wave of airships: just a fraction of Gorilla Khan's invasion fleet.

"Status report," he barked.

One of his lackeys, a simpering white-furred lowland gorilla, bounded up to the beast and clambered up the side. He hung to Khan's left, offering a placating smile of primate fangs.

"Most excellent, Mighty Khan, most excellent."

"I abhor your generalities. I demand specifics, Attaché Gonga. Not your mewling glad-handed bulletins." To confirm his disgust, Gorilla Khan threatened Gonga with the back of his hand—a hand that did not fall but stayed poised to strike.

"Yes! Yes. Of course." Gonga had this nervous laugh, a kind of wheezing, growling *heh, heh, heh*. It held little mirth, and whenever he made the sound, a sudden stink of fear rose. A smell that intoxicated the Conqueror Ape. "The invasion is going... ahh, swimmingly. The humans have begun to dispatch, ahhh, soldiers and police, but they are no match for our own warriors and agents, nor can they, ahhh, hold their own against our *technology*."

Technology. Yes. Khan longed to test their weapons on unwilling subjects. Hanging to the side of his Giganotosaurus was what looked to be a long wooden spear with a tip made from a gleaming multi-faceted ruby, a ruby as big as a human child's fist. But of course it was *so much more* than just a spear...

Well. Playtime would come.

Gonga continued: "The Centurions have been subdued. All the chapter houses have been taken; many burned to the ground. Those eager do-gooding spirits of the Century Club have been... ahh, sidelined and taken away by our, ahhh, new allies. The minds of the heroes are no longer with their, ahh, umm, *bodies*."

Their new allies, indeed. The saurian agents. Willing and able to serve with no interest in leading. A powerful force.

"Anything else?" Khan asked his inferior.

"There is, ahhh, one more thing," Gonga said, his voice lowering and once more offering that nervous huffing laugh. "We have hit a... a snag."

Khan roared. Bared fangs first to Gonga, then to the sky.

"*Explain*, Attaché Gonga."

"Some of the Centurions, a rare few—"

"Some of them *what*."

"A rare few remain, ahhh, unaccounted for, though we are sure that—"

Gorilla Khan backhanded the albino ape hard enough to knock the attaché off the side of his mount. The fool hit the ground and scrambled to once more gain his footing.

"Who?" Khan asked.

"I'm sorry?"

"I said, *who*! Who has escaped our grasp?"

"Ahhh." Gonga stood, dusting himself off. "Amelia Stone. Mack Silver. Benjamin Hu. Jet Black. Sally Slick. Ahhh. Reports are coming in of others. Just a few! Just a few."

Khan let go of the reins, and leapt off his mount.

He landed atop Gonga, once more knocking the pink-eyed simian to the ground. He grabbed tufts of white fur and pulled the weakling's face close to his own.

"What of my son?" Khan said, voice low.

"Ah. Ahhh. Yes. We have agents inbound as we speak."

"He's still there? Still at Oxford?"

Gonga nodded, obsequious smile firmly in place.

"Good." Gorilla Khan snorted. "I hate this place, Gonga. I hate the people. Their pink-cheeked optimism, their ugly utilitarian architecture, their disgust and misunderstanding of the natural world. But most of all I hate what they did to my boy. They... civilized him. Made him weak. I will change that. I will change him back. Awaken in him what has been awakened in me. For he is Son-of-Khan, and I am Khan."

The Conqueror Ape let his attaché fall back to the ground.

"Now, Gonga. We march." Gorilla Khan clambered back up into the custom-made saddle riding the ridges of the monster's back. He grabbed the reins and pulled them tight.

The beast reared back.

Once more the Giganotosaurus and the Conqueror Ape roared in unison.

CHAPTER SEVEN
OXFORD UNIVERSITY

Professor Khan never packed for an adventure before. What to take? Toothbrush and toothpaste, most certainly. Soap? Talcum powder? Grooming comb? Pomade? He felt the need to fritter the time away, poring over the problem as he did with any question: pros, cons, a long internal debate over how to design the optimal path through the problem at hand.

Adventurers and heroes do not debate, he chided himself, staring at himself in the mirror. *One has no time to pick through the details when danger is afoot. When it's time to throw a punch, it's time to throw a punch. Deep breath. Dive off the edge, old chap!*

He did indeed take a deep breath.

Then he swept all his toiletries into his leather satchel and exited his bathroom.

Toiletries. The first step toward adventure!

He reentered his office and library—his "lair"—and was met with quite a surprise.

"Son-of-Khan," said a voice from across the room. A gruff throaty greeting from another gorilla—this one wearing a black as night leather overcoat. The ape held in his hands a strange curved dagger the likes of which Professor

Khan had never seen—the blade itself forged not of metal but instead of a single jewel, light captured in flat facets. Something about it tickled the back of Khan's head, but he wasn't quite sure what.

"Another of my ilk," Professor Khan said. "Is this a friendly visit?"

"What do you think?" the other ape challenged, stepping forward into the room. Flanking him from the shadows came three more men—men who were not men at all, Khan knew, but the strange saurian interlopers whose faces were false. "Your father requests your presence."

"My father," Professor Khan said. He almost laughed. "Yes. Well. I don't think that's quite accurate, do you?"

"Do not sully the Conquerer Ape!" the gorilla warrior growled, and with both arms sent a reading table clattering into bookshelves. Professor Khan winced—harm to his books was a source of very real pain to him. The ape snarled: "You are son and successor."

"If you say so."

The warrior ape and the three saurians advanced. One of the agents hissed, cocking a confused head at the others the way a dog might. The warrior ape showed a single fang. To Professor Khan he said, "They cannot touch your mind. It is too primal. That is why the Conqueror sent me, Botu, his best warrior."

"Botu," Khan said, clucking his tongue. A clue, buried there. "Old Atlantean. Did my father name you? You may not know all you think you know about that name."

The warrior ape moved forward swiftly, his fists pounding the floor. A globe stood in his way—he shattered it with a fist. "Do not tell me about my own name."

"It's just—it doesn't mean warrior. It means *fated* to be a warrior." Khan's voice trembled. Where were those jungle drums now? Other heroes would know what to do here. They would have a plan. Or they'd just... wade in, guns up, blades out, fists flying fast and furious. But all he could do was lecture on the naming conventions of long-dead civilizations. "Fated. As in, I'm afraid, *not yet* a warrior."

Botu was not happy.

He pointed the dagger. The weapon began to glow orange, then red, as if a furnace burned within the crystalline blade. A thrumming hum rose.

"You shall pay for that," Botu hissed, baring teeth.

And then, most unexpectedly, Edwin came into the room.

He was dressed in a tweed suit and had a bag at his side.

"Professor, I'm ready to—oh. *Oh*. Oh my."

Botu and the three saurians turned toward the intrusion. "Kill him!"

When it's time to throw a punch, it's time to throw a punch.

It was, Khan knew, time to throw a punch.

He swung out a mighty—and, admittedly, clumsy—fist. Botu was nowhere near it. But that was fine; he didn't need to be.

The bookshelf, however, was plenty close.

Khan's fist clipped the side of the bookshelf—and internally, his heart sank as he committed this single act of violence against his beloved treasure trove of reading and research material—and it fell against another bookshelf—

And another.

And another.

Dominoes crashing into one another—

Until the final piece collapsed upon Botu and his saurians.

"Professor!" Edwin squawked.

But there was no time for celebrations. Khan bounded over the pile of shelves—and, by proxy, over the fallen bodies of the intruders—and pulled Edwin out of the door.

"No time, my boy. We must flee!"

Upstairs. Outside. Back into the courtyard. Moon and stars of early morning above. Already Khan could hear the bellow of his so-called "father's" warrior, a sound of certain rage. They'd be here soon—and then what?

As they stepped toward High Street and away from the Queen's College, the thunder of a motor and a blinding light suddenly greeted them. Khan held up his hands and Edwin, again, squawked—this time in wordless surprise.

A woman's voice called to them:

"Stop right there."

With it came the cocking of a revolver's hammer. *Cl-click.*

Khan held up his hands. "Yes. Of course. Apologies. Don't shoot."

"Wait. Professor?"

The erudite ape peered past the light.

The woman who stepped out of it—so she was no longer a shadow framed by a blinding edge—was a beautiful woman. Black, with long dark hair framing shoulders clad in the brown leather of a bomber jacket, swaddled in a white scarf.

She was quite beautiful.

The revolver in her hand went back into its holster.

"Professor," she said. "I'm Amelia Stone. I got your message."

"I wouldn't put that weapon away just yet, Miss Stone," Khan said, hurrying up to her and dragging Edwin with him. "We have a significant—"

Behind them, a door splintered open with a loud shattering crack.

"—problem."

CHAPTER EIGHT
NEW YORK CITY

The coldness of the water was like being hit by a fist—not just a single fist thrown by a single assailant, unless maybe that assailant was a skyscraper-sized giant with a fist the size of a Rolls-Royce Phantom. This felt like a hundred fists, *a thousand*, pummeling Mack's body as he dove into the waters of the Hudson.

Again he wished for the warm waters of the Pacific.

But at least he was away from Sally for a while. Even for a moment. The icy river forced him to clear his head. Get in the moment.

Reclaim Lucy and get far away from this town.

He sank beneath the water, fought against the current and swam down-river toward the nose of the plane—dragging himself through the gray, sightless nothing. He felt lost for a moment, but then caught sight of the mammoth belly of the Boeing clipper above him, a black shape cast against the shapelessness of everything else.

Most Clippers had one way in and one way out—you boarded the plane on a small buoyant sub-wing extending off the right side of the plane beneath the larger wing. But this wasn't your average everyday Boeing-314. This was a Sally Slick special.

She built in a second portal—a hatch right above the pilot's seat so that Mack could drop into the plane from above if need be. And today, that's exactly what he needed.

Mack felt his hands thump against the metal bottom of the plane, then pulled himself to the far side, the side where those dinosaur-faced mind-control mooks couldn't see him. A few moments of blind searching later, he had his knuckles wrapped around the rungs of a ladder and—quietly, gingerly, like a mouse trying to steal a cookie while Santa was laying presents under the tree—crept up the ladder to the top of the plane.

He slid his way along the roof on his belly—a worm's crawl toward the hatch. He peered over the edge, saw the... *configuration* of saurians still gathering at the dock, standing perfectly still and peering (thankfully) in the other direction.

Mack wrapped his hands around the hatch wheel. Tried to turn.

Stuck. Stubborn.

Up here, he had no leverage—no way to anchor himself and put his back into it.

Above him, screeching—two flying dinosaurs with their arrow-shaped heads circled like epic, featherless vultures. *Uh-oh.*

Again he made a go at the wheel. Hands gripping tight as they could, feet bolstering against nothing more than the rivets holding this hunk of metal together—

It gave. An inch.

And then another.

And then another.

And when it finally started spinning—

It made a sound like two boats rubbing together, metal against metal, loud as anything.

Double *uh-oh.*

From the far side of the plane, a cacophony of reptilian hissing rising in eerie simultaneity. Mack gritted his teeth, spun the wheel the rest of the way, and popped the hatch. A quick drop down and he plopped into his cushy leather pilot's chair.

Lucy's controls, presented before him. Comfortable. Familiar.

"Beautiful, really," he said to no one. Maybe to her. Maybe he said it to Lucy.

No matter now! Time to get this doll airborne.

Switches flipped. Buttons mashed. *Click click click.* Flip, flip, flip. All around him, little artifacts of the tropics he brought with him: a Samoan fishing net, fronds from a bottle palm, a little hula girl carved by some old wave-talker at a *heiau*—an old Polynesian temple and testing ground, and a bunch of bananas hanging in a sling between the two pilot chairs.

He grabbed a banana. Started to rip into it with his teeth as Lucy's two pairs of propellers whirred to life. Reached for the wheel—

Then: a bright light. His mind seized.

Saurian psychic waves, it seemed, did not care about metal or any other matter separating them from their target, for Mack's consciousness was suddenly a leaf pulled along a swiftly-moving river—

LEAVE THIS WORLD.

ESCAPE ITS GRAVITY.

COME WITH US.

The smell of tropics. He knew the smell. Loved the smell. The wet rain-forest canopy. Somewhere a lush fruit—like a pineapple but even sweeter— broken open and the cloying odor crawling up his nose. Wind in the palms. Warm air.

Just give in to it.

The propellers started to pull the plane forward.

But he didn't care. Didn't care at all.

THIS WORLD DOES NOT KNOW YOU, said the voice in his head.

BUT OURS DOES.

Mack gave in.

The plane began to move toward them.

Sally and Jet stood hunkered down behind the small sub-wall separating the edge of the city from the waters of the Hudson, and sure enough, the plane began to drift their way.

"C'mon," she said, climbing up over the wall.

"I can't swim," Jet said, in horror.

"*What*? I told you to learn."

"I didn't."

"I told you to *learn*," she said again, growling.

"I didn't! Okay?"

She scowled. "The earth is over 70% water."

"And a whole lot of sky above it," he said, sheepishly.

"I'm sorry."

"You're sorry? Wait. Why are you sorry?"

She continued to clamber up onto the wall.

"Wait!" Jet said.

Sally dove into the river.

Leaving him all alone.

What Mack saw, in the hollows of his own mind:

Dappled light filtered through the lush pleach of jungle palm.

Dark earth below beneath a squid-tangle of vines as big as a man's leg.

Rusted iron bars clanging, squeaking, swinging shut.

A flash of black claw—on it, blood and fur.

He felt himself fall toward these things even though they were in front of him—his entire center of being was wobbly, spinning wildly as if strapped into some kind of mad gyro machine. The loud voice continued to boom above and within him—

YOU ARE STRONG

TOO MUCH FOR THIS WORLD

A HUNTER

GIVE IN

LET GO

TIME MEANS NOTHING...

But then—

A hard shake and a shudder. The voices in his head were swallowed suddenly: did he just hear a gurgle? A cold saline rush washed over—no, not over, but *inside*—his skin, as if he once more plunged into the gray waters of the Hudson.

It was Lucy that saved him.

As the plane eased forward, the two high-gauge chains mooring her to the dock strained and stretched—and then held because, of course, those are chains. Pittsburgh steel! Each link as thick as the banana Mack shoved in his mouth just before taking a mental jungle vacation.

The dock, however...

The dock was made of wood. Wet wood—driven deep into river silt and clay, yes, but wood just the same.

Suddenly the dock wobbled, shifted, began to slide like lard in a hot skillet. The cluster of psychic saurians wobbled with it, still maintaining their telepathic assault on the weak-brained pink-skinned hairless ape inside the cockpit—

Until, of course, the dock collapsed.

Taking the saurians with it, and plunging them into the river. Thrashing. Gurgling.

And freeing Mack from his own chains.

For now.

It was like a dislocated shoulder popping back into place—suddenly there came a *pop* and Mack's consciousness was gone from the jungle and back to the cockpit of his favorite Yankee Clipper, Lucy. His hands shot out like lightning and grabbed the wheel.

Ahead, through the windshield, he saw Sally swimming hard overhand—no small trick with the heavy toolbelt weighing her down!—to meet the plane as it eased forward.

He didn't see Flyboy, but Jet was probably in there somewhere. Doggy-paddling, trying not to drown. Silly kid.

Good. Great. *Superb.*

Mack's heart leapt in his chest.

Time to fly.

Jet hadn't really ever told anyone this, but he was afraid of water. Water to him was the opposite of air—air was open, freeing, infinite. Water was an all-enveloping prison, a smothering blanket of liquid that would snake into your lungs and fill your gut and drag you into the depths fast as anything.

The sky was up. And light. And freedom.

Water was down. And darkness. And doom.

And so it visited upon him no small amount of horror to watch Sally Slick abandon him and swim toward the approaching Clipper.

He wrestled with what was happening. On the one hand, she'd always been there. Always saved him. Even when they were kids, growing up in the same nowhere part of Nebraska, she'd save his can from bullies. Or from that vicious dog from the Krumholtz farm. Or from his own homework, even.

On the other hand, the way he looked at her was not the way she looked at him.

He looked up to her.

And... well, she looked down on him. At least, that's how he saw it.

Maybe this was that. Maybe she was just plum *tired* of saving his hind-quarters from danger time and time again. Maybe she figured it was time to dump him like the ballast that he was, or let him go at the challenge alone.

In the water, Sally reached out, caught hold of the sub-wing, and hoisted herself up onto it just as the plane started to pick up speed.

She gave him a look.

Then, mysteriously, threw up a thumbs-up sign just before opening the door and ducking inside. With that, the plane accelerated, the props whirring and chewing air.

Lucy the Clipper cast up a hard spray of water and then lifted up out of the water, the magic of flight, an act that would never fail to impress Jet, would never cease to seem like a miracle of man's power, an emblem of his ingenuity and spirit to conquer the elements.

And here he was, on the ground.

Held fast by something so simple as water.

About ten yards down, hands shot up—twelve pairs of them, all at once, all in a line—and grabbed hold of the wall's edge.

The saurian agents began to pull themselves out of the Hudson, sputtering and gnashing their dagger teeth. They turned their heads toward Jet in unison.

CHAPTER NINE
OUTSIDE OXFORD UNIVERSITY

Amelia thanked her lucky stars that she remembered to bring the sidecar. Her bike, a 1928 Indian Scout Model 101—red as the cherry on a sundae's top—handily supported a second passenger, but not *two* additional riders.

Certainly not when one of them was a hulking ape in a professorial jacket and a tartan kilt. At present, that ape sat behind her, his tree-trunk arms damn near crushing the air out of her lungs as the bike bolted forward toward the airfield at Chalgrove. Some gawky student, by her reckoning—it was of some question whether or not the ape counted as a proper Centurion, but she with all confidence could say *that* human tangle of clothes hangers stuffed in a sleep-shirt wasn't. Whatever the case, that sidecar was a blessing—even if the kid wasn't here, she's not sure she could keep the bike up on two wheels alone with an ape riding behind.

Around them: the British countryside, splayed out. Above, pinhole stars in a black canvas—but looking ahead, she could see those darker shadows headed toward London.

Dinosaurs, she thought. *And blimps.* Reports were coming in that the same was happening all over the world—including her *de facto* home, Paris.

Being a member of the Century Club—even a new one who hadn't yet found her footing—was making for interesting business.

But it gave her a chance to do what she loved best: teach the thugs and bullies of the world that every action had consequences. She was no scientist, but she *respected* science, and knew that in the tenets of the physical world, truth could be found. That's why she had Newton's third law inked on the inside of her left arm:

For every action: an equal and opposite reaction.

You bully? You get bullied. You push? You get pushed back.

The Century Club gave her a chance to put that belief into practice: to make the theory a law, so to speak. The world was home to countless agents of evil and selfishness—sometimes it was smugglers in Paris, other times it was mad scientists with an army of floating brains. Who they were mattered little because their intention was always the same: to exploit the weak for their own gain. Hell with that.

"Miss Stone?" the ape yelled over the growl of the motorcycle.

"What is it, Professor?"

"I'm a bit new at this, as I'm not generally the *adventuring* type, and being attacked in my own office shook me up more than a little, I'm afraid, so—"

"Get to the question, Professor."

"Where are we going?"

"Up ahead," she said, "is Chalgrove airfield. Isn't much to look at but we've got a plane chartered and—"

She stopped talking. Her eyes squinted against the chill wind.

An orange glow on the horizon. It couldn't be sunrise already.

No. That glow. In the direction of Chalgrove.

It was then she saw the stars above swallowed by bands of black smoke.

Merde.

The airfield was burning.

"Change of plans," she said, seeing an opportunity to turn and taking it suddenly, stones popping and grinding beneath the sliding back tire of the Indian Scout. "I hope you have your sea legs, Professor."

The bike headed west, toward the Bristol channel.

CHAPTER TEN
HONG KONG

It all adds up, Benjamin thought, staring at the handprint-shaped receptacle in front of him, a receptacle that looked sculpted out of hematite—dark, smooth, almost mirrored. *I just wish I knew to what.*

The sum of the pieces—the culmination of the mystical equation—was something he'd been tracking for months, now. Snatching pieces of the mystery, snippets of the secret, catching them where he could and trying to piece them together.

The thefts from museums, all artifacts of lost civilizations stolen from the deepest of storerooms and antechambers.

The disruption of the ley lines: a stutter in the mystical geomantic power grid.

The disappearance of certain dinosaur fossils: not stolen, no, but quite literally gone as if they never existed.

And then the whispers of the spirits—ghosts and daemons and incubi, all hiding and running scared and saying the same troublingly vague thing: *The end is coming.*

Now, their warning seemed to prove true: dirigibles in the sky, lizard-faced "men" on the ground, dinosaurs stalking the streets and terrorizing people.

It happened in the blink of an eye, as if they had come out of nowhere. Or everywhere.

It didn't make sense. And that bothered Benjamin—like a hangnail you cannot stop picking, or a splinter that evades extraction.

This was what Benjamin Hu did. Not just for the Century Club—but for himself, for his missing parents, for the world around. Whenever he got his hands around a mystical mystery, he would not let go until it gave up its answers. Some called him obsessed.

He liked to think of it as "dedicated."

Here he finally tracked down one of the missing artifacts, an idol that looked not unlike the horn of the mythic unicorn—petrified wood with a wide base that tapered to a tip, the whole thing surrounded by a *helical edge*, like a screw.

He'd found the thief here in Hong Kong. An ape, one of Gorilla Khan's thick-skulled thugs, absconding with the key and heading toward *Kei Ling Ha Hoi:* Three Fathoms Cove. The ape was easy enough to subdue, given that Khan's "warriors" so frequently had the grace and elegance of a tumbling boulder. In fact, the ape gave up the key easy and fled.

The coward.

Benjamin was a dog with a bone: he could not let it go. And so he continued in the ape's footsteps, this (at the time) puzzling artifact in his hand—cold, and yet it vibrated as if with clandestine power. Hu descended down the cliff's edge along a walkway barely wide enough for one foot, much less two.

And there at the bottom he found a pedestal, and in that pedestal, a hole.

This enigma did not trouble him for long—a circle hole deserved a circle peg, after all. Besides, the inside of the hole was grooved. As if to fit an object with a helical edge.

Benjamin inserted the artifact into the hole.

It was, indeed a key.

But where was the door?

It didn't take long to answer that question. The ground rumbled and he heard the sound of stone gears grinding. Little stones bounded down the cliff's edge and rained upon his head—and then, right before him, cracks formed in the stone wall and the pieces began pulling back into the cliff, as if extracted piece by piece...

...revealing a passageway.

The chamber was not a deep one. Inside, Benjamin found a map carved into a flat rock wall, a map of the Earth before it belonged to man—the continents were shifted, as if the pieces moved by a child's hand and smashed into one another.

Carved lines connected the continents—lines which Hu recognized as the same ley lines that marked the world now. The land shifted, yes. But the lines never did.

Beneath the map sat another pedestal like the one outside, except on this stone pillar the keyhole was not so simple.

It was a handprint. Of hematite, as noted.

"Nothing ventured," Benjamin said, his voice echoing, "nothing gained."

He flexed his fingers, popped his knuckles, and eased his hand into the print. His right hand, for that was what the shape demanded.

It was cold. And smooth as glass.

And utterly inert, as nothing happened.

"I am the face of disappointment," he said with a sigh, and moved to retract his hand.

But it did not allow him that luxury. It happened fast—the hematite seemed to turn almost liquid, and his fingers sank into it as if sinking into mud. It formed over his digits and once more hardened. He pulled on his arm, but the pillar would not relinquish its grip.

An imperfect time, then, to host guests.

Behind him, two grunted chuckles.

Benjamin pivoted his body and met two trespassers: two more gorillas in long coats. One of them thinner and with bigger teeth and, as it turned out, also more familiar since Hu had only a half-hour before sent him scrambling away. The other was bigger, meaner, more silver in comparison to the other's merely gray.

"Greetings, gorillas," Hu said with a strained smile.

The larger gorilla dropped his knuckles to the ground and leaned forward, baring teeth. "If it isn't Detective Hu. Always sticking his finger in the nearest rat-trap."

The gray gorilla clapped his hands, hopping up and down.

"He looks to be trapped," the thinner ape said, ooking in delight. "Excellent, excellent."

"Perhaps," Benjamin began, "we can discuss our mutual discoveries like gentlemen?"

The silverback licked his chompers as the other drew a short-bladed dagger, its jewel-forged blade of familiar origin to Benjamin.

Both of them advanced on Benjamin as he tried again to wrench his hand free from its trap. "I suppose not."

They attacked.

CHAPTER ELEVEN
NEW YORK CITY

Jet ran.

He ran wishing he had his jetpack. He ran wishing he had a pair of pistols tucked into his forearm holsters. He ran wishing that his two friends and cohorts—or, at least, people he *thought* were friends and cohorts—hadn't just hopped in a plane and taken off for destinations unknown.

Most of all, he wished he wasn't afraid of water.

Because he was pretty sure that his hydrophobia had just cooked his goose.

River on his left, city on his right, he pounded pavement. In the distance he heard the screams of New Yorkers and dinosaurs alike. Other noises rose and fell: a bell clanging, the siren from a police car's running board, the thrum of dirigible engines as they anchored atop skyscrapers. And behind him came the sounds of footsteps.

The creepy thing: those footsteps weren't running. Not like he was. But they were chasing him just the same. Eerie human-faced saurians, a dozen of them, walking in stock step with one another—

It hit him. The feeling. The radiating pulse of warmth and greenhouse dampness and that voice echoing in his mind: WHY RUN? JUST LET GO.

The tension withdrew from his legs like snake venom sucked from a wound—they turned floppy and felt out of touch like he didn't have legs down there at all but just a pair of pin-wheeling fettuccine noodles.

That's when he saw the object in the sky.

At first he thought—*it's one of those flying dinosaurs come to swoop down and scoop me up in its lizard beak and carry me away to its nest somewhere*—but then the hum of the engines and the sparkling glint of the setting sun on whirring propellers became clear.

Lucy dropped back down out of the sky, flying over the Hudson and straight toward Jet.

The psychic waves washed over him like a tide, a tide with a mean undertow, and for a moment he couldn't even see Lucy at all. Couldn't see the plane, couldn't see the city, and instead he saw flashes of raindrops dangling from oversized leaves, saw iron bars thick as a baby's arm, saw a muddy footprint in soggy earth that was certainly not human...

But then he heard a sound: *POOMP.*

Followed by a: *CLANG.*

Everything snapped back to focus as he caught sight of Sally standing in the open doorway on the left side of the plane, a doorway that wasn't in the original Boeing design but that afforded her...

...well, a chance to do exactly what she just did.

She fired a grappling hook from a hand-made launcher. A bonafide Sally Slick special (though these days, weren't they all?).

She didn't fire at Jet directly. Rather, she blasted the gleaming steel tri-pronged hook at about ten yards in front of him. It clanged against the ground and, with the momentum of the plane, fast dragged along the macadam next to the river.

It whipped toward Jet lickety-split.

He had one chance.

Any normal man or woman might not have had a shot—but he was Jet Black, born at the turn of the century, the spirit of the sky made manifest. He was a Centurion. A hero of the age born with special reflexes and a gift for finding his way into the sky.

So as the grappling hook bounced across the ground toward him like a stone whipping across the surface of a pond, and as the voice continued throttling his mind — GIVE IN LET GO GIVE IN LET GO — Jet gritted his teeth and leapt.

His hands closed on empty air.

Oh no.

He'd missed his shot. His one shot.

But then suddenly, fast as anything, he felt himself yanked forward and drawn suddenly up into the air, passing swiftly over the heads of the saurian cabal—their mirthless razor-maw grins and dead gazes tilting toward him as he whipped past.

Upside-down.

One prong of the hook caught Jet and hooked his belt, the tip pointing down toward his thigh. He was caught in mid-air, wind buffeting his small body as the plane got lift and the island of Manhattan passed by. The booming voice in his mind faded quickly, suggesting that these mysterious malefactors of the mind operated by proximity above all else.

The closer the saurians were, the more dangerous they became.

Good to know.

But Jet wasn't able to savor this nugget of wisdom, for he was being dragged behind a Yankee Clipper by a grappling hook caught around his belt. A belt whose safety and stability was never tested under this kind of duress.

At least I'm flying, he thought.

The plane soared over the Hudson. Toward the Statue of Liberty.

A Yankee Clipper. Heavily modified, by the looks of it. A Hawaiian hula girl painted along the side, the fading image showing the girl laying on her side, thrusting out her coconut bra, offering the viewer a cartoonish and ever-obvious wink.

Gorilla Khan knew that plane. Rage bubbled up inside him like lava from an earthen fracture. He and his giganotosaurus had crossed the Brooklyn Bridge and were now poised over Battery Park when the plane flew past.

Something appeared to be dangling behind it. A person, perhaps.

The Conquerer Ape did not see a person, however.

He saw *bait.* A worm dangling on a hook.

Gonga called up from the ground—

"Should I call upon our, ahhh, our pilots? The biplanes are ready to detach, Mighty Khan." Gonga offered his obsequious smile.

"No," Khan growled. "I have a much better idea."

They must not escape, he said.

He told Gonga what to do.

Jet struggled to turn himself the right way, to extract the hook from his belt and hopefully use his arm strength to stay anchored, but the drag was just too strong.

And in facing the opposite way of the plane, he was the first to see.

A trio of flying shapes rising up from the city and falling in behind Lucy.

Not planes. Oh no.

Flying dinosaurs. *Pterodactyls.*

Impossible that they'd catch up to a plane with propellers, a plane like Lucy who was meant to move along at a good clip—

But perhaps they didn't have to. Because beneath Jet passed another three pterodactyls.

And he craned his head to see more coming at him from the front of the plane, too. They were all over. As the plane dove suddenly to duck an oncoming pair of the monsters, Jet realized all too late that they didn't *need* to catch up—

Because they were everywhere.

Pterodactyls swarmed. Sally manned her home-spun launcher, a launcher primed with a long tow-rope that dead-ended in a grappling hook—and, not coincidentally, a dangling Jet Black.

Flying dinosaurs swooped toward him—she couldn't *hear* their beaks snapping on open air over the sound of the props, but she could see. And with every duck and dive and swoop of the beasts they got closer and closer.

It wouldn't be long before one of them caught his head in their jaws. His helmet was tough stuff, she'd made sure of that, but she didn't know the bite pressure of those pterodactyls. More than a gator, surely, and that meant they could crush his skull like a grape.

Sally knew she had to do something now. Something crazy. *This is who you are. This is what you do.*

She marched to the front of the plane. The cockpit wasn't closed off like in most Clippers—she'd torn all that down and made sure that the only separation between Mack and the rest of the plane was the netting he hung there.

Sally threw open one of the lockers she'd installed there.

Mack called out: "What are you doing?"

"What I have to do," she said, withdrawing from the locker the prototype for a new jetpack she'd been working on for Jet. Wasn't just a jetpack. This was what she called a jet-wing: two boosters, yes, but also a pair of proper wings replete with flaps and ailerons like on a real plane. Was meant to give him more control up there in the sky—with a pack like this, he could thread a dang needle.

That was, if it worked properly.

Early tests had...

Well.

She didn't want to think about that now.

"No no no," Mack yelled after her. "Don't you even think about it! I'll get us out of this. I got skills, honey. You don't need to—"

But his voice was already lost to her.

Sally pulled a knife from her belt, hugging the jet-wing to her chest.

With a quick slash downward, she cut through the anchor rope on which Jet Black dangled.

Then with a running start, jumped out of the plane.

CHAPTER TWELVE
HONG KONG

Benjamin Hu did not merely *wield* his rapier.

The rapier was Benjamin and Benjamin was the rapier. The rapier was sharp, penetrating, incisive. It was not a blade in the traditional sense—it did not clumsily chop or hack away at a problem. It thrust forward, as direct as can be, perforating armor and cutting right to the heart of the matter. A philosophy Benjamin held dearly, a philosophy the blade spoke and believed.

His rapier had a hilt with a double-shell cup lacquered in silver. The design of the cup was cut with swooping metal calling to mind ghosts chasing ghosts around the base of the blade. The blade itself was signed by its swordsmith: TOMAS AIALA EN TOLEDO ANNO 1610.

It was an old weapon. But well-kept and totally restored.

The rapier leapt from its sheath with a whisper.

Hu used the tip of the sword to draw a swooping lemniscate in the air as the two apes approached—they were swiftly kept at arm's length by the blade point slicing molecules of air.

Benjamin's right hand remained firmly and uncomfortably ensconced in the handprint, however. The blade, then, held in his left.

The silverback advanced.

Again Benjamin cut ribbons out of the air. He clucked his tongue.

"It has been said that I could be a surgeon with this thing," Hu explained. "What shall we amputate today? Nose? Ear? Come closer. Perhaps I will surprise you."

The two apes stared at one another, nervous. The skinnier gray one grinned suddenly, the curve of fang over his lip, as he held up the short jewel-blade dagger, a dagger Benjamin could see was of Atlantean origin—the jeweled blade and bronze hilt gave it away. *Apes with Atlantean technology*, he thought. *It fits.*

The gray ape stepped into the breach, took a swipe with the dagger. The primate's attack was clumsy, telegraphed, more the motion of a woodsman chopping wood than a warrior executing an elegant maneuver. Hu easily blocked the dagger but the sheer power of it caused his blade to vibrate and the shockwave that traveled to his hand almost caused him to drop his rapier.

If for instance, his hand was *not* trapped inside an unyielding hematite receptacle—then that ape would've never landed a blow. Hu would've danced out of the way, back-stepping as the ungainly powerhouse struck only open air.

He did not possess just such a luxury.

Better to be proactive.

As the ape hooted and came in for another brash attack, Benjamin knew what he must do—squat thrust and lift the tip of his rapier, drawing an injurious line across the gorilla's wrist. The ape would bleed, his reflex would go off like a 21-gun-salute and the knife would clatter to the ground. Where Hu *might* be able to step on it and pull it close.

But the opportunity never presented itself.

The ape raised the blade—

And then froze. Staring at the wall. Jaw slackening. Eyes widening.

Benjamin found a warm blue glow at his back. He thought—*do not look, do not turn your back*, but when the larger silverback began to manifest the same wide-eyed awe, the itch was just too much not to scratch it. Benjamin *had* to see.

And see, he did.

The etched ley lines of the carved map began to glow with cerulean light. And at seven junction points of those lines, nexuses scattered around the world, a single image appeared repeated seven times—

It almost looked like a rune, like the Elder Futhark rune of Uruz—like an upside-down U or V with one leg longer than the other. Here, though, in the center of each were three diamond-shaped marks.

The glow grew brighter and brighter.

The nexus points, where the pseudo-runes appeared, did not correspond with any real world places—not on this map. This map was of an old world, a *truly* old world that physically did not exist anymore. But while the continents drifted, the ley lines did not—they were mystical lines mapped invisibly to the earth's secret power, and those lines never changed.

Which meant these nexus points still existed.

He just had to figure out where.

Benjamin fixed his eyes on the map. Let it burn itself into his brain—searing the memory upon the tabula rasa of his own mental canvas.

Then he shut his eyes tight, committing the map to memory—a final act like pouring cold water on a molten blade to confirm its shape.

As if on cue, the pedestal let go of his hand...

...just as the apes grabbed him and hurled him into the opposite wall. Benjamin's head cracked against a bulging rock and as the blue light of the mystical map faded to black, so too did the detective's grasp of consciousness.

CHAPTER THIRTEEN
SHARPNESS, GLOUCESTERSHIRE

They found him exactly where Amelia said they'd find him: at the Hind and Hare Pub, asleep at one of the tables, stinking of stout as an overturned pint glass sat beneath his bear paw of a hand. Drool collected in the wiry hairs of his salt-and-pepper beard.

Amelia tapped him. Gaining naught but a snort as a response.

She gave him a little push. The pint glass slipped out from under his hand, rolled off the edge of the table, and shattered.

Even *that* did not wake him.

The woman tending bar, a leathery old thing with narrow eyes and so many channels carved into her face she looked like the topographical map of a canyon seen from far above, grunted and waved them off with a dirty cloth. "He's asleep and he's blotto and like I said, we're closed. Now, get to scrambling."

"Captain," Amelia hissed in his ear. "*Captain.*"

Snort, grumble, a quick little belch that smelled of brine and ale.

Professor Khan and Edwin stood nearby, watching this scene unfold with some sense of curiosity and trepidation.

"Fine," she said, wiping her hands. She took a few steps back, and kicked out with a hard boot, toppling over the rotund man's chair—he hit the ground shoulder first, his old officer's hat rolling under the next table.

The man grumbled and reached up to the table to pull himself up—but the table tilted and flipped over onto him. He cried out in half-drunk rage, crawling out from the mess and just barely managing to get to his feet.

He rubbed his eyes. Saw Amelia.

"Oh. *You*."

"Captain Swale," she said.

"No," he said straightaway, gesticulating wildly with filthy, callused hands. "No! Not a bloody chance, no, no, never no, uh-uh, not happening, don't even *think* about it."

She smiled sweetly. "I haven't even asked yet."

"Well, whatever it is, no. Last time I got mixed up with you what happened? Half my boat, eaten by some kind of monster. And the time before that? Almost ended up with a hook for a hand after tangling with that wossname with the gears and gyros and diver's bell helmet."

"This one's easy," Amelia said. "Just a boat trip."

"Ohhhh, *just* a boat trip." Swale turned toward the ape and Edwin and threw up his hands. "You hear that, chaps? *Just a boat trip*. Heard that one before. Definitely... heard... that one..." His voice trailed off as he got a good look at Professor Khan.

"Hello," Khan said.

Swale turned toward Amelia. "That's a monkey."

"A gorilla," she corrected him. "Gorillas are apes."

"And he's wearing a suit."

"Mm."

"And a kilt."

"Also true."

"Am I still drunk?"

"You are.

"That's a big ape."

Amelia nodded. "And, point of fact, should you decide that you will *not* take us on what I assure you is a *very short* boat ride across the channel toward France, then I may have to ask that my gorilla friend use *his* powerful arms to rip *your* less-than-powerful arms out of their sockets so that he may beat you about the head and neck with them."

Swale visibly shrank, gulping loudly.

"Grr," Professor Khan said, mustering a poor facsimile of false animalistic bravado. For added benefit, he shook his wrecking ball fist.

It was enough. Swale winked. "Like I said, anything for you, Miss Stone. Anything at all. The Esmerelda is all yours and I shall captain it to your heart's delight."

"Then let's go," she said, gesturing toward the door. "Because time is of the essence."

CHAPTER FOURTEEN
NEW YORK CITY

One minute Jet was dangling from a rope by a grappling hook caught in his belt, pterodactyls swooping and shrieking at him, their bony beaks snapping just inches away from him. And the next minute he was unmoored, tumbling helmet over teakettle toward the waters below, the Statue of Liberty in the distance, facing away from him as if she were afraid to see what happened next.

He didn't understand. Did one of the flying dinosaurs sever the rope? His belt remained attached; couldn't be that.

Above him, the plane receded—or, rather, he receded from the plane but when you're falling toward earth (for the *second* time in just a handful of hours), one's perspective gets a little bit wifty. The pterodactyls continued swooping toward the plane and toward the rope—until realizing suddenly that the bait was off the hook.

And with that realization, wings turned downward and the flying monsters began to dive toward him—like gulls swooping toward a falling fish.

But then something else came shooting down out of the dark leathery wings and beastly arrow-heads: a familiar shape, limbs tucked in so that the body formed no less than a human dart.

Sally Slick hit him like a cannonball. His arms wrapped around her and suddenly it was not one of them falling toward the waters as the plane continued without them...

But *two* of them falling.

She was crazy, he thought. Certifiable. Those psychic saurians did a number on her brain, scrambling it like eggs in a skillet.

Then he saw: she had a present for him.

The setting sun glinted off the chrome and steel of the experimental jet-wing.

Jet Black let out a whoop, and tried to ignore the swarm of keening pterodactyls that dropped toward him and Sally.

It was time to fly.

Mack knew something was wrong, and that something was, he was worried about Sally. Not *normal* worried, either—no, normal worried was what he felt about Jet Black. Meaning, mostly, knew he'd be fine, had trepidations, ehhh, otherwise, out of sight, out of mind.

Sally, though...

He kept thinking, *I hope she's okay.*

And then he'd be mad at her for a moment: *What's wrong with her? Is she deranged? Did contact with those saurians leave her totally wobbly or what?*

And then ricocheting back to concern: *Please be okay, Sally.*

That's how he knew something was wrong.

Of course, that wasn't the only thing wrong. The throng of pterodactyls was just one in a long laundry list of issues, beginning with "psychic saurians" and ending with "I think Sally Slick just jumped out of a plane with a risky jetpack and also I think I have feelings for her but that makes zero sense and maybe I have the flu coming on or something."

All these thoughts were gumming up the works.

Time to shut all that down and focus—*focus, Mack!*—on getting clear of these squawking alligator-skinned parakeets.

Now, Lucy wasn't all that maneuverable—not like the Fokkers or the Hawkers or the Messerschmitts. Those were fighter planes. Lucy was either a boat with wings or a plane that floated depending on how you looked at it, but either way, it meant she wasn't particularly nimble in the air *or* in water. It was a trade-off Mack made because Lucy was comfortable, spacious, luxurious, and versatile (what with having conquered two of the elements—Mack dreamed of a day he could also slap some wheels on her and turn her into a driving machine, too).

Just the same, it didn't mean Lucy was without her tricks.

Mack popped the lid on a metal box found in the center of the pilot's wheel and thumbed the red button inside. He felt the plane shudder and then, depressing a hidden trigger on the inside of the wheel, heard the chatter of the two guns.

Sally had rigged it up. Hit a button and the very tip of the plane's tail popped off and revealed a pair of Fabrique Nationale belt-fed machine guns, each .30 caliber, each spitting bullets at whatever thought to come up on Lucy's six.

"Fill those damn iguana-birds with daylight," Mack growled, gleefully depressing the trigger. He hoped like hell he was giving Sally and Jet some cover.

Jet thought: *This is it. This is the time.*

He and Sally were bundled together, trying like the dickens to get the jet-wing straps over his shoulders and the belt cinched around his middle—but it didn't help that the wind was rushing up on them and they kept turning end over end over *end*, and that giant angry hungry flying monsters from oh-so-long-ago were swooping in and screaming at them.

They'd hit water in 30 seconds. Maybe sooner.

"Sally!" Jet yelled over the din. "Sally, I've got something—"

Whang.

A pterodactyl swooped in and Sally clocked it hard with her wrench. The flying reptile blinked and hurtled past, diving suddenly and unexpectedly toward the water.

He tried again: "—something I need to tell you—"

Above and ahead, Lucy started barking bullets out her tail-end—punching holes in those few pterodactyls that continued to trail her. Those monsters dropped like shattered kites.

Sally continued to cinch the belt, flipping switches around back.

The water below—now capturing the last pools of light before the sun set over the horizon's edge—was coming up fast.

"—Sally, I need you to know—"

He heard a *click-click-click* like a starter trying to get going and then, before he knew what was happening, *whoosh*. The jet-wing spit not fire but rather twin blasts of air. The wings extended and where once they were falling they were suddenly hovering in the air for the hair's breadth of a single second—

And then they shot up, straight up, through the swarm of dinosaurs and up into the clouds. Sally laughed and Jet hooted, and for this one mad moment, all was right with the world.

Mack felt a stab of something he hadn't felt in a long time: jealousy. He told himself that it was the aerial acrobatics—out there, Jet and Sally were performing ballet with that experimental jet-wing. Corkscrews and barrel rolls and Immelmann turns.

The way they dispatched the dinosaurs was art. This battle was about as one-sided as they came, like watching the Red Baron or Billy Bishop dogfight a sleepy pelican. The dinosaurs would chase. The jet-wing would suddenly turn—up, down, or reverse—and the dinosaurs would suddenly be slamming into one another, or would be suffering a blow to the cranium from Sally's wrench, or would get clipped in the face by a sharp pivot of Jet's wing.

Next, they set Mack up to finish the job like some mad badminton maneuver: Jet would rush straight out in front of Lucy, the half-dozen remaining pterodactyls in hot screeching pursuit. Then, just as the throng of flying reptiles were right out in front of the plane, Jet cut the engine and dropped swiftly downward.

Leaving, of course, a single precious moment where Mack could pull the trigger—the *other* trigger on his flight stick—and let fly with a chatter of bullets from the dual .30-cal Lewis guns mounted below Lucy's nose.

The pterodactyls shrieked as bullets tore through their prodigious wings.

They dropped together, a great big wounded cluster of flying reptiles. Plunging into the waters around Liberty Island.

They sent all the dinosaurs packing.

All, that is, but one.

One little flier. One little runt of a reptile.

A peteinosaurus clung to the underside of Lucy, a small collar of glowing fungus around the dinosaur's neck. Where the pterodactyls had a 20-foot wingspan, the peteinosaurus had only two feet from wing-tip to wing-tip.

The little creature, with its bony toucan-like beak and its small but razor-sharp claws, settled in and pressed its leathery belly against the metal of Lucy's underside.

The dinosaur had a mission. It did not understand this mission, not really—after all, the beast had a brain the size of a stunted acorn. But it did not need to understand the mission. It merely needed to complete it.

CHAPTER FIFTEEN
THE ESMERELDA

Fog clung to the water, crawling along it as if it had a mind all its own. In the distant and the dark, the shrieks of dinosaurs carried through the murk.

It bothered Edwin. Professor Khan could see that much. Amelia seemed to deny and defy her fear, while Captain Swale just pulled up the high collars on his sailor's coat and disappeared into himself as he steered the old steamer boat.

Khan, however—and he dared not say this to anyone, dared not even show such a thing for the crassness it presented—was energized.

This is most exciting, he thought, his heartbeat mimicking those jungle drums. With every screech came a jolt of adrenalin and with every jolt of adrenalin he felt woozy with exhilaration.

It was madness. He should be afraid. He should want again to be cloistered back at the university. Safe among his books. Comfortable nestled in academia's womb.

But here he was, out in the middle of the Bristol Channel on a rickety old steamer ship—what Swale claimed was one of the last operating steamboats in England—with no sign of shore, no sign of anything in fact but the stars above and the bands of gray fog.

And dinosaurs far off in the distance. Screeching and whooping.

Punctuated by the occasional dull *whumpf* of something exploding.

Amelia snapped Khan out of his reverie.

"You all right, Professor?"

"Oh. Well. Yes. I... think so." *I know so.*

"You're not suited to this life. Is that it?"

He offered a toothy smile. "Perhaps, Miss Stone."

"This life is all I know."

"So you are suited to it, then."

"Maybe." She popped a Zagnut bar from her pocket, tore the end off it with her teeth. Offered him a bite which he politely refused—he preferred a salad of leafy greens if he was being honest, and a sweet tooth was never really his thing. She spoke as she chewed: "Maybe it's just that I don't know any other way. Have you ever heard of *Le Monstre Aux Yeux Verts*?"

Translation: The Green-Eyed Monster.

He had, in fact, heard of such a figure—perhaps not a monster out of ancient myth but certainly a monster in the atrocities he visited upon the world. *Le Monstre* was a vicious crime lord. His face burned by fire. Rumor had it that he wore half a mask of pig iron to cover that side of his ruined countenance.

Professor Khan had studied Amelia's file. *Le Monstre* showed up again and again: her quest to find him bordered on the obsessive.

"I have not heard of this... monster," Khan said, unsure as to why he lied. Perhaps to see what she might say?

"I've been hunting him on and off since I was a child. My parents..." Her voice trailed off. She stopped chewing, the chocolate bar forming a lump in her cheek. "Anyway."

"So, how did you get out of London? You were there when the invasion happened?"

"Mm," she said, once more gnawing the sticky candy bar. "It was chaos. Above ground and worse, above the skies. I saw Khan's dread airship, the Blackspire, hovering above Parliament. A great light flashing down, siphoning bodies. That's how we were taken. The other Centurions. Vacuumed up into the belly of that beast."

"Really." *Khan. He of your genetic heritage. You knew he was involved.* Still. So much easier not to think about it. "I wonder what they're doing, there."

"I don't know. But eventually someone's going to have to get on that airship. Someone's going to have to go up and rescue all the..." She quieted and stared ahead with wide eyes.

Professor Khan followed her gaze.

Out there, on the water, a radiant green glow diffuse through the mist. No small glow, either—as they approached, they could see it rise higher and higher, the luminescent plume growing. In the ambient green light they could just make out shapes swirling. Flying pterosaurs—dozens of them ducking and diving inside the light.

Still a few miles away. But visible here just the same.

"What am I looking at, Miss Stone?" Khan asked.

Amelia swallowed the clot of candy. Her face wore the dueling masks of discomfort and curiosity. "I don't know, Professor."

Suddenly, she was off like a shot. Hurrying down deck to the ship's wheelhouse, where Swale stood hunched over the steamer console, puffing on a meerschaum pipe carved to look like Aeolus blowing heaving winds from his puckered mouth.

Khan followed after.

"Do you see what I see, Captain?" Amelia asked.

"I do, I do, of course I do. I've got both eyes."

"Both of them goggled behind cups of liquor," Khan added not-quite-under-his-breath.

Swale ignored the comment. "I'll steer us around."

"No," Amelia said. "Get us closer."

"Closer? *Closer?* Are ya daft?" He laughed but no mirth lived in that sharp bark. "Let me share with you a lesson about survival, little missy. Whenever one happens to see a strange glow out in the middle of the Bristol Channel swirling with creatures from before recorded time, it behooves one to go as far the hell around that as one can *possibly* manage. There you go. Little tip from your Captain. Take it or leave it."

"Leave it," Amelia said with a shrug. "Go closer, Captain. Don't worry, I don't want to get *that* close. But we need to see. We need to know."

Swale shot a look toward Khan. "You got anything to say, big fella?"

"Do as the lady demands," Khan said, trying to snarl as he said so.

Swale nodded, then, and rubbed his eyes. "Onward it shall be."

CHAPTER SIXTEEN
HONG KONG

A splash of ice water across the face did the trick—Benjamin Hu gasped suddenly and lurched into consciousness. Water down his face. Dripping off his chin.

He blinked away the water. The world resolved into focus.

Across from him sat a smiling man. Hawk's beak of a nose. Round broom-handle chin with a slight cleft in it. All in all a decidedly *long* man, lean and narrow as if stretched from the top of his slicked-back hair to the soles of his feet.

Benjamin tried to move. His hands were bound behind the chair.

Feet fixed to the legs of said chair.

"Ah," the smiling man said. His accent crisply British. "Welcome, Mister Hu. I have followed your work with great enthusiasm. You are a talented man. Keen of mind. Sharp of eye! The very epitome of mystical deduction."

"Deduction," Benjamin said. That word lolling about on his tongue. "Let me deduce, then. I see a man in a white suit with a pink rose in his lapel. I see a man with a broad smile and—ahh, yes, as my own eyes adjust I note that *yours* are green. And, that hand of yours. Right hand. The skin on the back rough, a patch of scar tissue that looks like the bumpy ground on an old pebble road. That *might* have been caused by, say, reaching foolishly into the mouth of a trapped Foo Dog statue left behind at—oh, I'm just conjuring this out of thin air—the mouth of a hidden tunnel in the Thousand Dragons Temple."

"Out of thin air, you say."

Hu decided to cut to the chase: "Gerard Spears. I wondered when we'd meet."

Spears. Long a rival to Hu's own efforts—a man constantly plundering archaeological sites and popping up on the blackest of markets and strangest of bazaars with mystical artifacts. Often sold quite cheaply and yet, curiously, sporting powerful effects.

"It is nice, isn't it? After all this time." That smile on Spears' face refused to waiver. "We almost met about three years back."

"The night market. If that fortune teller hadn't backed her donkey cart out—"

"I paid her to do that!"

"Did you now?"

"I did, I did." Spears chuckled. "Quite proud of that one. Timed very well. She was a horrid little woman. Had a tiny capuchin monkey with two tails. Rabid, I say. Always drooling and foaming at the mouth. So it goes."

One of the apes from before—the wormy one with the dagger—appeared through a small chamber door, carrying tea on a silver tray. A curious juxtaposition. "Tea?" Spears asked.

Hu ignored the question. "That night you stole a pocketwatch."

"Yes, yes. Made by Francois Leipine. Delightful little trinket."

"*Trinket*? It had the power to stop time."

"Mm," Spears muttered, dropping sugarcubes into his teacup and then urging the ape to pour the tea over it. The fragrant smell of green tea and jasmine leaves bloomed in the air. "With a kiss, if I recall. Open the watch, give the clock-face a little kiss and—time stops."

"You sold it for a pittance."

"Did I? I don't recall."

"Another deduction: you like chaos."

"An interesting theory!"

"You must come from wealth or have little interest in it. Because that's not why you're in this game. You're like a man taking joy in handing a child a loaded revolver."

"That *does* sound fun. I should try that some day!"

The skinny ape retreated from the room, tray in hand.

"You're a bad man, Spears."

"And you're a good man, Hu, and that's why we dance so well together. You win some, I win some, and together we weave and pirouette through the crowd."

"Why am I here, Spears? Why are we finally meeting?"

Long slurp of tea. "What, no more deduction? Mm. I may pout."

"I can deduce we're on a boat." The ground dipped and shifted beneath the chair—that feeling of being on the water was one where the brain seemed stable but the body did not. It was this disharmony between the two that gave one a measure of sea-sickness—Hu was not himself a sufferer but had seen even the strongest men chum the ocean with their vomit.

"Yes! An old Chinese junk, actually."

Hu attempted to undo his hands or unmoor his feet. To no avail. "And I can deduce that whatever is going on with these Atlantean artifacts—"

"Well-seen, sir, well-seen!"

"—involves the crass and clumsy hand of the Conqueror Ape, Khan. Which means you're tangled up in the same net as he. What I don't understand is *why*."

"You've already answered your own question," Spears said. "You said it yourself: I take pleasure in giving dangerous weapons to stupid children."

"Does Khan know you think so low of him?"

A twinkle in those green eyes. "Does it matter?"

"Why me? Why bring me here?"

"I wanted to meet you."

"When do you pull your pistol on me and kill me?" Hu asked. Seeing Spears' surprise, he further explained: "I can smell the gun oil. Recently cleaned, I assume?"

Spears pulled a revolver from under the table. A Webley Mark III .455 caliber.

Sure enough, the blued metal barrel gleamed with fresh oil.

Then—

Hammer drawn back. *Click.*

The barrel floated at chest level.

"I'm quite sorry, Benjamin. I don't *want* to kill you. I've enjoyed our time together. Our little cat-and-mouse. But those days are done, I'm afraid. The world as we know it is ending. The concrete jungle will be replaced by a very real one and from that jungle, a new empire will grow. I'm promised a very comfortable chair in that empire. You, however, were not."

"Don't you want to know what else I've deduced?"

Another flash in Gerard's eye. "Oh. A game. I like games."

"I thought you might. I smell something else beneath the gun oil."

"Do tell."

The gun still hovered, pointed at his heart.

Benjamin smiled. "I prefer to *show*, rather than tell."

He quickly shifted his body hard to the left, letting dead weight drop the chair onto its side—he did so just as a shot rang out from the Webley, splintering a beam at the back of the room. Many things needed to happen, and happen fast for this to work—

As his shoulder cracked hard against wood plank he jerked his shoulder and forced a piece of magnesium flint into the palm of one of his still-bound hands.

Time for an old magic trick, he thought.

Spears was up. Knocking his own chair back.

Hu let loose with his magic trick—

The Hands of Fire.

Not real magic. Nothing mystical about it. Just a quick bright flash of fire emerging from the magician's hands to startle and dazzle the audience. Entertaining for them.

And for an opponent, deliciously distracting.

But that was not the point. Not today.

Today, Benjamin just needed the fire.

Because what he smelled beneath the resin stink of gun oil was the stink of cordite—a smokeless propellant used these days to replace the gunpowder of old. They'd been making it in here—he could smell that faint acrid tang, that subtle stink of sulfur beneath it all.

It was all over the floor.

It caught fire.

Spears yelped like a kicked puppy as trails of loose and forgotten cordite burned like fiery snakes across the floor. It was more than just a distraction, though: as Benjamin twisted his body hard to snap the chair and free his legs, he could see from his vantage point on the floor the look of panic that passed over Gerard's face like a cloud passing in front of the sun.

Hu's adversary bolted from the room.

Not a good sign.

Hu had hoped for a distraction, but this was more than that: the serpent trails of loose powder burned swift toward a trap door in the corner.

The fire chased its own tail and disappeared through the crack—probably dropping a cascade of sparks and embers.

Time, then, for further deduction.

When Spears ran, he seemed to do so with little care of whether or not Hu died. Why? Because Hu was going to be dead anyway. *Why?* Because those loose trails of cordite weren't random. They were making cordite. Here. Then packing it in barrels, probably. And those barrels were almost assuredly stuffed below deck.

Thing about cordite was, it burned fast, hot, and bright—but it wasn't particularly explosive. It offered just enough punch to push a bullet out of a gun's barrel at over a thousand feet-per-second.

That was, unless the cordite was stuffed into tight-fitting containers.

The junkboat's belly was packed with one big boom.

Hu could not get his wrists free. Pumping his legs, he pushed himself across the floor—that gunpowder stink filling his nose—and slammed hard into the wall. But that let him get his legs beneath him, and he pushed himself to a stand like a wobbly infant.

Then he ran.

Shoulder through the door.

Out onto the deck.

Hu's vision was framed suddenly by a bright rectangle of sun that bled across everything, but he didn't have time to stop and figure out whether or not someone was standing there with a gun or knife pointed at his head, heart, or other parts.

Footsteps. Screams. Panic and alarm all around him as his legs churned forward. Already the sound of splashing rose up from every side: gorillas and sailors hitting the water.

Benjamin planned on doing the same thing himself.

But he didn't have time. Because the whole boat exploded beneath him and then the sea reached up to grab him and drag him toward its watery embrace.

CHAPTER SEVENTEEN
THE ESMERELDA

"That's Lundy Island," Swale said.

Amelia took the spyglass.

They all stood at the bow of the steamship, staring ahead. Barely believing what they were seeing. Ahead were the cliffs of Lundy, and above them—on the island itself—rose great spires of emerald light, but light that did not operate as light normally would.

It rose tall and straight until, some hundreds of feet in the air, the light began to bend—not smooth curves but calling to mind the way gems might stack upon or lay next to one another.

At times the space caught in the center of the light would pulse with a crackle of electricity and creatures would emerge from the portal. Beasts from before time. From before man. Perhaps from before *mammal*. Some flew. Some crawled. Some stampeded about.

Leathery things with large wings. Monsters with massive maws and tree-trunk legs and tiny arms. Creatures armored with scale and plate that looked more like rock than flesh.

The light illuminated them—in the view of the spyglass she could see these things. Dinosaurs, she knew. They did not belong in this place. In this time.

They were traveling a long way to get here.

Which made that thing—the great big maw of light—a gateway.

Lundy Island, Swale explained, was a curious place. Owned by self-proclaimed "king" Martin Coles Harman, who minted two coins of currency, the Puffin and the Half-Puffin, and further demanded that any traveling to the island pay a toll or tax. All that ended a few years back, of course: Britain was less than pleased with even the tiniest threat to its supremacy and empire.

Few lived there now. Folks manned the two lighthouses and St. Helena, the church. A few other estate houses dotted the island but, all told, fewer than 50 people inhabited Lundy these days. Most of them were eccentric and strange: wealthy iconoclasts who wanted a place to call their own away from the mainland.

"I wonder what happened to all those folks," Edwin said. Shivering against the cold.

"We have to help them," Amelia said. "Eccentric weirdos or no. Whatever's going on up there above those cliffs is very bad. It's the invasion. It's the source."

"You're all mad," Swale growled.

"Getting closer will let us find out more," Khan said. The jungle pulse throbbed in his veins. For a hair's breadth of a single moment he imagined himself scaling those cliffs by himself. Wind howling in his ears. His hands ready to grab, wrench, *crush*. But that balloon popped fast, lanced by a hard spear of pragmatism. "And yet..."

"And yet?" Amelia asked.

"... we're not particularly well-equipped. Edwin and Swale don't deserve to be thrown into the mix. I've never... been properly tested in the field. You're our only shot, Miss Stone."

She stared at him. He knew her response. Having read her file, he knew her modus operandi: evil was evil because it exploited good. The bad guys of the world were synonymous with bullies. They took advantage and they needed to pay.

Amelia Stone was a fighter. She took risks—wild, uncalculated risks.

She was about to say something. Khan could see that she'd reached a decision.

But then—

A distant splash.

She quickly tilted the glass downward just in time to catch something—a large dark shape, a glistening hump—sink into the mist-capped sea.

"Professor," she said.

"Yes?" the ape asked, idly stroking his chin whiskers.

"We can all agree that what we're seeing are dinosaurs."

"We can. Superorder *dinosauria*. 'Terrible lizard,' though, of course, dinosaurs are not strictly lizards."

"And some dinosaurs could fly, some walked on land—"

He finished her thought. "Some swam in the sea."

"We're not going to that island," she said. "You're right, Professor. We're not prepared. We need to..." He could see how painful this was. "Regroup. Swale, turn this boat around. Take us to France. We need to catch a plane. We need other Centurions. Because this is happening not just here but everywhere. This is an invasion. I believe our whole world is in danger and if we rush in now half-cocked we're just going to get ourselves killed, captured, or worse." She drew a deep breath. "Also, something is in the water with us, and I don't want to find out what."

PART TWO:
HEROES ATTACK!

CHAPTER EIGHTEEN
NEW YORK CITY

The room lay in ruins. Wrecked from corner to corner. A table splintered. Fabric torn from chairs, the wooden legs and arms marred with bite marks. Parts of the marble floor cratered. At the center of all this ruination stood the Conqueror Ape.

His chest heaved as he struggled to find some measure of calm. He wished for a moment that he could call for Gonga and have that simpering pale wimp bring him a trio of their psychosaur allies—if only so they could give to him a fraction of what they gave to all their captives from the Century Club and beyond.

But Khan knew that such a journey was not his to take. The psychosaur effect did not work on the apes. He didn't know why and didn't much care—it was what it was.

Serenity was outside his grasp. The best he could hope for was some rough semblance of composure. And any chance of that was ruined the moment Gonga stepped through the door.

Before the albino could speak, Khan growled: "If this is not good news, I suggest you turn around and go the other way." *Before I unmoor your head from its shoulders and eat it like a breadfruit.*

All this time, the bad news kept piling on. First, several Centurions escaped the psychic snare. Yes, fine, *most* of them had been dispatched, their minds neatly contained and awaiting what would come. But those who had escaped: Mack Silver? Jet Black? *Sally Slick?* Three of the Century Club's pre-eminent heroes. Figured it'd be them. Worse, they escaped the trap *again*—deftly evading the pterodactyl attack over the harbor.

Then, some second-stringers slipped the noose, too. That woman, the one who gave *Le Monstre* such trouble. What was her name? Amanda? Amelia? And then that mystic detective based out of Hong Kong. Who? Benjamin something-or-other. At least *he* appeared to be dead. He couldn't have survived that explosion. Could he? Then again, Spears claimed that no one found a body. And with these irritating heroes, you'd damn well better find a body.

Out of all of it though, the part that galled him the most was that Son-of-Khan was still out there. That operation had been botched from the start. Botu had much to make up for. His hide would be flayed if he did not correct the error.

My poor son, the Conqueror thought. *Domesticated. Enslaved. Doomed.*

The child would serve at his side yet. And then, when it was time for the Conqueror Ape to take off his helmet and give up this life—either by choice or by an honorable death—the boy would claim the seat of power.

"Ahh," Gonga began, spidering his fingers together. "Yes, yes, we have news—ah, *good* news, of course, Lord and Conqueror Ape, Mighty Khan. Plan, ahhh, *C* seems to have worked."

Khan's eyebrows raised. "Did it?"

"It did. The peteinosaur is... in transit."

"And the psychosaurs can track it?"

Gonga showed grinning teeth. "Yes. The... fungus makes it so."

"Excellent. Then we are close. The last flies will be plucked out of the ointment soon enough." Khan almost didn't want to ask but—"And word of my son?"

"...nothing, Mighty Khan. But soon! Soon I am, ahhh, sure."

Khan's mood darkened. His victories would remain bland and toothless until his son was by his side. Until they could together gaze down at this ruined, soulless world and claim it as their own with wild hoots and snarling barks.

"It is time to speak to the conquered city," Khan said.

"Of course!" Gonga clapped his hands. "Right this way, then, we shall clothe you in your ceremonial garb and you can speak to the subjugated masses from atop the—"

"No. No ceremonial garb." He lifted the armor draped across his chest to examine it—the nicks and scratches and little spots of mud and blood. Same with his helmet. "They need to be shown the face of war. The face of *wildness*. I will not clean myself for them."

It was then that Khan moved to the far end of the room, where the wind howled in through a broken window—a window he broke with a chair leg only ten minutes before. He gazed down over the city, a city splayed out before him like a precious kill gutted and flayed.

And then he jumped out, framed by the last glass shards and then taking them with him. His hand caught the lip of the window and then, roaring, Khan climbed down the side of the Empire State Building to speak to his slaves.

The street, choked with people. All of them shoulder to shoulder, elbow to elbow, quivering, wide-eyed, jaws slacked. A look of fear. A look of *defeat*. A look they would've worn naturally, Khan assured himself, but just to be sure, the psychosaurs stood placed every hundred yards or so. Each a psychic beacon—a net of sorts—capturing the throngs of humans.

Others hid in their homes and apartments.

And in the distance Khan heard the occasional *whumpf* as something exploded—a plane taken down by a pack of pterosaurs, a police car thrown into a bank by a quick jerk of a triceratops' head, a fire escape filled with fleeing humans torn down by ape soldiers.

The city was his. Pockets of resistance would soon be crushed.

And the age of the human would draw to a close.

First they dispatched those most exceptional specimens of the human race—the Centurions, yes, but also those Shadows who might seek opportunity in this time of chaos. Der Blitzmann put up quite the fight, and a handful of psychosaurs fell prey to his *electric* depredations. Still—for all the time that fool spent on building his electro-suit, none of it protected that most vulnerable of things: *his mind*.

The Red Wraith was easy enough to dispatch. So too were El Cid, the Duchess of Blood, and the Skull Flyer.

The true surprise was Doctor Methuselah. Khan's own creator. When they finally tracked him to his isolated Arctic lair, he had... changed. It was as if his thousand years were finally catching up to him. His flesh showed the deep canyons of age. His eyes sat sunken inside his head. He didn't have the strength. Didn't have the *fight*.

They didn't even need the psychosaurs to bring him in. He came willingly. Barely able to walk out of his own base. His so-called "mathemagic" failed him. Khan's wildness within finally triumphed. The old fool. Khan knew this day would come!

And now, the humans stood before him. Prey. Slaves. A workforce to build his new empire, and a food source to feed his dinosaur army.

Next to him, his Giganotosaurus—Mount-of-Khan—stirred, restless, appropriately hungry given Khan's line of thought. It wanted to lurch forward and eat. Before the beast waited a street full of appetizers and amuse-bouches. The only thing stopping the beast was the sheer lack of life, thanks to the psychosaurs. The humans weren't running, and so the dinosaur did not find the instinct to give chase.

Now was not the time.

This was the time for Khan to address his new subjects.

As Khan opened his mouth to speak, Gonga appeared suddenly by his side on the dais, shoving a tall microphone in his face. Khan stared at it like it was a rotten banana.

"I don't want—" his voice rang out over the crowd and he quickly clamped his hand down on the mic. "I *don't* want to use their technology. I do not require it. My voice is loud as it needs to be, Attaché Gonga."

"Ahh, yes, of course, but—not only will this amplify your voice so that those hiding may hear, it will also go out over the *radio*. So that any who tune in will know who has conquered them. Your voice, ahh, cast far and wide. Your conquest made *clear*. You see?"

Khan did see. For once, Gonga was good for something.

As a reward, he didn't cuff him behind the ear. He merely shoved Gonga off the dais.

And then, Khan spoke to his people as leader, conqueror, and monster.

CHAPTER NINETEEN
OVER THE PACIFIC

The whir of the propellers. The morning light gleaming on the Pacific like spilled diamonds. Lucy flying smooth with only a few bumps and shudders as they hit rare pockets of turbulence. Mack should've been happy.

But instead, he felt restless. His guts were like a trembling tower of tea-cups, each about to tumble over and spill their contents. He knew why. But he didn't want to admit it. Didn't want to think too hard about how *chummy* Sally and Jet had been since last night. Since the two of them came rocketing up on that brand spankin' new jet-wing, finally re-entering the plane and dancing around like they just won a Lindy-Hop contest.

The two of them were throttled on adrenalin. How could they not be? Those aerial maneuvers. Those damn dinosaurs. The ballet of bullets and screeches and wind rushing around twirling wings. Not even the most stalwart hero could pretend he wasn't a little juiced from the whole kit-and-kaboodle.

Mack adjusted his goggles, took a look at the fuel gauge.

Almost to the bare bottom. Drinking the last few drops.

That was a problem—or, *would* be, if Lucy wasn't retrofitted with a sec-ond tank. Made her a little heavier, sure, and also upped any fire risk. But just the same, it made sure they didn't have to stop for refueling on a long flight like this one—from New York City to the Hawaiian Islands, where the Century Club's final bastion awaited.

The idea for the two tanks came from, of course, Sally.

And she did all the design and work, too.

Sally, Sally, Sally. Everywhere, Sally.

Whatever. Fine. *Put her out of your head, Mackie Boy.*

Mack hopped out of his seat, stretched, took a nip of some ripple he had in a small flask stashed under the chair, and then headed to the back of the plane to flip the lever that switched the tank priority.

Down from the cockpit. Into the belly of the beast—he and Sally fitted ol' Lucy with all the amenities a good Centurion team would need: global map, conference table, kitchen, radio room, workshop. They had it all up here. It was, in its own way, a mobile clubhouse.

Jet sat off in the radio nook, earphones over his head. He had a glass of orange juice in his hand and he gave a friendly wave as Mack passed. Mack fake-smiled back and mumbled, "Yeah, good morning to you too, *ace*."

Back down another set of steps, Mack's feet ringing on metal stairs, hands sliding across metal railings. Through the cargo bay. Past the head.

Down to the fuel lever.

And there stood Sally, grabbing the lever with both hands and cranking it from left to right with a groan. She saw Mack coming, gave him a nod and a smile. "Morning."

"Uh-huh. I bet. What the hell are you doing down here?"

She cocked an eyebrow. "What does it look like? You know, I knew you weren't a morning person, but I figured I could at least get a thank you."

"Not from me."

"Well, how-do-you-do."

"Don't get smart with me."

"I'll get smart any time I damn well feel like it, Silver."

"I don't have to put up with this, *Slick*."

He turned heel-to-toe to march back to the cabin. Sally caught his arm, spun him around.

"What curdled your milk this morning?" she asked with a scowl.

"*You* did."

"Oh. Did I?" Her hands went to her hips. Fists planted there like deep-dug fence posts. She had that patented Sally Slick lean, a lean that said she was going to give you a good dressing down or maybe just clock you over the noggin with a wrench and knock you out cold. "Why don't you enlighten me, Silver. Tell me how I ruined your day."

"Well for one thing you, you, you—" He found himself stammering. Which was not like him at all. Curse this woman! "You *stole* my job. Here. Look. That lever, that's my job. I'm the guy in the cockpit. With the controls. I control things! That's... that's what I do, Slick. And here you are, robbing me of that." He leaned in, lowered his voice. "How the hell'd you know she was running low on Tank One, anyhow?"

"I could hear it."

"You could *hear* it. Like you got a sixth sense for it."

"Don't I?"

Damn, she's impressive.

"Yeah, yeah," he said, waving her off. "Pull the other one. It's got bells on it."

"You think I'm pulling your leg?"

"I do," he lied. But he was angry. So what?

"You're a piece of work, Silver."

"You're a pain in my neck, Slick."

She grabbed him by the back of the head and even when her lips found his, he was still half-sure she was about to slam his head into her knee or against the side of the plane.

But the only violence done was against his mouth—her mouth sought out his and he whirled her around to get a better grip. But then *she* whirled *him* around, too—a constant waltz of oneupsmanship. He heard his own voice inside his head: *I control things.*

He whirled her around again.

Just in time to hear someone clear their throat nearby.

Jet Black. Staring at them, pale as a sheet. Glass of orange juice trembling in his hand. "Sorry to... interrupt. I just thought you should come and hear this."

Jet felt rattled, topsy-turvy, like his jetpack had blown out and he was falling again, end-over-end, the ground rushing up to meet him—except here he sat perfectly still inside the Clipper's radio room, a comfortable chair beneath him.

He set his glass of juice down, took a deep breath. Flipped a switch.

"I was scanning the world band. Just to see—" He cleared his throat. "Just to see what was happening, what people were saying, if this whole thing really was global or what. That's when I found this."

He tuned into a frequency, cranked the volume.

"...the age of the human is now complete. You have done enough with this world. You have spread your foul influence, your diseases, your disruptive mechanisms across the globe—and now the end has come for you."

"Khan," Sally said with a sneer.

"Should've known he was behind this," Mack said.

"I for one am a little surprised," Sally said. "Khan's tried this before. Never successful. Between you and me, I don't think he's very smart. More warrior than strategist."

"Guys," Jet said, exhorting them to quiet down. He wanted to say more, wanted to burn the image of Mack and Sally kissing out of his mind with a soldering iron, but now was not the time. "Shhh."

The Conqueror Ape's speech continued:

"...your cities shall crumble and the primeval world shall rise anew. The beasts of land and sea and sky will once more dominate. Once humanity set its pink wriggling toes on the beaches of this world, your wretched civilizations came and pushed all the other creatures to the margins. Now it is *our* turn to push back. A dominion ruled by ape and dinosaur. The past into the present!" Here, Khan roared, and everybody covered their ears.

Mack started to say something but Jet punched him in the thigh to shut him up.

That felt good. And the glower on Silver's face granted Jet momentary respite.

"...but here we do you a mercy. We will not push you to the edge of extinction as you have with the other creatures of the world in your quest for supremacy. You can be a part of our new world if you choose. You can build our temples. You can pick the lice from our fur. You can fight in our arenas. And if you go against us, you can be food for the monsters."

Khan roared again. And then finished his speech with:

"I am Mighty Khan! I am Conqueror Ape! This world is *mine*."

And then the broadcast ended.

The three of them sat there. Looking at one another awkwardly. They knew they should be planning and plotting and trying to decode Khan's speech to see if they could suss out more information than what was merely spoken, but...

Silver barked a sharp laugh. "Well. Enough of that big dumb ape. Now we know whose finger is on the trigger of this thing. I've, uhh, got a plane to fly."

"Mm," Sally said, standing up, popping the wrench off her belt and giving it a quick twirl. "I, uhhh, have to go polish my tools. Oil them up. Hawaii. All that salt spray. Don't want them to rust."

"We good?" Mack asked—but the question was aimed squarely at Jet. Jet figured it meant more than just asking whether or not the meeting was over.

Best Jet could manage was a shrug with a muttered, "Peachy-keen."

Sally and Mack split, both going opposite ways. Leaving Jet behind with that topsy-turvy feeling inside his heart.

Onward, then. To Hawaii.

CHAPTER TWENTY
HAWAII

Professor Khan pressed his face against the porthole window. The breath from his nose steaming up the glass.

The island down there called to him. He saw black lava stone jutting out into the surf. Palm trees and wispy pine swaying in the wind. White sand beaches. Smoke off in the distance—from sugar cane production, most likely. The place had a wildness about it, as if it were the untamed heart of the island chain.

"Kauai," Amelia said, coming up alongside him and catching a glimpse herself.

"Yes," Khan answered, "I know. Known as Taua'i in old Hawaiian. Discovered by Captain Cook. Last island to join the Hawaiian Kingdom under King Kamehameha. Fertile earth. Good for growing all manner of fruits. Particularly good at growing sugar cane."

All facts, data, details. But that wasn't what was speaking to Khan's heart. It was the way the rainforest below seemed so untamed—or maybe the way the island seemed to will itself into existence, pushing up out of the ocean with jagged black rock framing its edges.

Ba-doom ba-doom ba-dum ba-dum.

Those jungle drums, pounding in the well of his chest.

"Beautiful, I suppose," Amelia said.

The plane banked right. They'd be landing soon.

The plane wasn't much to look at—a Ford Trimotor. Ten years old, maybe. Normally ten seats, not including those in the cockpit. Here, half the seats in the back had been torn out to accommodate Amelia's motorbike, an Indian Scout Model 101 (though they had to ditch the sidecar, to her grousing).

Right now their pilot, a beanpole Frenchman who went only by "Jean-Jean," was up front gleefully humming *Bolero* loud enough so it could be heard over the propeller.

"You don't seem impressed," the erudite ape said with a quizzical look.

"Islands aren't my thing. Too hot. Too sticky. Much rather be in Paris. Or Amsterdam. Or Chicago. Any city, really. Somewhere I can get a good black cup of coffee."

"They grow coffee here."

"Good," she said. "I need a cup."

"It's been a long journey. Not much sleep." Except for Edwin, of course, who sat a few seats ahead of them, curled in a ball in one of the front seats. Snoring like a grain thresher.

The Professor neglected to mention that he was not tired, not one whit. The adventure was still coursing through him like a saline rush. He'd been around the world, but not like this.

The journey to get here was by itself a small adventure. How Swale gave that steamship everything it had so they could escape the saurian that hunted the depths ("Possibly a Geosaurus," Khan said at the time. "An early forebear of the modern crocodile"). How they'd finally landed and made their way to an airfield outside Saint Pol-de-Leon in France—and how even there they could see the pterosaurs flying in the twilight of morning, how the dirt roads were stamped with massive reptilian prints. How finally they managed to find a pilot not too drunk and not too scared to fly them all the way from France to the middle of the Pacific Ocean, hopping from airfield to airfield in order to refuel the little Ford plane.

And now here they were. Blue skies. Hot sun. Kauai beneath them. The ocean all around.

"We'll sleep when we win," Amelia said simply—not a sentence spoken with bravado but rather a statement as plain as *water is wet* or *the pie is quite good*.

With that said, she sat back down in the seat across the aisle, and clicked her lap-belt shut. The plane banked again, then evened out, and from the front, Jean-Jean whooped:

"Hold onto your women and children!"

He cackled, then, and the plane suddenly dropped out of the air like a dead bird.

The door to the Ford plane popped open, and Professor Khan came stumbling out. The jungle drums could not outpace the fierce hoof-beat of his heart—his pulse was doing laps, his neck throbbing, his temples pounding.

Jean-Jean was a fine pilot, he was sure.

Landing was not his strong suit.

When the crazy Frenchman dropped the stick and the Trimotor slammed into the runway like a dropped brick, Khan almost bit through his own tongue. Edwin squeaked and then screamed. Amelia, normally stoic and stalwart as a sandstone cliff, was suddenly bracing her legs against the seat and squeezing her eyes shut so hard Khan was surprised she could open them again.

The plane skidded like a stone skipping across a pond's surface until finally it eased sideways and then stopped. The only sound remaining being the *tink-tink-tink* of the plane's engine and Jean-Jean resuming the jaunty humming of *Bolero*.

And now Khan was on his hands and knees, not kissing the earth but instead pressing his head against the cool grass of the makeshift runway.

That moment of serenity did not last.

He heard swift footsteps and then, just as he was looking up, felt something hard connect with his face, bowling him over. A voice cried: "APE ATTACK!"

Khan rolled. Pivoted his hips. Came up clumsily, but still managed to get onto his feet.

The world shifted, split in twain—two images slowly resolving back to one.

His attacker was coming at him fast—

Inside Khan's heart and mind, something snapped. Like a twig underfoot, a twig that just so happened to be the trigger for a deadfall trap.

The jungle drums went from a dull and distant throb to a fast and furious beat.

Khan tried to speak, tried to warn his attacker off, but all that came out was a harsh snarl punctuated by his teeth snapping together. His fists thrust downward against the earth and before he commanded his body to do anything at all, he found himself barreling forward—

Drums beating—

Heart kicking—

Fire in his veins, jungle in his heart, a curtain of red cast across his vision—

The two bodies collided. Khan picked up the attacker, hoisting him aloft, ready to slam him down and shatter his adversary into pieces upon the earth.

"Professor!" came a voice, a voice he knew was shouted only a few feet away but that sounded like it was a far-flung echo from another time, another place—and he realized then he wasn't even sure if the voice was talking to him. Who was he? Was he a professor? Is that what he was, how he would self-identify when all was said and done?

Another voice—"Jet! Jet!"—and suddenly the red curtain began to part, as if melting back to the sides of his periphery. The first voice called his name again and suddenly became clear. He knew then that this person was Amelia, and that Amelia was speaking to him.

Khan gasped, set his attacker down and backpedaled away—no longer with his front fists on the ground like a proper ape, but on both legs, standing straight, as a human would.

As a human *should*.

And he was human. Wasn't he? At the core of it all?

Laying before him was a figure he knew from his file. Jet Black. Fellow Centurion. And hurrying up to meet them on the grassy airfield was Sally Slick and Mack Silver. Further downfield sat Silver's famous Boeing Clipper, "Lucy."

Jet, rattled, managed to stand, and backed away, watching Khan suspiciously.

"Who's the ape?" Jet tried to say, but mostly croaked.

Amelia stepped into the breach, while Edwin hung back, looking like a mouse caught in the middle of two cats fighting. "That's Professor Khan."

Sally was first to catch up, panting. "Jeez, Jet, what got into you?"

"I dunno, I just, I thought—I was out here picking some fruit and then the plane landed and I didn't know who could possibly know about this place and then—" He gulped, wiped grass off his elbows and knees. "Then the first one I saw off the plane was a big ape. After hearing Khan's radio address—"

"My what?" the Professor asked.

"Not you-Khan," Silver said, strolling up with a toothpick in his mouth juggling from side to side. "Other-Khan. Conqueror-Khan. Big-Daddy-Khan."

"Ah," Khan said, the wind stolen from his sails. He knew his father was involved from when Botu attacked him at Oxford but until now he was able to... selectively remove that memory and think about the *fun* of it all.

But that, coupled with the fact he was a moment's notice away from ripping Jet Black into pieces, cast a grim pall over the proceedings. "I'm terribly sorry, Mister Black. It was not my intention and I don't know what came over me..."

Jet took a moment. Like he wasn't sure. Like he was the same as everyone else: suspicious of a big scary gorilla pretending to be human. But then a big smile spread across Jet's face and he thrust out his hand. "It's no big thing, Professor. It was all my fault, really. Going off half-cocked like that. It's just been a real whiz-bang couple of days, you know?"

The ape laughed, nervous. "Oh, I know."

"I've heard a lot about you," Jet said, Khan's hand dwarfing his own. "And I'm happy to see you here. It'll be a pleasure working together."

"Can the love-fest," Silver said with a smirk. "Mack Silver," he added, introducing himself not to the Professor, and certainly not to Edwin. No, he made a bee-line right for Amelia, who matched him smirk for smirk.

"Amelia Stone," she said.

Khan watched carefully—the other woman, Miss Sally Slick, seemed suddenly troubled. She hid it well, but it was like a dark cloud suddenly appeared over her head, raining on her parade. She walked up to both the Professor and to Amelia and offered her hand.

Introductions were made. Some tense. Others less so.

Edwin piped in with a peep: "My name's Edwin. Edwin Jasher."

But they were already heading down the airfield, leaving poor Edwin behind.

CHAPTER TWENTY-ONE
THE KOLOA CHAPTER HOUSE

"We've been here a couple days," Jet said as he headed toward the chapter house, which sat nestled in the shade of a massive monkeypod tree, its tangled branches reaching toward skies so blue Khan didn't know they could *get* that color outside a painting. "Took us a bit to figure out how to even... get in the darn place."

"Where are we, exactly?" Amelia asked.

"Near Koloa Town," Jet said. "Hub of the sugar trade around here by the looks of it. Town's about a five-mile walk that-a-way.

"Closer to the southern side of the island," Khan said. North end, he knew you'd find more rainforests and jungle and... for some reason, a small voice inside warned him not to go that way. *Don't shake the tree if you don't want to see what falls out.*

The chapter house was itself seemingly unexceptional—an open longhouse with walls of dark ironwood and a roof thatched with bamboo thicker than a baby's arm. The air hung hot and sticky. A centipede straight out of pre-history scurried across the floor in front of them, its hundred legs *clickity-clicking* on the wood.

At the far end of the chapter house sat a trap door in the floor with a red Oriental rug rolled up just behind it. Khan tottered over, and found himself staring at a most fascinating locking mechanism. Eight brass bolts and a polished steel X laying over the wood—and to the side of the trap-door, a flat square brass plate with a fixture jutting up the side that looked not unlike the periscope of Nemo's submarine.

Khan didn't quite know what to make of this. He could see no mechanism by which the side-bolts and cross-bolts would release the hatch, and even then, saw no handle. Behind him, the others gathered, watching.

"Just put your hand on the brass plate," Mack said, his impatience ill-concealed.

Khan grunted in assent and did just that.

His hand was larger than the plate itself (again that small voice, this time reminding him: *it was made for a human*) and then, when he pulled his hand away, the little periscope-suddenly hissed a blast of steam, and his handprint became illuminated in a faint cerulean glow that ran along the outlines and contours his hand had left behind.

The trapdoor made a groan and shuddered—*gung gung gung gung*—but then, nothing happened. Jet scratched his head and knelt down next to Khan. "Geez, it's supposed to open for us Centurions..."

"Oh," Khan said, standing up and dusting off his kilt. "I'm... I'm not really a Centurion." He offered a wan smile and pushed his spectacles up on the bridge of his nose. "I'm more, you might say, support staff." He tried to conceal the disappointment in his voice, he worried that such concealment was impossible.

Just the same, he added: "That is really quite wonderful, though. The trapdoor appears to operate via mystical metallurgy. Brass has many delightful qualities. Healing and protection. That's why it was used as a metal to make shields. How apropos, then, that this protective metal should itself protect the chapter house of... well. The protectors."

They all stared at him. "Sorry, was I rambling?" he asked.

Jet clapped him on the shoulder. "Not at all, Professor. It's just that kind of information we need because, I gotta tell you, we're flying blind over here."

Jet then pressed his own hand into the brass plate. Another jet of steam and *his* hand glowed not blue, but green. With the sound of invisible mechanism the brass rods and bolts disappeared, and a moment later, the hatch popped with a hiss.

For the first time, they descended, one by one, into the true chapter house.

Sally stood in awe.

She wasn't an architect, not really, but her fascination with structure went well beyond engines and machines. And *this* was fascinating as all-get-out.

Beneath the longhouse stood the Century Club's Koloa chapter house, and Sally in part had expected more of the same. Most of the chapter houses took on the look of the locale, so here she figured—well, it'd be traditional Polynesian or maybe something with a decidedly more colonial spin. But this was...

Well, this was different.

The entire subterranean chapter house was carved out of old lava tubes—tunnels sculpted out of the very ground not by the hand of man but by molten earth. Each featured striations and step-marks and coils of long-cooled rock.

Then, someone came along and built the chapter house into the tunnels itself—nooks for electric lights and desks and tables, a map bolted into stone, a radio and screening room sequestered off to the side. All of it connected by a series of conduits and pipes fixed to the wall with brass fittings. Sally hurried over to the pipe, ran her hand along it.

It was warm. It *hummed.*

"There's power here," she said, breathless with excitement. "Natural power."

Khan sidled up next to her. Rapped on the pipe with a knuckle.

"Geomantic energy," he said. "The native Polynesians believed that all things were infused with a magical energy, an *impersonal* energy, called Mana. Of course, cultural ego had the natives here suggesting that they had more of it than everyone else due to—well, various reasons, birth, war, bloodlines, choices made—but they also believed that these islands were receptacles of Mana. That they collected it. Might be something to that. These are some of the newest islands on the planet. Relatively speaking."

Sally heard what Khan was saying, but in her own mind sang the question: *What could you do with that energy, Sally Slick?*

Suddenly, she found herself jostled free from her reverie. Mack grumbled, muttered "Excuse me," pulling away as if he was afraid to touch her.

She pulled away, too. A reaction. No—an *over*-reaction.

But what else was she supposed to do? Mack Silver? The Silver Fox? What a horrible idea. *Don't go there. He's an unstable engine. Prone to blow up in your face.* Besides, he sure seemed to be making wolf-eyes at that Stone woman. And then there was Jet...

...the way Jet watched her. That look on his face.

He didn't trust Mack. That's what it was. Jet was like her brother and she could see the disdain on his face. Like it was transmitting a message in bright neon:

YOU CAN DO BETTER, SALLY.

Well, Jet was right. She *could* do better.

And it wasn't like she had time to worry about this anyway what with all the psychic dinosaurs and *not*-psychic dinosaurs and conquering army of Mighty Khan and the end of the world as all humanity knew it...

"Are you coming?" Professor Khan asked. The others were already heading down the twisting corridor cast in the glow from the pipe-powered sconces. Sally touched the wall one last time to feel the thrumming vibrations run down her fingers and up to her shoulder, and then hurried to catch up.

CHAPTER TWENTY-TWO

THE HOLLOW EARTH

Atok tasted blood as the bone club swung upward in a sweeping arc, connecting with the underside of his chin. His teeth bit tongue. The inside of his eyes showed a rain of lights, bright and pulsing. The crowd roared. The raft swayed beneath him.

And Ramtar pounded his chest. Gluttonous in his triumph. Fat, corpulent Ramtar. One of the strongest warriors of the Hollow Earth—some might say *the* strongest.

But that was why Atok was here, wasn't he?

Because he knew who the strongest warrior was.

He staggered to his feet. Far above their heads, the cavern mantle was lit by whorls and spirals of phosphorescent mushrooms that glowed in bubbled clusters. The lights played across the waters of the Sunless Sea, a vast subterranean body of water on which Atok and Ramtar currently bobbed, standing together on a raft that was feeling smaller and smaller as the fight drew on. And all around them on smaller rafts—many lashed together—were hundreds of other pale Neanderthals, whooping and howling and thirsting for blood.

The war council needed a war leader.

And this was not a democracy.

Ramtar saw that Atok was again standing and moved his blubbery body with alarming speed. The bone club crashed downward—

But Atok was no longer standing there.

The bone smashed into the raft, splintering the wood. Atok had to move fast—Ramtar, despite his size, was not like the Megatherium-sloth. And while his body was robed in fat, the bands of blubber only served to wreath powerful muscles.

Still—while Ramtar wasn't slow, he certainly was not as fast as Atok.

As the bone club struck the raft, Atok knew that Ramtar's hand would be stinging. Only for a moment, but a moment was all he needed; he stomped down on the club, causing Ramtar to lose his grip. And then Atok kicked the weapon into the waters where it disappeared down in the dark.

"No weapons," Atok said. He held up his hands, clenched them into fists. "With our hands. Unless your hands are too soft?"

Ramtar bellowed an incomprehensible sound conveying naught but rage. He lunged toward, knuckles popping as he took a swing.

Atok knew that he could end this now—his opponent had left himself open in anger, and a strike to the inside of the leg, or the throat, or even the groin, would end this. But that was fighting like one of the Night Crickets, a caste of mostly-female assassins. Deadly and deserving of respect but they were killers, not warriors.

Warriors fought with honor.

Ramtar swung a fist and Atok moved beneath it, pistoning his own punches up and down his opponent's prodigious flesh. Ramtar's fat body rippled with each hit.

But Ramtar just laughed. Then brought both fists down on Atok's head.

Another starburst. The front of Atok's skull crashed against the raft.

You're not thinking, Atok. Just because you fight with honor doesn't mean you cannot fight with wisdom and cunning.

Ramtar stomped. Atok rolled out of the way.

He has weaknesses. Everyone has weaknesses. What are they?

Ramtar took a swinging kick. Atok tucked in his midsection and the kick missed—barely.

He carries his weight all in the front. Like sacks of grain.

His back is exposed.

That is where you attack.

Atok caught the next kick, capturing the foot in his hands. He used his foe's leg to gain leverage and push up to a stand. Then he gave a heaving spin, moving Ramtar by a half-turn.

It was enough.

Atok rained down upon Ramtar's kidneys with a flurry of hard strikes. Like pillars crashing into the earth, like stones tumbling against stones. Ramtar's muscles seized as his nervous system lit up like the fungus above their heads. Then, the humongous warrior dropped forward. Almost upending the raft.

But it wasn't enough.

The audience cheered for more, more, *more*. Always more.

And the rules were clear: the raft was the arena. And to win, only one must be left upon the raft. Ramtar groaned, tried to cry out—

But Atok had no mercy because so much was at stake.

He planted his foot against the side of the blubbery body and *pushed*. It took all his might and his leg burned from the effort.

Ramtar flopped over into the water. Sinking for a moment but eventually bobbing to the surface, coughing and sputtering. Fat floated, after all.

Atok pulled his long raven-black hair behind him, winding a braided mammoth hair cord around it. The roar of the crowd declared him the victor.

The Elders sat at a table that was not a table but rather, a twisting root lined with softly glowing lichen. Atok waited, though his patience was wearing thin.

They stared at him. Judging him. Sizing him up. Gorleck the Blind—his eyes milky with fat cataracts—did not stare so much as he did *smell* the air, surmising whatever he could surmise from Atok's odor.

The five of them would occasionally make noises: *hmm, ahh, yes-yes, well.* Or loud breathing. Or tongue clucking. Lorzac the Healer smacked his lips—an irritating habit.

"You are the champion," Wirgen said. Wirgen, speaker for the Elders but not the eldest among them. That honor fell to Murglok. "You defeated Ramtar the Colossus."

"I did," Atok said, jaw set tight.

"And it was you," Wirgen continued, "that called the challenge."

"It was."

"You want to be war leader."

"I am war leader."

Wirgen chuckled. "But why? Why do you want to be? Why now?"

"We have not had a war leader for years and it is time for war."

Gorleck leaned forward, smelled the air again. "I smell your sweat, warrior. Hungry sweat, it is. You are eager to spill blood. Desperate to proclaim power."

"Quiet, Gorleck," Murglok said, his voice deep and guttural, the sound of two heavy stone wheels grinding together. "You insult the champion."

Gorleck bowed his head in acquiescence and leaned back. Next to him, Korsha—once a war leader herself—just stared out from behind the silver curtain of hair draped across her face.

Wirgen spoke again.

"You did not properly answer the question, Atok. Why war leader? Why now?"

"You've heard what the Upland scouts have said."

"I have. They say the Upland is in danger. An ape race with dinosaur slaves has claimed the surface world as their own. Subjugated the people—or, most of them, at least." Wirgen leaned forward, his eyes narrowing. "You want to save these people? Go to war for them?"

Atok almost laughed, but held his composure.

"No, Wirgen Speaker. I wish to conquer them."

The Elders all looked to one another. Even blind Gorleck appeared to cast them a look, though such display was only that. Shock and excitement and fear radiated from the five. Lorzac seemed the most rattled by it.

It was Korsha that spoke next: "We do not concern ourselves with the Upland. We are masters of the Hollow Earth. The surface is not our concern."

"With all due respect," Atok began, realizing that such a phrase usually preceded a statement that held little of the respect due, "it was not *your* concern when you were war leader taking us to war against the Huldrafolk."

"It is not the *concern* of the Hollow Earth, Atok."

"It should be." As Korsha opened her mouth to respond, Atok cut her off, eliciting gasps. "Once that was our world. But we were driven below by cataclysm and hardship but now it is our time to reclaim it. The human herd is soft and pliable like the sap of the warbling pine—"

Korsha hissed: "You are out of place—"

But Atok continued: "But we are hard and unyielding like the stone that surrounds us. By the Gods of the Dark, they have fallen prey to *apes* and *dinosaurs*! If the humans succumb to creatures we consider our prey, then that is a sign that they will fall to us, too. It is a sign that we must go to the Upland. That we must *retake* the surface world and claim it once more as our own." He grinned, now, because he could see he had them, just as he had Ramtar once he began pummeling the fat fool's kidneys. "We must no more hide down here, relegated to the below. It is time to go conquer."

It was heresy, he knew. The Below was considered sacred. The Uplanders always wanted to conquer high spaces—climbing mountains and building tall towers of metal and glass. But those of Hollow Earth took pride in going lower, deeper, down into the dark to find new creatures, new minerals and metals, new sources of water and food.

Just as apes once climbed down from trees to become Neanderthal, Neanderthal must then do the same, moving ever downward.

Atok knew the heart and the spirit of his people. In their heart and spirit was the same urge to conquer.

Wirgen looked to Murglok, for it was Murglok's approval that they all needed.

The old man leaned forward, his pinched and wizened face chewing on the problem the way one might chew on a shadow-elm seed. "Let it be known that Atok the War Leader shall take an army of warriors to the Upland and conquer it in the name of the Hollow Earth. Let our reign go as deep below and as high above as it must—from the burning heart of this world to the searing eye of the sun in the sky. Go forth, Atok. Earn a new name among those who dwell upon the surface. We may call you Atok the War Leader, but let them call you: Atok the Horrible."

CHAPTER TWENTY-THREE
THE KOLOA CHAPTER HOUSE

They asked him to speak and now here he was, standing before heroes that he, well, considered his *heroes*. Mack Silver and his intrepid Clipper! Jet Black, master of the sky! Sally Slick, with her boundless ingenuity! Amelia Stone, her two fists taking the bullies and malefactors of the world to task!

And, of course, Edwin. Not so much a hero, but—well. Nice enough chap?

Before him was what was left of the Century Club. Hundreds of Centurions sidelined. Captive or dead, nobody knew.

They'd been arguing for hours, late into the night. Trying to figure out something, *anything*, some plan of attack, some snippet of information they could use. They took periodic breaks, going up and outside and listening to the deafening hum-and-buzz of insects in the trees, the humid air growing cooler as thunder rumbled somewhere out at sea.

Then they said to Khan, it was his turn to speak.

And now he stood before them.

Shaking, a little bit.

"This is what we know," Khan said. "We know that... Mighty Khan, the originator of my genetic material but most certainly *not* my father, invaded the world with dinosaurs as his weapon—some might even say, as his soldiers. These dinosaurs appear to be from the past, transferred here through one or several enormous gateways. We know that some of these dinosaurs are humanoid, a reptilian atavism capable of enormous psychic energy."

"They steal your damn brain," Mack said. "It was like... like my mind was being taken on a ride I didn't pay for."

"I smelled rain and leaves," Jet said, staring off at nothing, obviously recollecting. "And I heard... sounds."

"Jungle sounds," Sally added. "At least, what I would imagine them to sound like."

Jet nodded, but didn't look at Sally—it was as if his gaze focused on her margins rather than meeting her eyes. Khan noted it, wondered what it meant, but filed it away as a question for a better time. More troubling was this connection to the jungle. What did that mean? Were the jungle drums he heard related? Had he been secretly affected by the psychic energy?

Jet said, "It felt good. I heard a voice. It wanted me to give up. Give in. And I wanted to listen. I almost did."

"What stopped you?" Sally asked.

Jet shrugged her off.

Khan continued: "I call these creatures *psychosaurs*, as they are plainly saurian and exhibit some—though not all—of the features we come to see repeated in most other dinosaurs. The psycho- prefix is of course a reference to their ability to affect the minds of humans."

"Of humans?" Amelia asked. "They don't affect you?"

"It does not appear as such, no. They seem keenly attuned to manipulating the mind of *homo sapiens*."

"Wait, wait, wait," Mack said, leaning forward as if suddenly interested. "Are we assuming these things came from back in time?"

"Possibly," Khan said.

"Then why the heck are they good at messing with *our* heads? What kind of survival tactic is that? They're only good at tweaking the gourds of a race of humans that won't exist until millions of years into the future?"

Khan scratched his chin whiskers. "Could've been a side effect. Useless then but useful now? Or perhaps they were capable of manipulating Neanderthal minds? Of course, Neanderthal man and dinosaur did not exist in the same time, but perhaps the psychosaurs persisted beyond the extinctions of their saurian brethren?"

"So they could head-shrink early humans, you're saying."

"Many believe Neanderthal man to be a subspecies of *homo sapiens*, but evidence—controversial evidence, I assert, but evidence I believe—suggests that man and Neanderthal DNA diverged a half-a-million years ago. Meaning, they are not the same. But perhaps the mind was close enough that the psychosaurs can touch the minds of modern man? I cannot say with any certainty."

"The only other option is that something quite sinister is going on." Everyone turned and, to their registered surprise, found Edwin to be the one speaking. Emerging as barely more than a squeak, but it commanded the attention of the room. "Something we, well, don't know. Some terrible manipulation."

Mack cocked an eyebrow. "Someone buy this guy a boat, call it the S.S. Obvious."

"No, no," Khan said. "He's right. There could be—and likely are—other factors we just haven't considered."

"That's life in the big city, pal," Mack said, standing up suddenly like someone lit a fire under his keister. "There's always something you don't know. This is time to act. Not to stand around and talk about our feelings. It's time to make some decisions and *do* something."

"But we don't have all the information," Khan insisted.

"So what? Information is overrated. We go with our gut. That's what we *do*. Professor, I appreciate the lecture, but here's the thing: sometimes you just gotta dive off the cliff without knowing what's in the water below. We don't think. We *do*. You'd understand that if you were a hero like one of us."

"Hey!" Sally said, standing up across from Mack and pointing her finger at him. "What's your problem with the Professor?"

"I got no problem here. No disrespect. It's just—he's an academic. An egghead. We're heroes. We use our brawn, babydoll." Mack looked to Khan, held up his hands as if to say, *sorry, this is just how it is.* "You're smart, Professor. But sometimes, to be like us, you gotta be a little bit dumb. Is it smart to run into a hail of bullets? To punch a dinosaur in the mouth? To jump out of a plane to save your buddy from gettin' eaten by a pack of starving pterodactyls?" At this, Mack shot a look toward Sally. "No. But we do it anyway. Because we're heroes."

"Babydoll," Sally seethed. "*Babydoll*?"

Mack rolled his eyes. "Really? That's what you took away from all the stuff I just said?"

"If we could all—" Khan started, but then—

The ground shook. Just a faint tremor. So light that no one but him seemed to notice.

"Everybody settle down!" Amelia said, raising her voice so it could be heard. Beside her, Jet just thumped his head against the table.

Khan was about to speak but then there it came again—

This time, the lights flickered. The rumbling was more distinct—a small quake.

Everyone froze. It was Amelia that said what they were all thinking:

"We're under attack."

Then—

The air lit up like it was on fire, or rather, like that firelight came reflected through an air suffused with hundreds of rubies. A deafening crackle left Khan's ears ringing and out of the nexus of red light appeared a body.

A body that dropped straight onto the table with a crash.

CHAPTER TWENTY-FOUR
NEW YORK CITY

Gerard Spears sauntered into Conqueror Khan's Empire State office—overlooking the city through its shattered window—like he owned the place, as if he had nothing at all to apologize for. Hands tucked in the pockets of his white pants. Fedora pulled low. Whistling a jaunty tune that Khan did not recognize.

Khan ended that tune by knuckle-stomping his way over to Spears and wrapping a hand the size of a canned ham around the gentleman thief's throat.

"You let Benjamin Hu get away," Khan seethed. Nostrils flaring.

Spears tried to say something but it came out mostly as: *Glurk*. His face was as red as a matchstick. Khan kept squeezing.

Red to purple. Again: *Glurrrrk*. Accompanied by a mousey squeak.

Khan longed to feel the man's trachea give way in his grip—it would feel like squeezing a small bunch of grapes into naught but skin, pulp, and juice.

But he let go. Spears gasped, dropped to one knee with his hand palm-down on the cool marble. Outside, bands of fog traveled over the city and licked at the shattered glass.

"Get up," Khan said, turning away and moving to sit on his desk.

Spears managed to stand. It was only a few moments where he looked rattled, disheveled, *afraid*—and then, as if by magic, he once more became the king of composure.

"Hu is dead," Spears said, finally. Now preening and filing his fingernails as if his head was not almost unscrewed from his body.

Khan stared, scrutinizing, looking for a sign of deception. "Is he, now? Last I heard no one had discovered a body."

"We found the body. Washed up on a rock. I'm no mortician, but I believe the explosion killed him. But some fish did have a nibble." Spears made a face like someone just poured vinegar in his tea. "It was really quite unpleasant. Anyway, I brought you a gift..."

Spears snapped his fingers and Gonga came loping in with a long black velvet cloth swaddling something. He handed it to Khan as Spears watched, equal parts satisfied and disinterested. Khan unwrapped it and pulled out—

A sword. A clumsy, stupid human sword. It looked like a sewing needle in his hand.

"What is the meaning of this?"

"It's a rapier, Mighty Khan. Hu's rapier. As sharp as he is. Or, was."

Khan made a disgruntled noise, threw the rapier on the floor in disgust. "I have no need for such petty, paltry human toys."

Spears massaged his throat. "What *do* you need then, my lord? I assumed you summoned me from halfway across the world to either kill me—which you did not do—or hire me for more work. Given how elegantly I came through for you in the procurement of certain... lost Atlantean keys to open certain... forgotten Atlantean archways."

"I need you to steal something else."

"Go on."

"I need you to steal my son."

Spears blinked. "I'm sorry. Surely you said, *the sun*, because I could probably swing that if you give me a few days and a good team."

"*My* son. Son-of-Khan."

"You want me to steal a person."

"*An ape,*" Khan snarled. "He is not—*not!*—a person."

"I meant it figuratively—ahh, he's quite large, is he not? Say, perhaps, very...*you*-sized?"

"So?"

"Well, it's just, I'm used to stealing smaller items. A brooch. A mummy's hand. Ancient Atlantean technology. That sort of thing."

"It's time to upgrade your services, then. Time to accommodate bigger targets, Spears."

"I'm not sure, Khan. Listen, I wonder if you might find someone better at this—after all, this isn't *theft* so much as it's *abduction*—"

"You'll do it."

"I'll... do it?"

Khan took both of his massive fists and ground them against one another. The knuckles popping on each. "Unless you'd rather us finish the earlier conversation between my *hand* and your *throat*. That conversation should settle matters."

"You know what?" Spears said, snapping his fingers. "I'm thinking about it and it looks like I have an opening on my schedule. And abducting—sorry, stealing, ha ha—a giant gorilla isn't that much different than stealing, oh, I don't know, a statue of a giant gorilla. Consider me the man for the job, Mighty Khan."

"I thought you might see it that way."

Spears smoothed the pleats of his white suit jacket. "So, you *do* know where this unruly child of yours is, yes?"

Khan offered a toothy smile.

"I do. I do, indeed."

CHAPTER TWENTY-FIVE
THE KOLOA CHAPTER HOUSE

Benjamin Hu dropped out of thin air and slammed hard against the table inside the Century Club's Koloa chapter house. His lungs pancaked and he struggled to get breath—but that didn't stop him from rolling off the edge of the table and waving around a dagger that appeared carved from a giant hunk of sapphire.

It cut through the air—*swish, swish*.

"Benjamin Hu?" said an ape nearby, an ape with tired eyes behind a pair of wire-rim spectacles, an ape wearing a houndtooth jacket and a tartan kilt. An ape who seemed to recognize him. Who couldn't be one of Khan's men, unless—

Ah. *Son*-of-Khan. Professor at... Oxford.

As his eyes adjusted and breath filled his lungs again, Hu saw other faces he recognized—other *Centurions*. Good. That was good. That meant the risk he took paid off.

He took the dagger and slammed it point down in the table.

And then promptly passed out.

The smell of coffee awoke him. That, and the hint of something sharp and sweet in the air. Benjamin sat up, head pounding, stomach lurching like a drunken sailor on a storm-swept boat, and had to steel himself against the tide of migraine and nausea.

All around him: a small bunkroom with grottos carved into smooth lava rock, wooden bunks held fast to the wall by cable and screws. On the wood: small cot mattresses. Ben was on one of these, and was alone, but only for a moment.

A figure he recognized—Jet Black, fellow Centurion, with his bright eyes and his morning cowlick—came into the room with two mugs in hand. One of coffee. Another of juice.

"Bean juice in this hand," Jet said, "guava in this one. Professor picked the guava, pulped it for us, too. The bean juice, well, Amelia and I took a ride on her Indian Scout to old Koloa Town, managed to convince some of the canefield workers to spare some coffee—what with the stuff growing on the island and all."

"So I made it," Benjamin said, each word a small, raspy misery. "This is Kauai."

Jet gave him a quizzical look.

Hu realized: he was speaking in Chinese. He tried again, said the same thing in English. Jet's mouth formed an "o" and he nodded. "Welcome to the Koloa chapter house."

He took the coffee from Jet, slurped from the hot brew. While the caffeine would not yet have had time to go storming through his system like a pair of wild stallions, the warmth and flavor of it still had an energizing effect.

"How long have I been out?"

"A little over 12 hours," Jet said.

Twelve hours. "Time is wasting. Gather everyone. I need to speak to you all."

Amelia watched as the Coconut Man rushed toward Professor Khan—foul aggressor, vile attacker! "Hit him. *Hit him!*"

Khan swung blindly, wildly, his massive fist connecting with the air in front of the Coconut Man's scowling face.

Whiff.

At which point the Coconut Man collided into the erudite ape and the "enemy" fell into his composite pieces: mop-handle body, palm frond arms, and of course, the coconut head with an evil face carved upon it.

"That was good," Amelia lied.

"No need to be nice, Miss Stone. Perhaps I'm just not the, erm, two-fisted type. I am, after all, not a proper Centurion."

She shook her head. "I don't buy it, Professor. I was there yesterday when you about broke Jet in half like a rib of celery."

A wind came and swept through the eaves of the monkeypod trees. In the distance, the green peak of Mount Waialeale disappeared beneath a band of hungry fog.

"I just don't... feel that same way right now," Khan explained. Amelia watched him. He seemed nervous. A little lost. She wondered then if what Mack said rattled him.

"I thought maybe the coconut would be a motivator."

"Coconut?"

"Your kind eats coconuts, don't they?"

"My kind?"

"Gorillas."

Khan laughed. "I'm a gorilla. Gorillas come from Africa, Miss Stone. Africa has no coconuts. And besides, I'm not even from Africa. Though gorillas are not generally meat-eaters, I am in fact fond of a good plate of bangers and mash."

"I'm sorry," she said, wincing. "I should think before I open my mouth. Certainly others have said things like that to me. I'm a black woman with a motorcycle. The things that people say sometimes..."

"I am sympathetic. They always assume I'm some kind of brute. Or that I'm a monkey, not an ape. Many seem to find it difficult reconciling that I am a learned man on the inside but a silverback gorilla on the outside."

"No worries, Professor." Amelia smiled. "We'll turn you into a brute yet."

He was about to say something when they both caught sight of Jet emerging from the longhouse. He yelled over to them: "Benjamin's awake!"

Finally. Nobody else was around.

There stood Sally, running some kind of... meter? (Mack wasn't sure what it was and he didn't much care) along the length of the pipes and conduits running along the lava tubes. The device had a little black needle that wobbled and waved, going nutso anytime she got it close to one of the fixtures.

Mack swept up behind her, sliding his hands around her midsection and spinning her around to meet him.

She whacked him on the head with the whatever-meter.

"Ow!" he said, rubbing his scalp. Lucky thing he was wearing his aviator's cap. "Touchy touchy, Slick. It's me. It's Mack."

"I see who it is."

"What? No smile? No kiss? No va-va-voom for the Silver Fox?"

"Leave me alone, *Silver Fox*." The way she said those two words—wait, was she *mad* at him?

"What are you all cranky about?"

"I don't have time for this. *We* don't have time for this. The world's in crisis. This time in a way far bigger and far worse than we've ever dealt with."

"Well, that thing with the Baron of Blavatsky was pretty bad. And don't forget when Der Blitzmann figured out how to commune with those... whatever the hell they were."

"Electricity elementals. And this is still worse than all that and you know it. I don't need the distraction." She looked up him up and down. "And neither do you. You got enough on your plate already, pal."

"What's that supposed to mean?"

"It means I saw you making eyes at Amanda Stone."

"*Amelia*."

"Oh, sorry, didn't realize you two were so close already."

"So close? What? Your coconut's cracked, girlie. Amanda—er, *Amelia*—seemed very nice is all. I'm not supposed to be friendly?"

"She seemed *pretty* is what you mean."

"I am nothing if not a man who appreciates beauty." He narrowed his eyes. Oh. Ah. Suddenly he understood. His face split into a wide smile. "You're jealous."

"I'm no such thing. I don't do jealousy. Like I said: it's a distraction."

She pushed past him. Moved to the next conduit. Brought the meter up against it and again the needle jumped.

"You kissed me," he said.

"Energy spike," she said, tapping the meter. "The energy traveling through this is strong as a bull. It's like a river of power. If only we could harness that..."

"*You* kissed *me*," he said again. He wasn't letting her off the hook that easy.

She spun around. Whacked him again with the meter.

"Ow!"

"And that kiss won't happen again. I'm not going to waste my time on this. Because that's what it is, Mack Silver. A big giant waste of time. Time I don't have. Time *you* don't have. I'm at least doing something." She gave him a hard shove. "What are *you* doing, exactly? Sniffing around like a dog looking for a treat? You gave the good Professor a mouthful last night—why don't you live up to your own idea of a hero instead of barking up this tree again?"

"You're an ice queen, Sally Slick."

"And you're an idiot, *Silver Fox*."

"What we did was a mistake," he said.

"You're damn right," she agreed.

He grabbed her again and kissed her.

She sucker-punched him in the gut.

"I thought—" He croaked, coughed. "—we were flirting."

Suddenly, Sally's eyes darted past him. He leaned against the wall, clutching his midsection. They had an audience. Not Jet this time. Benjamin Hu.

"If you two are done doing..." Benjamin seemed to search for words. "...whatever it is you're doing. I'm ready to tell you all what happened."

Mack forced a smile. "Lead the way, Benji."

"Benjamin."

"Benny?"

"No. Benjamin."

"Fine. *Benjamin*. Don't get your knickers in a knot. Let's do this. Sally?"

She grumbled and pushed past him.

There, back at the table (with the shimmering blue dagger still stuck in the ironwood), they all looked to Benjamin to understand what had happened.

It was then that he told them his story.

CHAPTER TWENTY-SIX
BENJAMIN'S STORY

I should be dead.

The boat I was on—the boat of one of my many enemies, Gerard Spears—exploded beneath me when I set fire to it, fire that ignited the barrels of smokeless gunpowder in the belly of that boat. My feet were free but my hands were still bound behind my back with a braid of hemp rope knotted by expert hands.

The waters were dark. I could not see. And I was sinking fast.

All around me pieces of the boat either bobbed above my head or sank with me.

I struggled. But I was dizzy. Confused. My shoulders aching with my hands unavailable to me. The light above began to fade.

A momentary digression—

Did you know that the waters around Hong Kong are home to dolphins? Pink dolphins, as a matter of fact—the pink coming from a bloom of blood beneath their skin, allowing them to thermoregulate their body temperatures.

It was down below when I first caught sight of one of these pink dolphins. A flash of pale color, a swish of bubbles. The dolphins must have seen the boat and thought it a fishing trawler, the pod of them arriving in the hopes of accompanying the ship and getting a taste of the bounty.

But they did not find fish. They found me, instead.

I see the looks on your faces. You think here that the dolphins are going to save me and carry me to freedom—that somehow they, friend to every sailor, let me ride them the way one rides a pony or a motorbike.

Not quite, I'm afraid. But the dolphins still did save my life, have no doubt of that. They came up and took their short, hard noses and began jabbing me—in the stomach, in my side, in my chest. Not only did it have the effect of startling me and bringing me fully back to the awareness of my situation, but they also juggled me up, up, up—closer to the surface.

And it was then they saved me in another way:

They became my model. I knew that the only way to swim with my hands still bound behind me was the dolphin kick—to swim as they swam. Whip-kick my legs, push myself up and up and up until I finally again broke surface. I saw light. I felt the wind. Air filled my lungs.

I saw the husk of the boat some hundred feet away, slowly sinking. Apes and men and barrel halves bobbing.

They hadn't seen me, but they would.

I sank again.

And then I swam. I swam hard, kicking out my legs and occasionally rising back to the surface to catch a breath and to tread water—no easy task with your arms tied, and it wasn't long before my legs began to burn like they were on fire.

But I managed.

The dolphins swam with me the whole way.

I ended up on an outcropping of rock south of Kau Pei Chau. I was close to land. I wriggled myself onto the rock and rolled over, sawing my hands back and forth on the jagged earth, cutting through the wet rope.

I laid there for a time. Just breathing.

Evening crept ever-closer.

And then I sat up and I saw it.

A gate. Made of multi-faceted light—like an archway made of jewels, but insubstantial, unreal. It stood far off in the South China Sea. Rising tall from the half-moon shape of Waglan Island, easily dwarfing the lighthouse. In the light I saw the winged dinosaurs circling.

I had to go there. I had to see.

But I knew I could not swim and so I found a fisherman's dinghy tied up on the far side of Kau Pei Chau and... liberated it. I left some coin on the post. With the way things were going, it wasn't like anyone was fishing—normalcy had gone the way of the dodo once dinosaurs were born anew into our world.

It took me an hour to row out there. Just as long to creep up around the far side, on the side of the lighthouse, to get a better look.

And I did indeed get a better look. The archway of light rose out of two stone pillars, pillars lined with old symbols—Atlantean symbols, symbols from a fallen civilization. It looked as if these pillars, which rose as tall as two men, were dark with fresh earth.

I was not alone on this half-bitten fingernail of rock.

It was swarming with creatures.

A pack of raptors jogged the margin, leaping from rock to rock, trailed as they were by another larger pack of much-smaller creatures: compsagnathus, the little scavenger dinosaur. Above me orbited pterodactyls. Chained to each pillar was a Tyrannosaur, roaring into the night.

And apes. Soldiers and scientists knuckle-walking about. Khan's army.

Many of them kitted in Atlantean garb.

It was then that it clicked: Atlantis is the key. I had heard the rumors that Atlantis resurfaced—but, like with my searches for Quivira and Cibola or Lemuria or the entranceway to Agartha I was never able to discern its location.

It became clear then that not only was Atlantis real and it had returned—or, perhaps, never left—but that the Conqueror Ape had claimed it for his own. Thus explaining why he had been silent for the last half- decade.

Just then, the gate crackled and a massive warrior ape, a plume of peacock feathers jutting up from his scaled helmet, emerged from the gate, momentarily confused. But he regained his stride and pulled on a long rope whose other end disappeared into the snapping tendrils of electricity.

From the gate the ape warrior pulled a cart on wooden wheels, a cart with a bamboo cage. And then I saw—the psychic saurians stood within this cage, standing stock still and shoulder to shoulder. A dozen of them. Maybe more.

As they appeared, they shimmered and my image of them slipped away like an oily spoon tumbling from my grip—they suddenly wore human masks and bodies, the costume complete.

That was not a good thing.

Because they sensed me there. They knew I was hiding behind a rock, watching.

They turned their heads as one and began screeching. Their needled maws snapping at the air and instantly I felt their presence heavy in my head, the booming voice of their hive-mind crashing down upon me like beams of timber.

I pulled a thought of my own out of the morass and it was that I had to escape, had to do whatever I could do to flee—

And for a moment I thought about diving backward—if I timed it right and angled my body just so, I would tumble into the surf, hopefully breaking their psychic grip.

If I timed it wrong or twisted my body this way instead of that...

I'd be broken.

But in that moment I had my own reptilian response, a response that was all flight and no fight and yet to any looking from outside would have looked the opposite.

I did not dive. I ran.

I ran straight toward the danger.

My feet felt heavy. My mind was sinking into the mire.

I no longer smelled the sea. I smelled the jungle.

I snatched the dagger from the hilt at the ape's waist.

I heard birds screeching in a canopy of trees that did not exist in my present.

I passed the cage as the ape warrior struggled to unlock it and loose upon the world this fresh batch of saurian agents—

I smelled rain and sweat and lushness.

I leapt.

I leapt through the gate and I felt it tear me apart.

CHAPTER TWENTY-SEVEN
KOLOA CHAPTER HOUSE

"You look okay to me," Mack said to Benjamin, leaning back on his chair, ignoring the sour look from Sally sitting across the table.

Benjamin continued: "I thought for a moment I'd made a terrible error. Yes, I could no longer feel the chains of the psychic saurian around my mind dragging me to wherever it was they wanted my consciousness to go, but I was lost, bodiless, thrown through a prismatic oblivion. But then I realized— I could feel time shifting all around me. I knew that this was a space connected by two points in time: *Now,* and *Then.* 'Then' had a specific point, a point from which the dinosaurs were being pulled into our world—this gateway was one door and it must surely open up at the other end at a time potentially millions of years ago—

"And then I could see. I could see these tunnels of time like strands of black thread—seven strands, to be exact, and then I realized: I had seen the archway before. In fact, in a manner of speaking I had seen *seven* such archways before, on an old Atlantean map. These gates appeared at crucial nexus points where ley lines—lines of mystical energy—meet.

"They met at a single point, a point at which I was racing toward at incalculable speeds. That told me these were not merely temporal gates but spatial gates, too."

Khan cut in: "Engines not just of time travel, but of teleportation."

"Exactly." Hu smiled. The ape understood. "It was then I thought of the Piraha tribe—"

Again Khan spoke, this time truly excited: "Yes. Yes! They do not have language for time—they do not tell stories or histories of the past, they do not remember their ancestors, they for all intents and purposes live as animals do: in the present."

"Indeed. Some have said they are limited and unevolved but they have a surprisingly sophisticated view of time—that it all exists at one point, converging together with all moments happening in bold simultaneity. It told me that I was not forced to keep to this path. That if I truly wanted to, I could go anywhere and at any point."

"So you came here?" Mack asked. "Oooh. Bonehead move."

It was Benjamin's turn to shoot him a look. What was this lout's problem? He was acting out. Like a child. But, one problem at a time.

"I took the dagger in my hand and I carved a slit in the very matter of time the way a pirate slices into a sail with his cutlass,. The rift opened and I pictured in my head a place—and that place was here." He sighed, happy to have told his tale.

"I suppose I should be doubly happy I did not teleport into the middle of solid lava rock."

The room laughed.

"I hate to agree with Mack," Jet said, "but while all this is well and good, it seems to me like it's time to figure out a plan. We can't sit here on our hands while the rest of the world sits pinned beneath Khan's thumb."

"I have an idea," Khan said. "May I?"

Benjamin stepped aside, and the erudite ape took the floor.

CHAPTER TWENTY-EIGHT
KAUAI, HAWAII

Edwin ambled about, kicking stones into the trees. None of the Centurions even noticed he was gone, surely—he slipped out through the hatch and wandered away from the longhouse and not one of them came to find him, see if he was all right or if he needed tending to. Even Khan was so wrapped up in being surrounded by his heroes he forgot all about poor Edwin.

He was, to them, *persona non grata*.

And that was quite lovely, thanks for asking.

He caught a whiff of ozone followed by a sulfurous pocket of magic residue. The monkeypod trees shuddered, shedding a few leaves, and on each leaf Edwin was *sure* he saw strange numbers inscribed there—numbers that faded as soon as he saw them.

A figure emerged out of the trees from the direction of the kicked stones.

"Well, hello... Edwin," said Gerard Spears. Eyes twinkling. Mouth tweaked in a playful smile. "Nice to see you again. Mister Jasher."

"Of course, Mister Spears. Nice to see you too."

Spears tucked the flat of his hand in his trouser pockets and toddled about, whistling. "How's everything? Things going well with our little friends?"

"I think so. The Chinaman just showed."

"Hu? Ah. Good. Glad he's not dead. Was a bit worried about that. Him doing a whirling *ballestra* off this mortal coil might complicate things unnecessarily."

"Ballestra?"

"Fencing move. Interesting that I know that."

"Interesting, indeed, Mister Spears." Edwin offered a sheepish smile— really, the only kind of smile he knew how to offer with this borrowed face. "So what brings you to the Hawaiian islands?"

"Ah! Well. Khan sent me to kidnap Khan. More specifically, Khan Prime—Daddy Khan—thinks that I should abduct Beta Khan. He further believes that the other ape is his son rather than his rough genetic equal. He's not particularly bright for having taken over the world just now, is he?"

"I suppose not. Ironically, Son-of-Khan is very smart. Smartest I've seen in a long time."

Spears clucked his tongue. "Well, like I said, a *rough* genetic match. Those who are the same are not always the same, isn't that right, Edwin Jasher?"

"It is, Gerard Spears, it is."

"I'm of course not really going to kidnap Son-of-Khan. The Professor is quite safe where he is. You may continue to be his keeper."

"Oh, good. I thought, but wasn't sure—as you said, those who are not the same and all. What are you doing here, then?"

Spears snapped his fingers. "Right! Of course. I've come to fetch a pet."

"A pet, you say?"

"A pet. Walk with me, Edwin."

Edwin did as the man asked. Why wouldn't he? Together they sauntered down the stone-step path leading to the longhouse and stepped out onto the airfield. Spears pointed at the Boeing Clipper, the plane Mack Silver called "Lucy," and saw something duck behind one of the tailfins.

"I just saw something," Edwin said.

"Yes. Let's get a closer look." Spears took a knee, and began to upend a small pouch of white dust—like powdered chalk—into the matted battered grass of the airfield. Then, around the edges of the circles he began to drop playing cards, except these cards did not feature suits of hearts or diamonds but instead were like flash cards. On them were odd symbols and numbers that Edwin would best describe as "non-existent" or "downright imaginary."

Then Spears uttered a series of numbers—like an equation, of sorts—and from behind the tailfin of the Boeing Clipper came a little puff of black smoke.

A half-second later, a similar puff of smoke erupted from the middle of the circle.

Out of that smoke dropped a tiny dinosaur with a collar of phosphorescent fungus around its outstretched neck. The little lizard with its arrow-shaped head squawked and hissed.

Spears reached out and caught it by the neck.

The dinosaur made a gurgling noise and thrashed about like a captive turkey.

"There we go!" Spears chirped, giddy. "Now, to plant this little fellow... elsewhere."

"Will it work?"

"Probably. Mostly. If not, it's of little concern. What's happening is what's happening and what's done is done. The Conqueror's time draws to a close—if we can delay his realization of that for a time, then all the better."

"Anything I can do?" Edwin asked.

Another twinkle in Spears' eye. "You know what? There is."

And then Gerard told Edwin just what needed to be done.

CHAPTER TWENTY-NINE
NEW YORK CITY

Mighty Khan, Conqueror Ape, went for a walk.

He did not go alone. He went flanked by a contingent of stomping ape warriors, snarling dawn tyrant dinosaurs, and quietly creeping psychosaurs.

On his walk, he gazed upon a city that had fallen to him. A city where men and women cowered in windows or were rounded up and locked in cages and basements. Where buildings stood smoldering from the wreckage of fighter planes. Where dinosaurs roamed the streets and skies and tunnels, and apes held their leashes. Where the human herd had finally assumed its proper role: as prey, as slaves, as the weaker species.

Khan's chest swelled with pride. New York City, once-dominant human enclave, fallen. Like so many other cities. London. Berlin. Moscow. Chicago. Yes, of course some standouts still held firm—the entire middle tract of the American country was hard to rein in, for instance, hard to even get a handle on, but what did it matter? It was a dust-blown dry-bone dead zone and the people there would soon tire of their battles with the invading creatures and lay down their stubborn resistance. It was good they fought back. That was the way of nature—the prey often fought or fled the predator.

Besides...

It wasn't about controlling all the world. It was about controlling its most critical points.

And New York City was chief among them. He imagined this city given over again to the trees and the beasts—vines choking skyscrapers and pulling them back down to the ground, Central Park allowed to explode with life and escape its confines, the endless tunnels below the city filled with all manner of strange, non-human life.

Khan clapped his hands. Gonga came bounding up next to him.

"Ahh. Yes. Yes. Greetings, Splendorous Khan, King Khan, All-Conquering-Khan. What can, ahhh, Gonga do for you *today*?"

"I want to rename this city," Khan said.

"Good, ahh, very good." Gonga reached in a satchel that hung by his side and withdrew a small steno pad and pen. "Ready."

"New New York," Khan said, testing the words. "No. I don't like it. My name should be in there. It should be rewritten in homage to me."

"Khanapolis?" Gonga asked, and for his suggestion received a cuff to his head.

"I hate it," Khan growled. "The polis was the birthplace of democracy. I have no interest in democracy." And under his breath he added: "It also sounds stupid."

"Ahh, yes, stupid, stupid, so stupid."

"New Khan City," Khan said, finally.

"New Khan City! Yes. Glorious. Wonderful." Gonga hopped up and down, quickly scribbling the name. "I shall alert the generals, tell the soldiers, broadcast to the humans—"

Khan silenced Gonga and stopped walking.

They'd come upon an intersection—Broadway and 57th. Over there, a deli—a small fire inside still burning. Across the corner from that, a Rolls sat overturned, drowned beneath the spray from a busted hydrant.

No birds. No apes. No dinosaurs.

In the distance: a throaty reptilian bellow swiftly cut short.

Khan turned to the trio of saurian humanoids standing there, staring ahead, seemingly unfazed. He shook one. "What do you sense? Do you sense anything? Tell me!"

Damnable creatures. Plucked from the doomed cities of their ancient civilization and they were still harder to read than cardboard.

"Sir," Gonga began, "Ahh, if they sensed something surely we'd know? They'd grow, umm, ahh, *agitated*."

"Something's wrong," Khan asserted.

"All is well!" Gonga said, making that awful rasping half-laugh, *heh-heh, heh-heh*. "See? The city is—"

Gonga's head snapped back. An arrow thwacked into his eye and the white ape tumbled backward. Khan's blood boiled and in the deep well of his barrel chest he felt the jungle drums of his own rage-fueled heartbeat kick into a panicked, pounding rhythm—all at the same time another two arrows flew true, one jutting out of the chest of a saurian, the other piercing the throat of one of the restless eotyrannus.

The saurian crumpled. The eotyrannus listed and fell over.

And then they appeared.

They came from everywhere. Men, but not men. Long hair. Short, thick bodies. Broad faces and thick brows. Wearing skins and leathers or nothing at all. They poured from windows, came up from out of the manholes, and swung down from rooftops and awnings and balconies.

They were coming.

They were coming *for him*.

An arrow snapped against Khan's armored chest and bounced off and landed on the ground, its flinty shaft catching the fading light of the afternoon.

His ape soldiers leapt into battle, rushing forward to meet the clashing subhuman horde.

The Conqueror Ape spun toward the two remaining psychic saurians. Both of which stood, panicked like spooked cats, hissing at nothing. Khan screamed at them: "Do something! Reach out with your minds! Save me!"

A stone-bladed hatchet whirled through the air, caught one of the saurians dead in the chest, dropping him like a brick. An arrow took down the other one.

The eotyrannus shrieked and ran the other direction.

Which suddenly seemed like a very good idea.

He had to flee.

Had to run.

Khan turned tail and bolted.

Atok had little understanding—and, frankly, little *interest* in understanding—exactly how the infrastructure of a human city worked. The ins and outs mattered little. He didn't know or care that the tunnels beneath the city were built by sandhogs and that many of those tunnels went very deep. All that mattered was such tunnels provided a very thin membrane between the Upland and the Hollow Earth and that with minimal effort, Atok and his Neanderthal army were able to break through and enter the city.

And now, only an hour later, Atok already had one of their primate leaders—if not *the* leader—on the run. Bounding away from his invading throng. Climbing up the side of a building and disappearing around its side.

Atok twirled his basher, a mace carved from the bones of a blind cave mammoth, the head of the weapon a tangle of tusk-tips curving this way and that.

He called to his warriors, who numbered in the hundreds.

It was time to hunt an ape.

CHAPTER THIRTY
THE KOLOA CHAPTER HOUSE

Jet sat at the far end of the table, listening to Khan put up a dizzying laundry list of Things To Do To Save The World—save the other Centurions, find the location of the lost city of Atlantis, defeat the Conqueror Ape—but, in reality, he was only barely tuning in.

Mostly, he was watching Sally.

And trying to make sure that no one was watching him watch Sally.

She was beautiful. Tough, yes, but soft, too. Eyes like glittery opals. A mouth that spoke its mind and did so with the hint of a pretty smile that wouldn't go away, not if you covered it in a blanket, threw it in a trunk, and dropped it on the bottom of the sea.

They grew up together. They were *always* together.

And he loved her. Maybe he always had.

He knew that, now.

And she didn't feel the same about him.

Not yet. Maybe not ever.

And then there was Mack. *Mack Silver.* Jet couldn't help it—just thinking about the self-proclaimed Silver Fox felt like bugs crawling up the back of his neck. And he *liked* Mack. They were buddies. Er, in theory. Mack and Sally didn't have any place together: Mack was a globe-trotting, liquor-swilling ladies' man. Sally needed more than that. She deserved more than that.

Suddenly, before he realized what was happening, the whole room was staring at him.

"Wh..." he began. "What?"

Amelia spoke: "I asked if you had any ideas?"

"Oh. Right." He cleared his throat. Averted his gaze from Sally. "I, uhh." He struggled to find something, anything, that was pertinent to the discussion. He instead tried to divert: "Whatever we do is going to be awfully hard with those psychosaurs playing games with our gourds, you know?" There. Whew.

Except, then a small voice spoke up from the other side of the room. A clearing of the throat and a slight, "I may have an idea."

They all pivoted their heads. There stood Edwin.

Khan smiled and stepped aside. "Edwin? You have something to say, my boy?"

"I do," said the diminutive Brit—Jet was not himself a big guy, but Edwin Jasher made him look like the Colossus. "It would seem that the problem first and foremost is, as Mister Jet suggested, the psychosaurs. It is their mind control that stands in our way above all else."

Khan lifted an eyebrow. "And what do you propose we do about it, boy?"

"It was something *you* said, Professor," Edwin chirped. "Mystical metallurgy. Brass as a protective metal."

Both Khan and Benjamin looked to each other at the same moment, their eyes lighting up. Like they both realized something big at the same time.

"We can use brass!" Khan said.

"To block the signal," Benjamin added. "*Of course.*"

"The psychosaur alpha waves would—" Khan paused and scratched his head. "Well, where in the brain would they affect? The amygdala, most assuredly, but how to block just that one little walnut-sized piece of brain?"

Benjamin paced. "No, you're thinking of the brain. We need to be thinking of the *mind.*" Jet watched the two of them orbit one another. They were quite the match, these two. "Brass is a mystical metal, and so we must assume that all the mind should be protected. The *mystical* and psychic mind. When telekinetics and healers work their mind magic, they touch their temples. The crown chakras. Yes! That's it. The temples. We need to protect our temples."

"The brass fittings," Sally said, pointing to the pipes and conduits. "They're all held there with brass. I can rig something up. Something with some tension, something that holds the brass from around the back of the head."

"How long will that take?" Amelia asked.

"I might need some help prying them off the walls—and it might mess with the power down here in the chapter house—but five or six hours, tops." As if to demonstrate, Sally spun the wrench and smiled. Jet's heart spun and smiled along with her.

"So, then what?" Jet asked. Seemed a smart question, after all.

"We split up," Amelia said. "We each tackle a different problem. Khan. Atlantis. The other heroes. Three teams of two."

"Makes sense," Sally said—but did Jet hear a grudging tone in her voice?

"Oh," Khan said. "I don't know—I don't know that I belong with you all—"

Jet stood up. He wasn't going to hear another word of it.

"Professor, far as I'm concerned, you're as much a Centurion as any of us. Without you we'd all still be knocking ourselves in the heads with coconuts." Jet shot Mack a look. "Ain't that right, Mack?"

"Mmm," Mack said, forcing a smile. "A real hero. Total Centurion. Happy to have you and all that happy hullaballoo."

Amelia nodded. "Right. Solves that. So, who's with who and who's doing what?"

Mack grinned. Looked to Sally. "I'm with Sa—"

"He's with me," Jet blurted out. A horrible idea, maybe, but there it was.

"Whoa!" Mack said, blustery. "Hold up, Flyboy, that's not what I was gonna—"

"We'll hit Khan in New York," Jet said. "It makes sense. We're both airborne, both versatile, and can wreak havoc on his dirigibles."

"Wait, *wait*," Mack protested, "I was thinking that maybe Sally and I—"

Sally interjected: "I'd like to travel with you, Professor. I think I'd like to see what kind of technology Atlantis has to offer, but I think I'll need your big brain to understand it."

"Agreed!" the Professorial primate said. Jet felt a small moment of triumph—while he wouldn't be with Sally, neither would Mack. It felt a bit like falling on the grenade: painful, but perhaps worth the sacrifice.

Amelia walked and offered her hand to Benjamin. "Looks like it's you and me, detective. You good with that?"

"Quite," he said with a smile.

"Only one problem," Amelia said. They all looked to her. "We have three destinations and two planes. That makes this math a bit tricky."

It was like someone stole the air out of the room. Before that it felt like everything was in motion, plans were forming, teams were made. Now it seemed suddenly hopeless again.

"I have a new idea," Sally said. "This chapter house is fueled by a very strange power source. I'd like to track that power to the source. And then I'd like to use it."

Benjamin asked what everybody else was thinking:

"Use it for what?"

"I want to build a teleporter. That's how we're getting to Atlantis."

CHAPTER THIRTY-ONE
NEW YORK CITY

Mighty Khan's muscles ached so bad he thought his tendons were going to snap like guitar strings—climbing up the side of the Empire State was murder on his body, and a dread voice in the back of his mind whispered: *You're aging, old gorilla.*

'Old gorilla.' Can't be. Won't be. He could go toe to toe with the youngest among them. That's why he was the Conqueror. The ruler of all had to be ready to stand and fight, to demonstrate his leadership—

And that's why you're running away from some caveman?

He chuffed out loud as the wind whipped past his face, barking at his own interior doubts. "I'm pretending!" he said to no one but himself, most of his growling voice lost to the air currents up here. "*Pretending* to flee so that they become overconfident and make mistakes."

Yes. Yes! That was it. He wasn't weak. He was *surviving*. Using guile and trickery. Signals of a higher mind. A mind far more advanced than those... primitives.

Who *were* those warriors who thought to invade this city? *His* city!

New Khan City!

No time to think about that now. He finally reached the lip of the ledge outside his war-room and swung himself up into the open space.

Inside, Botu and a cadre of other warriors had a map of the city laid out and were ooking and grunting over it. Caught in the throes of some strategy argument; the map was marked with a series of red circles and X's—circles and X's that did not matter.

They saw him enter and immediately panicked, each of them shuffling to the margins of the room as if to make way for Mighty Khan's not-so-mighty entrance. The ape-lord stood, frazzled, unsure what to do next. Again that doubting voice: *you've never made it this far, have you? Atlantis was one thing—they barely fought back. But this, the entire metropolis of New York City? The entire world? How do you expect to hold onto the globe when you can't even control the city in which you stand?*

"Shut up!" he shouted, though no one in the room spoke. They all bowed their heads further. Khan stormed over to the map, flattened it back out and began stabbing at it with the flat of his ape-finger. "Look. I *said*, all of you look!"

Botu and the others hurried over. Khan bared his teeth.

"We are under attack. By... someone new. Primitive man. They came here, from the direction of Central Park. We need to stage a counter—"

Somewhere outside, echoing over the city, the sound of a dinosaur screaming. A Tyrannosaurus Rex, perhaps.

Just then, the doors to the war-room burst open. Rutah, one of his war generals, stormed in, her eyes wide and wild. "Mighty Khan!" she cried, hurrying before him and bending knee. "We are attacked. From the south. By men. Men that came up through the earth. Through the holes in the street. Through the subway tunnels!" She cried out, a lamentation to her weakness. "We must strike back. You must ride the Giganotosaurus and lead us into battle!"

"No, no, no," Khan mumbled. None of this was happening. They were coming from the *south*, too? Where was Gonga? "Gonga!" he cried out, but only his own internal voice answered: *He's dead, don't you remember? Your old gorilla mind is becoming feeble.*

The doors opened again. Another silverback came shouldering through. Khan didn't even know this one's name—thick, almost reddish fur, and as if to mock him, *old*. The gorilla's face a mask of cavernous lines and wrinkles, like an apple left out to dry in the sun.

"Glorious Khan," the old one said, "I was hoping to meet with your attaché..."

"Who are you?" Khan barked. "Get out of my chamber!"

"I am Koku. And I have news, Ape-Lord—"

"Yes, old ape, I know. We are under attack."

"It's not that, sir. It's the tracker. The..." He tried to form the word with his wrinkled simian lips: "Peta... peto... peteinosaur."

The peteinosaur. With its little collar of fungus—the same fungus found on every dinosaur here in the present. A critical component, in fact. That fungus was the high-energy food-source of the psychosaurs and in fact they seemed to share something of a psychic connection with the stuff. They smeared the material around the necks of other dinosaurs—or at the base of the head—and that gave them control over the beasts same as a leash gives a man control of his dog.

That was the thing—Khan did not control the dinosaurs. Not directly.

The psychosaurs did that.

But Khan controlled the psychosaurs.

Didn't he?

"What about it?" Khan asked. *Tell me you found my son.*

"It... moved."

"The heroes are on the move?"

Koku shrugged. "It would appear so. It would be better if I gave this news to Gonga and Gonga could tell you—"

"Gonga is not here!" Khan said, lips wet with froth. "Just tell me. Where is the little creature now? Where have the heroes gone?"

"They've gone to the Blackspire, Mighty Khan."

"The Blackspire." He said it, but it barely registered. The command dirigible. The biggest airship in Khan's fleet. Captained by Pilot Mozo. And home to the majority of the captured Centurions—all of them vacuumed up into the sky and kept in storage, their minds lost, flung to the margins of time itself. "You're telling me the heroes have gone onboard our most capable craft. Our incredibly *well-defended* crown of the fleet?"

"If I could just meet with Gonga—"

"This is good news," Khan said. Outside, he heard the shrieks of pterodactyls, saw their shadows swoop past the window toward the ground. That meant those missing links were here, with their bone clubs and flinty arrows and crooked spears. But Khan didn't care. Because if the heroes were aboard the Blackspire, that meant his *son* was aboard the Blackspire. "Where is the Blackspire now, Koku?"

"The psychosaurs say it's over the West Coast, Mighty Khan. Los Angeles, I believe." How did the heroes find it, anyhow? The psychosaurs made it easy for Khan to track—all those reptilian freaks had to do was stand around a map and just *point*. Long as they had some of that glowing yellow fungus to interface with, it was deliciously simple. That's how they knew where the peteinosaur was. Simply ask them and they point. And probably hiss. And stare blankly.

Such strange beings. No spark of wildness, no predatory *hunger*. Not a surprise they were going to go extinct, Khan thought. Before he stepped in and conquered them, of course.

"I'm going to the Blackspire," he declared.

Rutah's face fell. "But, Mighty Khan, the barbarians are at our gates—"

"And the *heroes* are about to strike a blow against our greatest airship," Khan seethed. He neglected to mention that he didn't expect that the heroes had a snowball's chance in the Devil's own hands and that the only thought galloping through his mind was that he was finally going to see his son again. It didn't seem... pertinent. "You're the war general of New Khan City."

"New Khan what?"

Ah. Right. They weren't there when that was decided less than an hour ago.

Khan snarled: "It's what we're calling it now. The city. This city. New Khan—oh, never mind. Just fight back the damn half-men and restore order to my prize metropolis." He spun around and met Koku's wrinkled visage. "Ready my biplane, Koku. I must leave at once."

"Mighty Ape-Lord," Koku said, bowing his head and hurrying off fast as an old gorilla could manage. *That is an old gorilla*, Khan thought, suddenly feeling young again.

CHAPTER THIRTY-TWO
THE KOLOA CHAPTER HOUSE

Benjamin spread out the map and closed his eyes. In his palm he held seven rocks—little porous hunks of solidified lava taken from the ground outside the longhouse.

"Seven gates," he said, envisioning the tunnel of time and space which he had used to teleport himself here to the Koloa chapter house. He further imagined the map he'd seen on the cave wall, the one with the seven glowing runes, each representing what he believed was one Atlantean portal. The thorny bit was trying to place *that* map—a map of a very old planet Earth where the continents had not all separated out—as an overlay above the map beneath him. "I know that one of the gates is outside Hong Kong. Waglan Island."

He thunked down one of the rocks at that location. Eyes open.

Amelia spoke up. "Another on Lundy Island. Bristol Channel."

"Yes," Benjamin said, plunking down another piece of lava. "That's two." He let one of the stones hover over the eastern coast of Africa. "They must be using the gateways to move their armies and stage invasions—whether from Atlantis proper or from the far-flung past. Further, it is safe to assume that each gate is on an island given the Atlantean propensity to be out at sea, and moreover, I have already deduced that the gateways lie at the points of nexus for powerful ley lines. Which means this gate is…"

He dropped the stone.

"Moheli. Indian Ocean. French protectorate, but only barely."

"That's three," Khan said, standing on the far side of the table.

"Given the invasions of New York City and, as seen on the televisors, Los Angeles, we can construe that America is framed by two more gates—and that fits with my memory of the original stone map. But where, exactly?"

"When we flew out of the Big Apple," Mack said, "we didn't see squat along the Jersey side of things."

"North, then." Benjamin tapped the map. "Here. Block Island. Northeast of the tip of Long Island. Matches the others. Few people there. Lighthouse. Agreed?"

Nods and mumbles all around. Only two missing were Jet and Sally—Jet was off helping her with the brass fittings.

"West Coast?" Khan asked. "The South Farellon islands are off of San Francisco."

"Yes, and that would work," Benjamin said, his hand hovering over a tiny little pinprick west of the City by the Bay. "But! It's awfully far out. And my memory of the stone map has it further south…"

"By Los Angeles, then," Edwin said, a quiet mousey squeak.

Khan clapped him on the shoulders. "Sensible, my boy."

Edwin smiled a mouth of crooked British teeth.

"Channel Islands make sense," Amelia said. "Not sure which one, though."

Benjamin *hmm*ed. "Probably doesn't matter but let's assume the furthest flung—San Miguel island." *Thunk.* Another rock on the map. "Only two more to go."

He dropped one rock east of Brazil.

He dropped the other somewhere north and east of Papua New Guinea.

He said, "This one is somewhere in the Marshall Islands. Could be on one of a hundred islands even in this little cluster. Rough guess? Majuro. Here. It was here many of the gods of the region were born—it's a sacred space and makes sense that such stories might have risen up around one of the Atlantean gates, even if it wasn't active."

"Mythology could play a part," Khan said, suddenly lost in thought.

"And here," Benjamin said, tapping the rock off the coast of South America, "*Ilha dos Buzios.* Past *Ilhabela*, the beautiful island. Or maybe *Ilha Comprida*? Not certain."

"That's seven," Mack said.

Amelia gave him a nudge in the ribs. "Good. You can count."

"Har, har."

"It all adds up," Benjamin said. "All strong loci of ley line power. And the line running from the Marshall Islands gate to the gate just outside Los Angeles would cross..." He tapped a small cluster of islands. "Here. Hawaii. The same energy that's powering up this chapter house and providing the light by which we see."

"So, now what?" Amelia asked. "Sally and the Professor will just start building a teleporter?" To this, Ben shook his head.

"No, for that we will need to know the precise location of the ley lines. The energy must form a nexus somewhere. A line that might also connect the Brazil and Hong Kong gates. But I do not yet know how to pinpoint that."

"I have an idea," Khan said. "*And* I have an idea to help us locate Khan's dirigible."

"Do not keep us waiting, Professor," Benjamin said with a smile.

"You're quiet," Sally said, using a pair of metal snips to bite through and cut off pieces of brass from the fixtures they pulled down. Jet worked further down the lava tube "hallway" (really just a tunnel), using a screwdriver to pry the fixtures out of the rock.

"Just busy."

"You think this is really going to work?"

"I dunno. Maybe."

"That doesn't sound like the glass-half-full guy I know." To this, he said nothing. Like a bird, she kept pecking. "Okay, so what's wrong?"

"Nothing."

"It's about Mack, isn't it." It came as a statement, not a question.

She studied his face, saw the answer telegraphed there even before he said it: "Yeah. Yes. Jeez. It's about Mack."

"You don't like that we..." *Oh, just say it, you wilting lily.* "Kissed."

Jet took the piece of curved brass he held and idly turned it over and over again. "I'm not a real big fan of the idea, no."

"I kind of figured as much." She crimped a small square of brass—luckily, the fittings weren't more than a couple millimeters thick, like tinfoil folded over a few times—and used some stiff wire she found inside one of Lucy's toolboxes to wrap around the notched squares. "You want to talk about it."

"I, uhh." He stepped over to her, then turned back around, and then turned back around *again* so that he was facing her. "What I want to say is, I, uhh."

This was hard for him. She could see that. "I'm not going to make you say it."

"You're not?"

"I'm not."

She smiled, took his hand in her own.

He looked down at it. Whispered: "Oh."

"You think Mack wasn't right for me."

"That's... that's true."

"That I can do better."

"That too."

"I appreciate you looking out for me."

He smiled. "You always look out for me."

"I do." She gave his hand a little squeeze. "It's because we're family. You're like my little brother. You had my best interests in your heart all along. I knew how you were feeling and I just didn't want to admit it. You're right. It's stupid to get involved with another Centurion like that. Like we're not busy enough I have to have my head all dizzy around some silly romance?"

"Silly," he repeated, in a seeming daze. "...yeah."

"That's what you were going to say, right?"

He pulled away. Offered her a smile, though for some reason she could've sworn it wasn't all that happy. "That's exactly it."

She gave him a little fake punch to the shoulder and smiled. "Here. Put this on." She held up the headband with the brass squares. It fit like a pair of reverse eyeglasses, almost. "Pop it on around the back of your head. The wire should sit over your ears, but it's flexible, too—" She helped fit it on. "There you go. Just a couple tugs here and there and... ta-da. How's it fit, Flyboy?"

"Good. Fine. Snug as a bug in a rug."

Sally gave a little yawp of triumph, then kissed him on the cheek. "We might just save the day yet. Go tell the others. I've got more of these to make."

"Mythology could play a part," Professor Khan said, reiterating what he'd said earlier (and mostly to himself). "If we look at Hawaiian myth—and history!—what do we find? We discover that one place is chock full of *heiaus*—or temples—more than any other here in the islands. That place is Waipio Valley, the so-called Valley of the Kings. It is a place supposedly protected by a healing energy—the waters of every tsunami fail to reach Waipio, and those who are sick sometimes take pilgrimages there. It is said that in the valley, Mana collects there."

"How do you know all this?" Mack asked, either dubious, impressed, or some strange mixture of both.

"I read a lot." He neglected to add, *And my brain is larger than yours.*

Mack leaned over to Amelia and with a smirk muttered: "Maybe I should start using books for something other than propping up my cockpit chair."

"Waipio's on the main island," Benjamin said. "All the myths tend to originate there. Pele and Kane-milo-hai. And it's the only island in the chain with a still-active volcano—Kilauea." Benjamin stood up, started speaking with his hands as well. He brought his palms and fingers together and then back apart, mimicking a volcano rising and erupting. "Such dramatic earthly activity generates a lot of mystical energy." He paused to consider: "Though perhaps it's the reverse. Perhaps the intense energy gathering there results in cataclysmic movement? Well. No matter. I think we have a place to go, then."

"Still doesn't help us find the Blackspire," Mack said. "That damn blimp could be out there anywhere. With all the best heroes in its belly."

It was then that Jet came in. Khan noticed that Jet's normal *get-up-and-go* seemed to have *fallen-down-a-flight-of-stairs.* Crestfallen would be the word, Khan thought.

Jet held up the brass-and-wire circlet. "Sally made the first prototype. She's got more coming, but it works. Or, at least, it fits."

"That Sally," Mack said. "Always coming through in a pinch."

Khan wasn't sure if Silver said it sincerely or with some measure of bitterness. "Finding the Blackspire," Khan said, refocusing the discussion the same way he would with his students at Oxford, "is no easy task. After all, we have all the skies above the whole of the Earth that could be home to that one airship—which is not so much like finding a needle in a haystack as it is finding a mote of dust floating around a darkened room."

"Ugh, metaphors," Mack said. Everyone shot him a look.

"But we can make some, as Benjamin would say, deductions," Khan continued. "We can deduce that the Blackspire is near to one of the seven Atlantean gates. It most likely uses those to travel between parts of the world. Further, that means it's likely near to a ley line nexus, just as we are. If you look at some of the Centurions who have been made captive, some of them have strong psychic capabilities. The Mentalist, or Charmaine Krikoshki, or—"

Benjamin said it with him: "The Projector."

"Assuming that the teleportation device Sally builds works, then we can use that to teleport to the psychic signal of a hero like the Projector. It should take you right to the Blackspire. Further, Mack and Jet can teleport directly to New York City. If we are truly able to access the ley lines as a transportation—well, I hesitate to use the word 'grid' given the tangled skein of these lines—then we are as good as gold."

"That's making an awful lot of assumptions," Amelia said.

Mack showed her his wolfish grin. "That, my dear, is what we do. But me and Flyboy over there will take our chances with Lucy. Direct flight and all that. Besides, we don't want to get in Sally's way. Ain't that right, Jet?"

Jet gave a nod. "Sounds right. Mack."

"So, it's settled," Khan said. "The rest of us go to Waipio?"

They agreed.

They go to Waipio.

PART THREE:
IT'S A TRAP!

CHAPTER THIRTY-THREE
WAIPIO VALLEY

It had been two days, and the teleporter still wasn't working.

"It works on paper," Sally said again and again, pointing to her notes and blueprints. The idea, after all, was relatively simple: at the most sacred of Hawaiian temples, the heiau of Pakaalana, Sally would dig deep and tap into the mystical flow of energy the same way one might tap into a maple and access the sweet syrup inside.

From there, the energy would feed into a pair of homespun Tesla coils— except here the coils were meant to produce an outpouring of mystical energy rather than the alternating current of electricity. The energy would— *should!*—be directed onto the crumbling stone platform (like the base of a pyramid if the majority of the ruin had long been sheared away) and create there a gateway, beaming anybody standing on said platform into the occulted network of ley lines.

In theory.

Alternatively, it might rip apart the atoms holding together the human body and incorporate them into the Earth's mystical energy.

Not that it mattered, because, as noted, the teleporter still didn't work.

Mack and Jet had flown them all to the coast, where the waves crashed and the riptide hungered, and then Lucy was gone again.

Soon after, it started to rain.

And it had been raining since. They took cold comfort in the fact that at least they did not have to descend into the valley the hard way—coming to Waipio from the rest of the island meant traveling over a thousand feet into the valley, down muddy trails and past sheer rock walls cut into by the razor-sharp erosion of needle-straight waterfalls.

The valley itself was beautiful, even in the rain—taro patches and fish-ponds and a color green that none of them had ever seen before, as if the plants of this place thrived on the energy that pulsed beneath it all.

But the rain was—if you asked locals—a sign of bad things to come.

As they pushed forward into the valley from the beach, hauling their gear and Sally's equipment from the beach down the mud-slick trails toward Pakalaana, a man caught up with them—a bare-chested native holding a taro leaf over his head. "You should not be here," he said in English. "The others sent me to speak to you. Turn around. Go home. Go back." He kept his eyes on Khan above all others. Nervous, darting eyes.

"It'll be okay," Amelia said to him, reaching for his shoulder to comfort the man. But he pulled away.

"It will not! Whatever you come to do, you come to ruin. You always come to ruin."

And then he fled again, bounding down another trail toward a longhouse in the distance.

"We may want to stop," Benjamin said. "It may be time to consult with his people. To speak with the *kahuna* and find out what we're up against—"

"No," Sally said. "I'm sorry, but we just don't have time. He says crazy stuff most of the time but here I have to agree with Mack. The time for talking is over. This is the time for doing."

"I agree," Amelia said, shielding herself from the rain.

Khan nodded, too. "I... I also agree."

Benjamin nodded. "Then we push on."

They pushed on. When they got to the heiau, they used hand augurs to dig deep as Sally built the coils and placed them to the sides of the stone dais, and as they worked the man with the taro leaf over his head would show every few hours. Usually saying nothing. Sometimes accompanied by others who stayed further away—one time he even brought a few children as if to set an example of what not to do, or perhaps what the boogeyman looked like.

One time he said something even more ominous: "If you do not quit," he called over the rain, "then you will find your flesh in the mouth of Nanaue."

And then, he fled. Again.

Now, after these two fruitless days, the teleporter still wasn't working—the most they'd accomplished was a few violet sparks, each ethereal and ephemeral, before the coils again went dark. The rain never quit. The valley was growing sodden and their feet were sinking into the mud. Everything was looking hopeless.

It was about to get a whole lot worse.

Echoing through the valley came a terrible sound—a shrieking cry that sounded as if it originated from a man but then changed into that of a beast.

It was distant, far off, but the threat was clear.

"Dinosaurs," Amelia said.

"No," Khan responded. "They don't sound like... that."

"Nanaue," Benjamin said.

Amelia turned toward him, narrowed her eyes. "You say that like you know what it means."

He gave a sheepish look. "I... do."

"Care to enlighten us?"

Everyone huddled around Benjamin.

"I thought it just a myth," he said.

"What's just a myth?" Sally asked, wiping her hands on her overalls and squinting against the knife-slash rain that fell.

"Nanaue the Shark-Man," Benjamin said. "A cannibal—an eater-of-men. Cursed by his people to become half-shark and to protect this valley."

"That's what the native was talking about," Amelia said. "Flesh in the mouth of Nanaue."

Another half-man cry over the din of the falling rain.

"He's hunting us," Khan said. "He'll find us eventually."

"Not if we find him first," Sally said, picking up a wrench and whacking it against her hands. "We know what's going to happen here. He's going to come for us. And if we're not careful he's going to tear apart what I've built. I say we go to him, first."

"I can get behind that," Amelia said.

Benjamin nodded. "It may be the wisest course of action."

"I'll stay here," Khan said. "I won't be much good to you out there. I can keep working on Sally's design. See if I can't figure something out."

"Professor," Edwin said, "if I may? I think you should go. I think... well, sir, I think it's time you accepted your role as a man on the frontlines, not as some lofty academic hiding in the back. You're a hero, sir. You're my hero. And I believe that they're going to need your help out there if you care to give it."

"Edwin," Khan began. "I don't know, my boy..."

Amelia clapped Khan on the back. "He's right. Join us."

"I... I will." Khan's lips curled into a smile, revealing a mouth of very sharp teeth. "Let us hunt this Shark-Man before he hunts us."

Edwin, of course, stayed behind.

He sat there on the stone dais as the day advanced and the hours passed toward another evening in the Waipio Valley. Across the valley came the shouts of the Centurions and the occasional roar of the Shark-Man.

He did not know who was winning. He could only hope.

Eventually, he caught the scent—again that whiff of ozone, and when he closed his eyes he spied a sudden burst of strange symbols written in light in the dark behind his eyelids.

Gerard Spears sat next to him. Appearing out of nowhere. As was his way.

"They still haven't quite got it yet, have they?" he asked. Edwin found himself suddenly taken out of the rain as an umbrella opened with a *fwump* above his head.

"No, I suppose not."

"Sometimes, the universe needs a nudge."

"It does."

"Why do I have to be the one to nudge it?" Spears asked.

"Because you're the one with the magic."

"I am, I am. Well, three things need to happen for this teleporter to work. Do you know what they are, Edwin?"

"I do but I have a feeling you're going to want to hear yourself say it anyway."

"True enough! First, they must defeat the Shark-Man. It is his will that rules this valley. Second, one of them must spill blood. I don't know which one will suffer—maybe all of them, who can say? If I had all the answers this grand design would not be much fun, would it?"

"It wouldn't."

"And the third thing is—they've dug in the wrong spot, silly gits."

"Have they?"

"You can't sense it." It was a statement, not a question.

Edwin shrugged, gave another hangdog smile. "As we've established, you're the one with the magic."

"Right-o. Right-o. Anyway, yes, they've gone and missed the spot by—" Spears got up, forcing Edwin to hop up and follow lest he once more be drowned like a rat in the rain. They both went to the hole where a series of copper wires disappeared into the mud.

"Less than a foot, honestly. I suppose you can't blame them. Being what they are and all."

"They're not you, is what you're saying," Edwin offered.

"Well, to be fair, they're not you, either."

"I suppose not." Edwin kicked a clump of dirt into the hole. "What can be done? Must we wait until they figure out their error and fix it? Oh my, that could be days. I have a sense that things are moving much faster, now."

"They are. And so the overall equation must be... massaged, my little friend." Spears again removed from his pocket a satchel. This one rattled with stones white and black, like those stolen from an abacus. He took a palmful of them, poked through them with a probing finger. Those strange symbols—like the ones Edwin saw burned into the backs of his eyelids only minutes ago—were etched onto each pebble.

Spears tilted his hand, let the pebbles rain into the hole.

A puff of black smoke.

And then the hole vanished, only to pop up an instant later—six inches to the left.

"There we go," Spears said, snapping his fingers. "Lickety-split."

"And the other problem?" Edwin asked.

"They will have to deal with the Shark-Man on their own. I have other things to do."

As if for punctuation, the Shark-Man's wretched cry came again, echoing over the valley and through the storm. Edwin turned toward it, and when he turned back around—Gerard Spears had gone.

CHAPTER THIRTY-FOUR
NEW YORK CITY

This was not what either of them expected.

Jet Black blasted through the steel and glass canyons of New York City, wind rushing past his ears and inflating his cheeks—the jet-wing was faster and cleaner than anything he'd ever flown, able to turn on a pinhead and perform dazzling aerial feats. He felt like one of the barn swallows he used to see back home, flitting through rafters and between barn boards and ducking and diving like the very laws of physics had no place among those birds.

Good thing, too, because otherwise, he and Mack might be already dead. Another stone-tipped spear sailed in their wake, missing them by inches, not feet—it was spears and arrows and sling-flung marbles of hematite, all fired with alarming speed by—

Well, by Neanderthal men, from the looks of it.

New York City was embroiled in a war. But not the war Jet would've figured. This was chaos unlike anything they'd ever encountered. The streets below them lay choked with half-men and gorilla stormtroopers and screeching dinosaurs. Just moments ago Jet soared over the head of a T-Rex as it ripped a Neanderthal right off the street and pitched the primitive warrior through a café storefront.

The war raged in his ears—the hoots and screams of apes, the ululations of pale Neanderthals, the shrieks of dinosaurs.

Still wasn't enough to drown out the screams of Mack Silver.

Jet held Mack under the arms and thanks to Sally's forethought had a leather strap to bind the two Centurions together at the chest.

Since they took off, Mack hadn't stopped screaming.

Jet had to admit: it pleased him. He wasn't proud. But he *was* happy.

Up ahead—the gleaming spire of the Empire State Building. *Back again*, Jet thought. Irony was alive and well. After landing in the river and managing to interrogate one of the gorilla sentries protecting the edges of Manhattan ("New Khan City," the ape said through clenched teeth), they found out all they needed to know: the city had fallen to Khan's army; a new invasion force had arrived from, if the ape was to be believed, "down beneath the ground;" and Khan's central command center was the Empire State Building. Go figure, Jet thought.

Right where it all began. For him, at least.

"Coming in for a landing!" he yelled to Mack.

"Land! Land! *Land!*" Mack screamed. Not, Jet believed, unlike a little girl.

The observation deck. Perfect.

Jet sailed over the fence, shot straight up—another delicious yelp from the so-called Silver Fox—and then floated back down again. An elegant landing, Jet thought.

Mack, panting fast, unclipped the belt and dropped to the deck on the flat of his hands. He pressed his forehead there and cooed like a pigeon.

"I love this observation deck," Mack said, rubbing his cheek against it. "I love you, concrete. I love you, ground."

Jet knelt down. "Thought you liked flying the friendly skies?"

"Suck an egg, Pally," Silver said.

"This a bad time to mention that we're still almost 900 feet up in the air?"

Mack finally got onto his hands and knees. "You know, none of this would be a problem if you didn't drag me along on your little adventure. Why couldn't you go with the monkey?"

"The ape. He's an ape. And you know why."

"Oh, we're gonna finally talk about this? After two days of keeping your clap shut *now* you're gonna open up like a damn oyster?"

"She's not right for you."

"Maybe she gets to decide that."

"Maybe she does," Jet said. "But maybe she's not hip to your lies. Maybe she thinks she's different. *Maybe* she thinks she's gonna be more than just another port-of-call for the island-hopping Mack Silver. But we both know different, don't we?"

Mack, still on his hands and knees, didn't say anything. Something flashed there across his face, though—something Jet wished he never saw. Jet squeezed his eyes shut, then offered a hand. "Here. Get up."

The pilot stood on wobbly legs.

"Really?" Jet asked.

"She *is* different," Mack said.

"You think that now. But what if you're wrong?"

"I..." Mack's voice trailed off. "You don't know me, Flyboy. Maybe I got a heart, you know? Maybe I'm up for doing something different with my life."

Jet set his jaw. "Not this time, you don't."

"Oh, Flyboy's grown a pair." Mack's fingers curled into fists. "Let's see if you—"

Just then, the door to the deck popped open.

Two apes. Decked in chainmail. Trailed by a pair of psychosaurs—for the moment they looked human, but Jet and Mack both knew the truth. Jet saw the face shimmer—sometimes it melted away like fast-oozing candlewax, revealing the emotionless (and noseless) saurian face beneath before the face flickered and resumed the mask.

Before Jet could say, "Save it for later," Mack was already redirecting his anger. The ape on the right never saw what was coming—Mack's fist crossed left like a rocket flying in front of the moon, and the ape attacker tumbled backward into one of the psychosaurs. Jet leapt in, gave himself a short boost from the jet-wing's air boosters, and delivered a sharp flying kick under the chin of the other ape.

Leaving one psychosaur.

The creature hissed.

That's when Jet felt it—like fingers probing at the edge of his mind, looking for a crack, hoping for a way to find a gap and pry back the invisible door.

But the grip was oily, uncertain, sliding off.

The headband worked!

Mack smiled. "Nice job, Sally."

"She does know her stuff," Jet said.

Together, they stormed forward. They grabbed the psychosaur under the armpits and the creature hissed and flailed, trying to bite at them with its needled maw now that its psychic attack was foiled by a couple pairs of flattened brass. They hurled the psychosaur against the fence and the creature slid downward—*lights out.*

"C'mon," Mack said. "Let's go wrangle ourselves a megalomaniac ape."

The old ape winced, a thin trail of blood trickling from his prodigious nostril. He'd put up a good fight—threw Jet back, broke the map table, damn near flung Mack out the window—but the two heroes came back good and strong, putting the ape on the ground.

"He has gone!" Koku cried. "Mighty Khan has left the city."

"You're *lying*," Mack said through clenched teeth, rearing back another fist.

"No! I am not lying. He said—he said you had gone to the Blackspire. To rescue the other lost Centurions."

The tension left Mack's fist.

He and Jet shared a look, and the message conveyed in that alarmed gaze was the same: *How would he know that was part of the plan?*

Outside, they heard a clamor—apes ooking and screaming, things breaking, the murmur of voices and again, an all-too-familiar ululation.

Jet knew what that meant—and his suspicions were immediately borne out as a tide of Neanderthals spilled into the room, spears out, arrows nocked, bone axes and clubs held aloft. Jet immediately backpedaled toward the shattered window, knowing he could just drop out and into open space. But as Mack moved to join him, all arrows pointed at him.

"Move and die," one of the pale half-men said, grunting. The dozen or so warriors—many of them beaten, battered, bloody—parted to let the one who spoke through. This one had the air of a leader about him. He carried himself, chest puffed out, chin high.

Mack lifted a foot to take a ginger step backward and Jet could hear the tension in a half-dozen drawn bows *creak*.

"Mack," Jet cautioned. "Don't. Move."

The leader nodded. "Arrows. Poison. You move. You die."

"No problem," Mack said, offering a false smile and surrendering hands. "You speak English, then."

"I speak tongue of the weak. Plan for this day."

"A forward thinker," Mack said. "Good for you, buddy. No need to be a pill. Just tell your goons there I'm not going anywhere. My name's Mack, Mack Silver. Behind me is my buddy, Flyboy McGee."

Jet rolled his eyes.

The Neanderthal thumped his chest. "Atok. Hollow Earth."

"Good to meet you, Atok."

"Where ape?"

"Wereape? You're a wereape? Like, a man who can become an ape? Or an ape that becomes a man? Are full moons involved? Because it's late afternoon—"

Again the bows pulled back. The warriors took a step forward, ready to bash Mack's brains in, but Atok held out his mace—a gnarly looking thing made of various tusk tips. Getting hit by that, Jet imagined, would give you one hell of a headache. The kind of headache a couple of aspirin won't fix.

"*Where ape*," Atok reasserted, looking none too happy about having to do so.

Jet hissed: "He wants to know where Khan is."

Koku, still on the floor beneath Mack, started to crawl to the margins of the room. An arrow flew fast and, suddenly, Koku slumped to the marble. An arrow jutting out of his head.

"That wasn't him," Mack said.

"*Where ape*."

"He's gone!" Jet said. "He fled the city when you attacked."

"Take me to ape."

Mack laughed. "No can do, Atok. We're not his buddies."

"We don't know where he went," Jet lied.

"Destroy ape army," Atok said. "Destroy ape leader. Take me to ape."

"We can't!" Mack yelled. "He's our enemy, too! We're on the same team, chief."

"Then you die," Atok said.

Under his breath, Mack tossed Jet a look and said, "All right, maybe we're *not* on the same team."

"We challenge you to hand-to-hand combat," Jet said, suddenly. It made sense. "Man to, ahh, man. Warrior to warrior."

"Battle?" Atok asked.

Mack mumbled, "Kid, you're off your feed. You can't take this guy."

"Battle," Jet continued. "And I nominate Mack Silver—" He pointed to Mack, just to make it clear. "—as our champion. Champion of all humanity."

"Kid, I hate you so bad right now," Mack said.

Jet shrugged.

Atok stretched his neck. Bones popped. He lifted his bone club. "Battle."

"If we win," Jet said, "we leave here unharmed and you have to go back to wherever you came from. If you win... well, gosh, I guess you can do as you please."

Of course, Jet knew Mack couldn't win.

But that was all part of the plan.

CHAPTER THIRTY-FIVE
THE BLACKSPIRE

The Blackspire. The crowning airship in Khan's fleet—a thousand feet long, blacker than the night, fitted with a massive undercarriage seven levels deep. The Blackspire was home to dozens of elite gorilla soldiers. That was not to mention the resident psychosaurs and the hundreds of captive Centurions comatose in their coffin-like compartments, their minds not just figuratively gone but *literally* gone—each consciousness thrown into another time, another place, and another body entirely.

Normally, the halls would be bustling with activity—apes running drill-laps, guards walking the halls, gorilla scientists studying the various artifacts they'd pilfered from their conquest of Atlantis (a once-disappointing collection of spoils, truth be told, or *was* until they discovered the seven keys and seven gates that let them move backward to the dawn of time).

Further, when Khan stepped onboard the ship he should've been greeted by a royal contingent of obsequious warriors, each falling over one another to help him moor his plane in the docking bay and clamber up into the belly of the zeppelin beast.

But the Blackspire was a ghost town.

Khan climbed up the ladder from where his black biplane hung. No one met him there. He ascended into the zeppelin's A-Deck, which accounted for the living quarters of those within the Blackspire—and again, nothing.

Dead. Inert. No movement.

Until—

A psychosaur appeared at the end of the hall. Just one. Stock still. Smiling. Though, when you saw through the human façade, it always looked like they were smiling, didn't it?

Khan approached.

"Where is everybody?" Khan asked.

The psychosaur hissed.

Khan grabbed the mute freak, shook him so violently the thing's neck almost snapped. "Show me! Show me where they've gone!"

But again, nothing. It just stood there. Breathing. Staring.

Worthless, Khan thought. An investment that had paid itself out and would soon need to be shut down. He saved them from extinction in the past but knew that the future would eventually catch up to them. Their value was fast receding.

The Conqueror Ape had fleeting visions—fears of what happened here. The heroes had come and... well, what, exactly? Somehow destroyed hundreds of battle-tested apes? The crème-de-la-crème of Khan's shock troops? Hardly made sense.

The pilot. Pilot Mozo would know. The Blackspire was still flying, after all, the Pacific Ocean glittering below, with Los Angeles to the east and the Atlantean gate glowing tall to the west (even in the day you could still see its light, though night was when the portals' majesty truly made itself clear).

Khan pushed past the psychosaur and knuckle-walked over to one of the ascent tubes—the Blackspire needed no stairs or elevators given its normal crew. The ascent tubes were lined with steel bars and made it easy for the apes to climb up and down from deck to deck whenever necessary.

Khan began his ascent to Deck G, but then he saw something below him—

Peeking out from Deck C was the face of a tiny dinosaur. A collar of glowing fungus around its neck.

The peteinosaur.

"You," Khan growled.

The dinosaur *gleeped* and disappeared down Deck C.

Khan let go of the bars and dropped down to the doorway of Deck C, and swung his way onto that floor. Deck C—the prison level. Neatly sandwiched between all the other floors so that those hoping to escape would have to go through apes either way.

Apes that were, at present, not here.

Another ghost town. Lifeless.

Except for that irritating dinosaur. Khan didn't know what he was hoping to find and had no idea how the dinosaur would help him—he envisioned some mad notion of grabbing the damn thing and forcing that lone psychosaur to read its memory—but in reality, Khan was driven by rage. He wanted to grab that thing and snap its tender little body in twain.

The dinosaur fled down the hallway, past row after row of empty cells. The Blackspire's current prisoners—the Centurions—were two decks up in specially-built chambers to keep their bodies alive and in stasis (if entirely mindless).

The peteinosaur ran away, then took flight, then ran along the wall, then darted left in mid-air—sailing into one of the open cells.

"Got you," Khan said, storming forward, hoping to catch the thing before it realized it had just trapped itself. He ducked into the cell, saw the thing clinging to the wall and trembling, the beak-like bone mouth opening and squawking. "You little crumb—"

The steel bars of the cell slammed shut with a reverberating clang.

Khan wheeled.

He was trapped. Caged like a common *animal*. He felt the drum-beat of his fury kicking hard in his neck, his forehead, his wrists.

From down the hall came a jaunty whistling.

With the whistling came a song sung in an all-too-familiar voice:

"Yonder stands a pretty maiden, who she is I do not know, I'll court her for her beauty, let her answer yes or no..."

"Spears," Khan snarled, lip curling high.

Sure enough, there walked Gerard Spears. White teeth spread in a happy grin.

"Oh, hullo, Khan," Spears said. He gave a cheery wave in which he waggled all of his fingers. "Didn't see you there."

"Spears! What kind of joke is this?"

"Joke? Not sure I understand, O-Mighty-Ape-King." Spears acted almost as if he wasn't paying attention—smoothing out the wrinkles in his jacket, scrutinizing his fingernails.

"Let me out."

"Would that I could."

"Spears, you common brigand, I swear, if you don't open this cage I'll break each of your bones and grind them into dust—"

"Really? Will you? Because I don't think you will. It's not that I doubt your strength, of course. I mean, cor, *look* at you! You could tear a man limb from limb. The problem isn't in your body, old man. It's up here—" Spears tapped his own head. "You're daft as a shoe. All this time you've been led around with a pair of fingers hooked in your nose and you haven't once opened your eyes to see it. And here you sit, a gorilla in the zoo. Ruler of the world for, what was it? Less than a week? Really quite sad."

"My son," Khan croaked. "What did you do with my son?"

"I let him go, you big poof. More specifically, I didn't even encounter him. He's off doing his own thing, you see. Fulfilling another part of my—well, I dare not call it a *plan*, because this isn't so much an orchestrated series of actions as it is a delightful cascade of dominoes tumbling into other dominoes."

"Who are you?" Khan said, pressing his head against the bars and baring his teeth.

It was then that Spears showed him. Only for a moment.

"But you're..." Khan didn't even have to finish the sentence.

The man—his enemy, his maker, his master—laughed.

And Khan roared in rage.

CHAPTER THIRTY-SIX
WAIPIO VALLEY

Khan howled in fear.

The closer they got to the Shark-Man, the worse the weather got—the rain came in hard and fast, a gray curtain of steel knives; the wind keened and wailed; lightning tore a hole in the sky and thunder shook the earth.

At first, the Professor thought, *I can do this.*

But now the only thought that paraded cruelly in his head was: *You're going to die.*

He ran through the tall grass of the valley, bolting through a copse of hala trees with their exposed tentacular roots—when last lightning had flashed he saw Benjamin using some whipcord branch as a rapier (his Atlantean dagger stuck in the earth ten feet away) just moments before the mystical detective was flung through the air like he weighed no more than a woman's purse. The monster standing in his place was only peripherally human—Khan saw a human face streaked with mud, but a body lined with protrusions and pro-tuberances, each fleshy lump and muscular hillock dead-ending in a shark's mouth. The many shark maws snapped at the air.

That's when Khan ran for his life.

He tried to find the jungle drums, tried to hear them beyond the hammer-fall rain and the ground-shaking thunder. But all he could hear was his own heartbeat: fast not because he was mad or because he was ready to be a hero but because he was scared out of his wits.

He heard Amelia yelling.

He heard Sally screaming.

The ape climbed fast into a flowering tree, shaking loose white rain-drenched blossoms that plodded to the muddy earth below. And there Khan curled around the central branches and pressed his face against the tree and wished it would all be over soon.

Sally brought the wrench down hard on one of the Shark-Man's razor mouths—this one jutting out of his back, gray and plump. The cannibal had Amelia pinned to the ground, sharp grasses rising up around them, his chest-facing mouth about to snack on her face—

But Sally's wrench turned the monster's attention elsewhere.

Its half-dozen mouths screamed in unison with the man's own mouth—his native face a rictus of torment, a twisted mask of both fear and rage—and then it bounded after Sally with renewed vigilance.

She ducked low and ran fast, knowing just the right moment to take a little hop-skip-and-a-jump over the boar path she was using.

Shark-Man did not know to take such a little jump, because *he* didn't know Sally had set a trap there for him. His splay-toed foot caught on a wire strung between the roots of two hala trees and before he knew what was happening, a heavy branch swung from his left like a baseball bat right at the level of his human head—

In the matter of a moment the Shark-Man's human head became, only for that moment, a shark's head—a great white half-moon mouth open wide and catching the branch, biting it clean in half. Sally blinked again and saw that the human guise had returned, the shattered stick still in his mouth as if he were some kind of Labrador retriever.

The Shark-Man spit out the branch—*ptoo*—and came charging for her.

It was Sally's turn to trip. She moved to run, found her foot trapped on one of the exposed roots and her world went topsy-turvy. The ground punched the air clean out of her lungs. Suddenly a greasy gray body was atop her, teeth snapping together. Blind and dazed, she swung her wrench up hard, only to have one mouth bite down hard on the tool. The shark-head twisted and the wrench pulled from her grip and was gobbled down one of the beast's many throats. The beast's weight was heavy. It screamed in pain and with great wrath.

All of its mouths opened and it was then Sally knew she was a goner.

Lightning split the air above her—a crackling blue fork that lit up the sky.

And above all of it, frozen in that moment and emblazoned upon her vision, was a massive figure leaping forth.

An epic shadow shaped like a gorilla. In a kilt.

Suddenly the Shark-Man was bowled aside by the heavy weight of a pouncing ape—gone was the erudite demeanor and the reserved disposition. Sally scrambled backwards to see the Professor Khan glimpsed back during that scuffle with Jet on the airfield—the ape tore open his white Oxford shirt and pounded on his chest like it was a set of booming timpani drums. Lightning flashed again and she saw Khan's teeth, bright and pink and with canines the size of a human finger.

Shark-Man regained his footing and came at Khan.

The ape got under him and with both hands used the monster's momentum to lift him up and over Khan's head and back down to earth on the creature's head.

But Shark-Man wasn't down and out—though upside-down, both of his kicking feet suddenly became sharks, biting and snapping at the air. Khan backpedaled, the dual mouths nearly taking a bite out of his face and neck.

Shark-Man leapt to his feet.

Khan again beat his chest, and then cocked a fist—

The Shark-Man ran toward Khan and Khan ran toward the monster—

The beast's many mouths opened in unison—

Khan leapt and threw a dread haymaker—

And the two gargantuan combatants collided.

The Professor screamed in pain.

And when lightning lit up the world again, Sally saw why: Khan's fist had indeed connected with Shark-Man, but the fist was buried in the razor-tooth maw that jutted forth from the monster's chest. Shark-Man bit down and blood ran along Khan's arm.

Sally knew that this was it. They'd all bitten off more than they could chew. Some of Mack's cockiness—*we're heroes,* his voice said in the back of her mind, *ain't that enough, doll?*—had infected them and now they over-stepped their bounds.

As a result, Khan was surely going to lose that arm.

But then, the erudite ape's head snapped forward. Focus returned to his eyes, pushing through the pain. She saw Khan plant both feet in the muddy ground and thrust his shoulder forward with a twist of his hip.

The Shark-Man shuddered. Khan tightened his arm again, and the Shark-Man gave another violent shudder before sliding off of Khan's arm and plop-ping into the earth like—well, like a dead shark hitting the dock.

Khan's arm was a bloody mess. The fur slick with red.

But held in the hand was Sally's wrench.

"Miss Slick," he said, voice hoarse. "I think you dropped this."

She took the wrench.

And then Khan passed out.

Two hours later they came staggering out of the tall grasses, beaten, bedraggled, more than a little bewildered. But the rains had stopped and the sun managed to peek out from behind the bands of dark ocean-swept storm-clouds above. Khan, once again conscious, plodded along between Amelia and Sally with his bloody arm hanging limp by his side. Benjamin led the way back to the temple dais.

None of them looked good. Benjamin's brow was gashed open. Amelia looked like she had been nearly drowned in a pit of mud—it was already cak-ing over and turning clay-pale. Sally just looked shell-shocked.

But Khan, at least, was smiling.

Their battle with the Shark-Man was over, and he was the one who ended it.

Out in front of them Khan suddenly saw a head bobbing above the foliage—a face that lit up as soon as they approached. Edwin. Smiling like a goon. Waving his arms excitedly as if he were the happiest drowning man one ever did see.

"Professor! Mister Hu! Miss Slick! Miss Stone!" Edwin dashed toward them, making a sound that Khan could only describe as a giggle. "Oh, you must come. You must see!"

And then he bounded away like a jackrabbit.

The heroes looked to one another, and shrugged. They followed after.

They heard it before they saw it. The static crackle, the metallic snap. Khan's spirits lifted even further, and once they saw it he about fell over laughing.

The teleporter worked! The two coils to each side of the dais pulsed tendrils of violet light; atop the stone platform a rippling gate formed, blue waves of what looked like flame radiating out from the center. As they approached, the sound from that gate grew louder: *waah-waah-WAAH-WAAAAAH*.

It was Sally who broke first.

She pulled away from Khan, staring at the gate. Then she laughed. And then she cried. Though the erudite ape was not entirely familiar with the depth and breadth of human emotion he could see that her tears were ones from a fount of joy and not grief—though certainly the raggedness and fatigue from their fight with the Shark-Man contributed.

Sally bit her lip and turned to the others. "We did it."

Benjamin bowed and winked. "*You* did it."

"We all did it," she asserted, wiping tears. "All of us."

Khan swept her up in his one good arm, taken suddenly by the feeling of triumph. He spun her around, and again her tears turned to laughs.

"I hate to break up the party early," Amelia said, flakes of dry mud falling away as she spoke. "But the clock is ticking. We'd better get ourselves through that gate."

The spinning stopped. Reality took hold like an ice wash or a sudden spike of sobriety. Khan knew that just because a crackling blue portal hovered above the platform did not strictly mean that the portal did what it was supposed to do. Sally's "*It works on paper!*" assertions were all well and good, but what happened when someone stepped through that thing?

Amelia and Benjamin started packing what little gear they were bringing. "We'll go through first," Amelia said.

Khan set Sally down and hurried over. "Are you certain? We don't... we don't know what will happen. You could be thrown backwards in time. Or teleported to the wrong gate. Or, or, disintegrated into your component molecules, or—"

Amelia placed her hand on Khan's shoulder. "It'll work. We trust Sally. Besides, this is what we do. Sometimes we jump and build wings on our way down."

"Well," Benjamin said with a playful smile, "I prefer to build my wings before I jump. But Amelia is right. I trust in Sally's design. Wish us luck, Professor."

Benjamin shook Khan's hand. Khan swept him up in a hug. Then he pulled Amelia into it, too, nearly crushing both of them with his one good arm and his bloodied other.

And then, together, Amelia and Benjamin stepped into the gate.

One minute they were there—and the next, they were gone in a blinding flash.

"I hope they're all right," Khan said.

"Me too," Sally answered.

"Me three," Edwin added with an awkward smile.

The ape shifted uneasily from foot to foot. "It's our turn."

"That it is," Sally agreed.

"This is how heroes act," Khan said, as if reminding himself.

Sally corrected him: "This is how *Centurions* act."

"Shall we, then?"

Sally nodded.

Edwin wiped his sweaty palms on his pants.

Together, all three of them gathered up their things—just enough to carry, tools and Khan's pack and assorted Sally Slick doohickeys. And then they stepped onto the platform and into the portal and like that, their bodies and in fact their very beings were ripped apart.

CHAPTER THIRTY-SEVEN
NEW YORK CITY

This wasn't the first brawl Mack had been in. Brawls were kind of his thing—well, brawls, drinking, island girls, daredevil flying, and also, drinking. Go to a bar, get in a fight. It's what he did. It's what he *liked* to do. It was all in good fun (except when some poor palooka ended up getting a bottle broken over his gourd).

This, however, was not fun. Not at all.

Jet had pushed him into a fight with this Neanderthal—initially, Mack thought, *You know what? I have a shot at this. This guy's short. Pale like he hasn't seen the sun in years. Dumb, too, because, c'mon, he's basically one broken DNA chain away from a chimpanzee.*

But then Atok threw a fist that damn near knocked Mack's brains through the back of his head. All Mack saw was a field of stars erupting—like fireflies glowing bright against broad black nothing. When finally his vision resumed he saw the caveman's epic bone mace crashing down toward his face—an attack that would shatter his skull like an egg.

Mack rolled over just as the weapon cratered the marble floor only inches away.

"Cripes!" he cried. "You trying to kill me?"

"Yes," Atok said, and took a swinging kick for Mack's head. Mack caught the foot, gave it a twist, and almost toppled the caveman—but the Neanderthal caught himself.

Just the same, it gave Mack time to get to his own feet.

"I thought we were being gentlemanly about this," Mack said, putting up his dukes.

"Do not understand," Atok said, and took a swing with the mace. Mack ducked it—but barely. Behind him, the restless throng of cavemen—and quite a few cavewomen, Mack noted—hooted and grunted, hands pushing him back into the circle. He looked over their heads, tried to spy Jet somewhere in the thick of it, but couldn't find his ally's tell-tale helmet anywhere.

"If it's gonna be like *that,* then I'm about to let loose with both cannons you musky-stenched, pale-skinned, Missing-Link-looking sonofab—"

Atok headbutted him. It felt like kissing a cannonball.

Fine, Mack thought. *You want to play like that? Let's tango.*

The mace whiffed through the air. Mack ducked it. Then kicked out a leg and kicked Atok right between the legs.

The caveman staggered backward, doubling over.

The crowd of gathered Neanderthals gasped collectively.

Mack dusted his hands, cracked his knuckles. "Now it's a brawl!" But the caveman straightened up and backed away.

"You fight with no honor," Atok said. "The battle is over."

"I won?" Mack asked, gleefully incredulous. "I *won*? Ha! Ha ha!" He started doing a little Irish jig, elbows out, feet stomping about. "Jet! I won!"

But then he noticed—the crowd of cavemen began closing in on him. Teeth bared. Weapons drawn. They began pushing him toward the back of the room.

"Wait, what? I won. Battle's over."

Atok stepped through the crowd. "Fight with no honor, lose with no honor."

They continued to come at him. Pushing him back, back, back.

Toward the open window.

"Hey," Mack said, hands up. "Guys. Ladies. Cave...people. We can talk about this, can't we? Seems like there's a conversation. Maybe I can get a mulligan? A do-over?"

An arrow whisked by his ear. Close enough to let him hear it. A purposeful miss.

"The honorless dog die honorless death," Atok said.

The back of Mack's head hit the top of the window frame. His feet against the lip. The caveman kept coming. He looked again for Jet—but saw nothing.

The little crumb had deserted him.

"Now you fall," Atok said, and swung with the mace.

But suddenly, a pair of hands curled under his arms and yanked him backward through the window. Once again, Mack screamed like a little girl.

Jet rocketed forth, twisting his body so as to do a sharp turn between two skyscrapers in order to duck away from a pair of pterodactyls headed their way.

Mack finally stopped screaming about thirty seconds later.

"How did you know that would happen?" Mack yelled, incredulous.

Jet laughed. "I didn't."

Let him chew on that for a while, Jet thought.

They headed back toward Lucy.

Lucy was set further out from the city—about a quarter mile out in the bay so as not to attract quite so much attention, but not so far out they couldn't get back to her in time if they needed to. Jet eased the two of them toward the water, his air-boosters on the back causing the water beneath them to ripple and churn.

He dropped Mack on the subwing and followed after.

It wasn't long before Mack was in the cockpit, grumbling and grousing. Jet tossed him a compress for his face.

"That caveman gave you what-for," Jet said, trying (but failing) to suppress a laugh.

"Uh-huh. It's a real chucklefactory, kid." Mack pressed the compress there, started up the props. Lucy started to growl and hum. "I'll get him next time.

The whole thing took me by surprise is all. Didn't help that he had all his Missing Link buddies there distracting me."

"Sorry I threw you into that," Jet said with the uttermost sincerity. "I knew I didn't have a shot and couldn't risk having the jet-wing take a hit. We've no idea how stable this thing really is yet and didn't want to find out then."

Jet went to the subwing door and moved to close it.

"I hope I get to see that Atok again *real soon*," Mack said as Lucy started to move through the water.

As Jet started to close the door, he looked up.

"I think you're going to get your chance real soon," Jet said, throwing closed the door just as something heavy landed hard atop Lucy with a *thud*. "Because he's here."

Atok did not like being played for a fool. He barked orders to two of his warriors, speaking once again in the tongue of his people—"Grozen, Londar. Get me a glider. The honorless cur must not be allowed to escape so easily."

Minutes later, his two warriors produced for him one of the gliders they used to sail the great caverns of the Hollow Earth, a collapsible bone glider with wings made from the leather of the eyeless Fungus-Eating Moon-Bat, one of the many denizens found down below.

Atok set his tusk-mace aside—it was too heavy for this trip—and grabbed the heads of a few of his warriors, pressing his forehead against theirs.

"For the Hollow Earth," he said.

"For the Hollow Earth!" his Neanderthals chanted.

Atok leapt out of the window, unfolding the glider as he fell. Wind caught beneath him and he soared like a pterosaur.

Out in front of Lucy, Mack saw what looked like some kind of rickety bat-wing glider plunged into the bay only moments after hearing the thud above.

"What the hell was that?" he said, urging Lucy to pick up the pace.

"It's him," Jet said, hurrying up the steps and into the cockpit. "It's Atok."

As if on cue, Atok's face appeared at the windshield, upside-down.

He pounded on the glass with a fist.

"We need to *go*," Jet said.

"Lucy's not a horse," Mack said. "I can't kick her with spurs to make her go faster."

Atok's face disappeared from the window. They heard footsteps above—*whomp whomp whomp whomp*—heading toward the middle of the plane.

Lucy was going at a good clip now, rocking and bouncing atop the water.

At the subwing door, a heavy pounding: *wham wham wham*.

"He's trying to get in," Jet said.

Lucy started to lift up out of the water. There came that momentary sense of weightlessness as a plane leaves its earthly mooring. Mack grinned.

"Let him try. That door's built like it could withstand a bomb. You can be sure that Sally built it to be caveman-proof—"

From down below, the sound of that door being wrenched open.

"You were saying?"

"Okay. Okay. *Okay*." Mack rubbed his brow. "Go take care of him."

"What? Are you nuts?"

"I'm flying the plane!"

"My jet-wing's already stashed! And I still don't have my pistols back."

Mack rummaged under the seat. "Here you go."

Into Jet's hand he slapped a wide-mouthed flare gun.

"This is it?"

"That's it."

Jet broke the flare gun barrel open to make sure it was actually *loaded* with a flare.

From mid-plane came a booming voice: "Honorless d—"

Mack pulled back on the stick and Lucy shot upward, cutting short Atok's battle-cry. This was Jet's chance, so Mack elbowed him. "Go! *Go*."

As Jet disappeared out of the cockpit, Mack started to formulate a plan.

Khan had gone to the Blackspire.

So that's where they were going, too.

CHAPTER THIRTY-EIGHT
THROUGH THE GATE

It was the same, but different. Benjamin felt like he'd felt when he leapt into the Atlantean gate before but this time could not see the scope of the seven tunnels twisting to a single point—further, he had no sense of time here, only movement. His body was gone but his soul and mind were present and tangible. Near to him he felt another presence: Amelia, he hoped. The energy of the ley lines was warm and electric; he thought for a moment about giving in to it, about becoming part of it now and forever. He'd long appreciated the mystical wherewithal of the planet and mused on how perfect and pure it would be to merge with that, to become not merely an outsider but a participant in the fundamental make-up of the cosmos.

But then he remembered—they had work to do. They were not part of the cosmos; they were outside of it. As heroes must be.

Benjamin sought out the minds of other Centurions, heroes who were by all reports captive on the airship Blackspire.

He sought out the minds of those he knew—

The Cerulean Devil.

John Shade.

The Orchid.

He looked for the minds of those he'd never met—

The Projector.

Jenny Greenteeth.

The Gray Mantis.

And he could find none of them. It was like reaching up from inside a pit and searching out handholds and finding nothing there but a smooth wall. He felt Amelia beside him casting out her own psychic feelers—and yet she remained.

All the heroes were gone. Their minds, lost.

In here, despair felt like a real thing—it weighed upon him, dragged him down deeper into the mystical trench. Benjamin embraced the warmth. Wondered if perhaps it was best to get lost after all. The channel of bright light had stripped away part of who he was and it was eroding more of him away, bite by bite, until he no longer tried to reach out at all.

But then, one mind shot through the empty energized space like a perpendicular bolt of lightning. A mind and a face and a soul.

It made no sense, this face; it had no right to be here. It felt like a crass intrusion, a violation of the mystical order. It was a face *known* for violating the mystical order.

Benjamin grabbed out, found Amelia, held her there.

Then he reached for that face, that *mind*, and pulled himself toward it with all his psychic might.

"Was this what you were looking for?" came the voice.

Benjamin sat on his knees, doubled over, trying not to retch—and, more importantly, trying not to black out. He tilted his head, saw Amelia on her side next to him, eyelids fluttering.

And behind her, a wall of compartments. Like space age coffins, all aluminum curves and bulging rivets. In each, a Lucite porthole, and through each porthole, the face of a Centurion. Benjamin searched those faces, saw many he did not recognize, but just as many that he did.

Passive. Empty. Like embalmed corpses. And if his gut spoke true...

All of them, without their minds. Without any flicker of consciousness.

"Centurions in repose," came the voice again. Benjamin lifted his head. Saw Gerard Spears standing there in his white suit coat and white pants, fingers twisting the pink rose in his lapel. "It has a beauty to it, don't you think?"

"If I had my blade..."

"If you had your blade you'd what? Cut me to little bits? Oh. That's not nice. You play at being refined—Benjamin Hu! Thinker and deducer!—but you're really just a brute like the rest of them, aren't you?" Spears twiddled his thumbs. "Anyway, your lovely rapier is probably somewhere in New York. I gave it to the ape but if it's not a bunch of bananas he doesn't know what to do with it."

Next to Benjamin came Amelia's voice—she spoke while still laying curled up on her side. "Does your boss Khan know you talk about him like that?"

"He's never been a particularly good boss," Spears said. "I think it's time for a *regime change*, don't you?"

"You don't have what it takes," Benjamin said, managing finally to stand— though the way his vision swam and dipped he didn't know how long he had. "And you don't have an ape army. Or a gaggle of psychosaurs. *Or* dinosaurs. So good luck with that, my old nemesis."

"Oh but I *do* have all those things. I'm the one holding Khan's leash, after all. And he's the one holding all the other leashes." Gerard leaned in, spoke *sotto voce:* "Though let's admit, that makes me all a bit lazy, doesn't it? What an opportunistic slugabed I turned out to be!"

Benjamin moved fast. He lurched forward, onto his feet, his one hand drawing the Atlantean dagger from the back hem of his pants—

He drew the blade. Threw it.

The sapphire dagger spun through the air.

And stopped about six inches in front of Spears' nose.

"Sorry, that's not part of the *equation*," Spears said. He snapped his fingers and Benjamin saw a burst of bright light that spit strange symbols onto the wall, written there as if in molten lava (before once again fading away). The dagger was gone.

That word.

Equation.

It ping-ponged around Benjamin's head like a ricocheting bullet.

What Spears did was plainly magic. And yet spoke of math as in

Oh, no.

Spears. *Spears.* It was a ruse. A dread and deadly ruse!

"Doctor Methuselah," Benjamin said.

The man-called-Spears grinned his too-white teeth. "Figured it out, did we?"

Methuselah. It meant man of the spear. Referring to the oldest man in the Bible—this man was not that man, no, but *this* one stole *that one's* name as rumors said he was far older than any Centurion or Shadow could ever be. He was the worst among the Shadows, the most powerful and confounding, harnessing some heretical combination of magic and math that he called the "mathemagical equation." He often borrowed puzzles and ciphers to cloak his schemes and yet, by purposefully putting those ciphers out there he was teasing the heroes, goading them into finding him. Egomaniacal. No—*megalomaniacal.*

Amelia groaned, and Benjamin helped her stand.

"Spears," Benjamin said. "Man of the spear. The clue was there all along."

"Among others," the Doctor teased.

Among others.

Benjamin's mind worked through it—like flipping through a hundred books at once, he radiated out from what he already knew. *Spears. Man of the Spear. Methuselah. Mentioned only one time in the Bible—Genesis. Extra-Biblically, where? Book of Enoch. Book of Jubilees. Book of...*

Jasher.

"Edwin Jasher," Benjamin said, his heart sinking in his chest.

The man-who-was-Spears clapped his hands together and did a fancy twirl, laughing. "Yes! Yes, yes, yes. Edwin Jasher. Protégé to your Professor Khan who is himself an almost replica of my own creation, Mighty Khan. Good show, Benjamin."

"Who is he? One of your cronies?"

"He is *me.*"

"But..."

"I broke off a piece of my persona years ago. Implanted it in the thief you know as Gerard Spears and the witless twit known as Edwin Jasher. To what end, I did not know—but I learned fairly recently that for all the pieces of the equation I can see, there exist just as many variables I cannot. I learned to let go, Benjamin. To let chaos be chaos and let the dominoes fall as they may, only nudging here and adjusting there. And now…"

A trio of psychosaurs stepped in behind Benjamin and Amelia. And a trio stepped in behind the Doctor, as well.

"I think you'll find they have a hard time controlling us," Amelia said, her face plastered with a defiant grin.

Not-Spears shrugged. "Oh, your minds are not to be cast away, not yet. The others were not part of the equation, so I sent their minds back in time, back to the start of all this. But that's a story for another time. You know what else is a story for another time? Where I've been hiding your old friend, the Green-Eyed Monster, all this time."

Amelia snarled, tried to bolt forward.

Not-Spears snapped his fingers again and she tripped forward, turning just in time to land on her shoulder and not her head. Benjamin raced to her side.

"No, I need the both of you around. You're still dominoes that have yet to topple, I think. So in the meantime—" He moved his finger as if he were drawing symbols in the air and then, nearby, the doors to two of the coffin-like containment units popped open. "Will you please secure yourselves for the remainder of the trip?"

Benjamin helped Amelia up. He tried to see his way past this. Best vulnerability was behind them—

"Stop looking for a way out," Not-Spears grumbled, and then with another gesticulation Benjamin and Amelia found their Sally Slick circlets pulled suddenly off their heads and crumpled up like a wad of tinfoil. "Now if you will take your place? The final act is about to begin as we transition to the lost islands of Atlantis."

Benjamin helped Amelia into one of the pods.

"We won't let you destroy the world," she said.

"Oh, my dear Amelia," Not-Spears said. "I don't want to destroy the world. I want to destroy all of time itself."

Even the closed doors of the pods could not stifle the sound of his laughter.

CHAPTER THIRTY-NINE
ATLANTIS: THE CRYSTAL DOME

They dropped out of the energy channel and into a magnificent city on an island encased in a massive crystal dome—moonlight shone through the facets of the crystal, multiplying moonbeams and throwing over everything a soft light, luminous and eerie.

And all around was like a smaller, far stranger version of a human city—tall buildings made of crystal or sculpted gems; massive brass gears turning mysterious machines; canals of iridescent water shimmering as if topped with chips of perfect glass; twisted conduits that pulsed and hummed and thrummed; no stars above but rather an orrery of little mirrors redirecting what light came through the crystal dome.

The ground beneath them seemed to throb with energy.

It was beautiful.

Sally only had a few moments to take it in before the wave of nausea and dizziness washed over her like a tide, drawing away any strength she had in her legs.

Next to her, the Professor and Edwin were suffering the same effects. Edwin was flat on his back, moaning and whimpering. Khan did not seem quite as affected—his massive head hung low as if he needed a breather, but he still stood mostly upright.

"We have..." he said between breaths, "... company."

Sally lifted her head and saw that, indeed they did.

They were surrounded by warrior-apes. Not just gorillas, as comprised Khan's army out *there*, but others, too—a long limbed orangutan with a crystal breastplate and codpiece, a rangy gibbon with his head beneath a crystal helmet, a chimpanzee ducking behind a brass shield. All of them held weapons—jeweled knives, strange wide-mouthed pistols, swords that looked carved from the same crystal that formed the dome above.

Behind, the apes milled.

"The Atlanteans," Khan said, and Sally heard in his voice great reverence. They were frail humanoid slips, tall and wispy, so pale their skin was almost blue—and Sally realized suddenly that their flesh was nearly translucent. All their features seemed exaggerated, too: cheekbones and fingers and chins, all longer and quite pronounced.

They stayed in the background, many emerging from the crystalline structures or peering out from windows high above. Just watching.

Sally couldn't tell if what she saw on their faces was placidity or a fear with which they'd simply grown comfortable.

Above their heads, above even the crystal dome, Sally saw something floating up there in front of the moon—but she could not make out what, as the facets of the dome distorted it wildly. Still, she was fairly certain it was some kind of face.

"You have invaded the Dome City," ooked one ape—a massive Siamang ape whose neck bladder puffed up with every word he spoke through puckered lips. He seemed different than the others—decked out in a full suit of crystal armor, the helmet on his head sporting the plumage of some strange and forgotten bird. "I am Captain Chirrang. Identify yourselves, criminals, or be executed and chum the waters around Atlantis."

Sally tried to find her footing, but still fell to one knee. She tossed a look toward Khan. "We're in a bit of a pickle here, Professor."

Khan nodded. He turned toward Chirrang and spoke.

"I am Professor Khan. Also known as, Son-of-Khan." The gorilla took a deep breath. "I am here at my father's request to serve by his side. So turn your weapons away and do not threaten me again unless you hope to invoke his wrath."

Wow, Sally thought. And when the apes pulled back and began to confer with one another in a series of mutters, gibbers, and shrugs, she thought, *Double-wow.* Even more amazing was how completely the Professor assumed that role.

A tiny thought wondered whether she needed to worry about that.

The apes did not put away their weapons, but at Chirrang's urging they did stop pointing them directly. Chirrang frowned, waved them on. "Mighty Khan, King of Atlantis, is not here. But I can take you to his chambers. There you can meet with Vizier Hooben."

A phalanx of apes formed behind them and in front of them and suddenly, like that, they were walking (or in Sally's case, slowly shuffling until her brain and body properly reconnected itself) through the streets of a civilization mankind had long forgotten.

CHAPTER FORTY
LUCY

Atok threw Jet headlong into the radio room. The flare gun spun away as Jet crashed into the receiver and then tumbled over it, into the chair and table beyond. Everything went woozy, but Atok wasn't done. The caveman moved with purpose, walking in slow strides that seemed somehow inevitable, as if he would not be stopped by any means found in Heaven and Earth and Jet thought, *Well, maybe I should just lie down and have a nap.*

Atok had other ideas, it seemed.

The Neanderthal warrior hoisted Jet up and shook him.

"Show me honorless dog!" Atok demanded.

"He's... not... *urk*... available right now," Jet said.

Atok hurled Jet out of the radio room and into a set of lockers.

Jet scrambled to open one of the lockers as Atok stormed forth again. His fingers felt numb, his arm almost detached from the body—

He got the locker open—

Atok's hand clapped down hard on his shoulder—

In the locker hung the jet-wing.

Jet hit the booster ignition and rolled to the side as the air-boosters blasted a cannon's breath of air that hit Atok in the chest like the fist of an invisible giant.

The caveman bowled backward.

Jet ran, dove, grabbed the flare gun.

He stood. As did Atok. The two, dizzied but not down, circled one another like a pair of predatory cats. Or, rather, Atok seemed like a panther. Jet felt...

...well, mostly like a housecat.

Jet held out the flare gun with one hand, wiped a line of blood from his nose with the other. "I don't want any trouble, buddy."

"Too bad," Atok said.

The plane shifted a little—an altitude adjustment. Downward, not up.

"You're getting pretty far away from your..." *People* didn't seem quite like the right word, Jet thought. Instead, he went with: "Army."

That gave Atok pause. His eyes darted to the open door. Puffs of cloud whizzed by as the sky darkened into evening.

"Cannot let honorless dog lie. Must bring back. Or Atok lose honor instead."

"So, we're not going to be able to figure this out, then?"

"You *friend* of dog. Also honorless. Also dead."

"So be it," Jet said.

Atok leapt, and Jet fired the flare gun.

A red phosphorus fireball punched Atok right in the chest. It hung there like the cherry on a lit cigarette, burning. Jet smelled scorched hair. Atok hit the ground, rolled over and leapt back to his feet, swatting at his chest like all he had to do was crush the bug that had landed there.

But it didn't work. The flare kept burning. Atok growled, then his growl morphed into a scream, and as he backpedaled, Jet saw his chance. He darted forward, shoulder low, and slammed Atok hard—

Right out the subwing door.

Atok tumbled out of the plane and disappeared.

Jet collapsed, panting.

Mack's voice came over the intercom.

"You alive, kid?"

Jet crawled his way over, pulled himself up the wall, and hit the button to speak into the com. "I'm here. He's... not."

"Ehh, lucky. I bet you couldn't have taken him back at the Empire State Building, not with all those Missing Link mooks and him with that big damn—"

"This isn't a competition," Jet said, exasperated. "I got lucky. Now what is it?"

"I found one of those gates."

"Okay."

"Hong Kong Hu was right. Block Island."

"What's your point?"

Jet felt the plane dip lower.

"I'm going to fly into it," Mack said.

"What?!"

"I'm going to fly Lucy into the gate. Looks big enough."

"Mack, I don't know if that's such a hot idea—"

"I'd buckle up, Flyboy, because I have no idea what's gonna happen."

Ahead, through the windshield, the darkening sky gave way to a massive shimmering gate thrusting up out past Long Island.

Mack knew that flying into the heart of that gate—with pterodactyls filling the sky and psychosaurs on the ground and god-only-knows-what in the unseen heart of the thing—was a move that was dubious at best.

But he didn't see any other choice.

Khan was gone. Off to the Blackspire. Benjamin and Amelia were already there and—well, what he really meant was that *Amelia* was there, and he suddenly wasn't sure if he actually cared about that or whether he was just thinking about Amelia to distract himself from thinking about whatever danger *Sally* might be in and—

Ennnh. *No time to think about that,* he told himself.

You're in this to save the world, not a couple of broads.

And if Khan is out there somewhere, and he's the head of this thing, then that head needs to be cut off. *And I'm the one who's gonna hold the hatchet.*

He had no idea what was going to happen when he dropped Lucy through that portal. Maybe he didn't need to know. It was like he told the Professor when he—regrettably, he could admit that now—got on the erudite ape's case. *Information is overrated. We go with our gut. Sometimes you gotta dive off the cliff without knowing what's in the water below. Don't think. Do. Sometimes, to be like us, you gotta be a little bit dumb.*

Heck yeah.

The gate was coming up, now.

Mack dropped the stick.

The plane plunged.

His control wobbled—not like he was hitting pockets of air but like Lucy was resisting him, which didn't make any sense since she wasn't *alive* or anything. He tugged harder on the stick. She'd listen to him. She was the one woman that always did.

Every part of Atok's body hurt. The air up here was cold and cut like a ghost knife slicing clean through him—he held onto a part of the iron bird (its tail, best as he could figure) as the beast dipped down toward a massive portal made of pure light. *Some human trap, some foul conveyance of their crass magic called 'science,'* Atok thought. It didn't matter. Let them bring him to it. He would defeat it. He would defeat them all with his bare hands if he had to.

He knew he should just let go. But he had an honorless dog to punish.

And that gave him all the strength in the world, even as the pterodactyls dove screaming for the iron bird, even as the metal beast pitched suddenly downward and Atok's guts felt like they were still a thousand feet above his head, even as the plane disappeared into the crackling light and was tossed into the continuum of space-and-time like a paper boat on a storm-tossed sea.

CHAPTER FORTY-ONE
THE BLACKSPIRE

Mighty Khan the Conqueror Ape wasn't conquering much right now except for maybe the rut he was wearing into the floor of his cell.

Back and forth, back and forth. Pacing. Occasionally pausing to scream in rage, or punch the bars or shoulder the weight of his body against them.

They didn't budge. Nor should they. He had them designed to withstand enormous strength—even his own.

Methuselah.

The name hung in his mind like a black cloud.

Khan was a fool. A fool to believe that when they captured Methuselah in his Arctic lair he was truly that wizened and withered. That wasn't even him in his entirety—it was mostly just his body and enough of a consciousness to stay behind and grant him the motor skills and the mumbles, enough to seem like he was the gutted rag-doll Khan believed him to be.

Khan believed it because he *wanted* to believe it. He adored that his maker and mentor had finally fallen. That it was Khan's time to rise. That the good Doctor's long-suffering quest to solve the mathemagical equation and unravel all of time was at an end.

The ape wanted temporal power. He wanted control over the mortal world.

Methuselah wanted something far stranger. And Khan never understood that.

And now? The Doctor had used him. Khan didn't know how, not yet, not *exactly*, but he had been led around by the nose like a circus animal. Methuselah had encouraged him to take Atlantis years ago. Khan thought the old man was just shoving him somewhere far away so that he couldn't get in the way of the Doctor's plans, but it was the opposite, wasn't it?

The Ape-Lord was initially disgusted by the spoils of the lost—or, rather, *hidden*—civilization. Yes, the jewel knives were pretty and oh-so-sharp. The sonic cannons were effective, but not exactly a brand new paradigm in weaponry. All their doo-dads and gew-gaws were useless to Khan. Best he got out of them was the technology to create more airships and to let his dirigibles float higher and move faster.

But then he found it. The secret of the Dome City. The pulsing heart not just of Atlantis but of all creation—a vortex of space-and-time linked backwards through history to a single moment: the moment Atlantis was created.

The Atlanteans had been at war with a psychic race of saurians and Khan went through the portal with a contingent of ape soldiers and handily turned the tide of war. He pushed the Atlanteans back into their crystal dome (which, given the coming meteors, must have been to protect them from such cataclysmic skyfall) and subjugated the psychosaurs. The psychosaurs feasted upon this strange glowing fungus and used that very same fungus to turn dinosaurs into slaves.

Khan thought how elegant this was. The predator-and-prey chain of being in perfect harmony. The psychosaurs enslaved the dinosaurs. So Khan enslaved the psychosaurs.

Little did he realize, he was not the top of the totem pole.

Methuselah was above him. Tugging *his* leash.

Though, to what end, Khan was not sure.

Now, Methuselah had the Blackspire. And had, if he was to be believed, literally unwritten the contingent of apes on this ship out of existence, as if ripping a page out of a book and tossing it in the nearest wastebasket. Methuselah's math was cruel.

And Khan would surely soon meet the worst of it.

All he knew was, right now, he wanted to see his son.

Suddenly, the Blackspire shuddered.

Where were they going?

Gerard Spears—really, one third of Methuselah's consciousness thrown into a body once possessed by a man called Gerard Spears—piloted the Blackspire through the San Miguel gate, throwing the entire airship into the space-time continuum.

If he let it, the ship would simply travel backwards in time to the point of the portal's origin—the dawn of the Atlantis Dome City—but the insidious Doctor had little interest in going anywhere through time. Dome City, yes. A million years in the past, not so much.

All he had to do was think of where he wanted this ship to go and—

Voila.

The dirigible shuddered and its nose-cone punctured a hole in the side of the continuum, emerging in the sky within the crystal dome of Atlantis, above the city beneath. Beyond the facets of the dome, the other islands of the hidden archipelago were spread out across the ocean in a half-moon pattern, the moon and stars revealing their shape if not their scope.

Above the dome floated an airship whose belly was a crystalline carving of Mighty Khan's angry ape face. Hard to make out here, but Methuselah knew what it was.

Such an egotist, that Khan. A fine protégé for a time, Methuselah decided, but his usefulness had gone the way of the dodo. Concerned overmuch with mortal concerns. Territory and wealth and—*ugh*. Though, what else would an ape care about? Not a higher mind, that one.

His son, though. His son had promise.

Too bad he chose the side of good.

For now.

He looked forward to what was coming. The culmination of unexpected sequences—of dominoes falling, of invisible levers and pulleys and better mousetraps, of secret fractions and imaginary numbers never before seen—was going to unmoor this universe from time itself and make him the master of all. For when time was gone he would no longer age. And entropy would end its erosive, corrosive influence on the great equations—all would be not just constant but *The* Constant, a constant he controlled.

It was what he always wanted.

And all he had to do was put a few things in motion and let the joyful chaos of the universe take care of the rest.

"Oh, chaos," he said to no one, steering the ship with a trademark Gerard Spears smile on the stolen face. "How I love—"

The air in front of the Blackspire crackled. Lightning shot out from a rent in space and time. Belching forth from the hole came a plane.

A plane named "Lucy."

Methuselah hit the deck as the Boeing Clipper crashed head-on into the decks of the Blackspire, the wing tearing a vent in the dirigible, the propellers ripping apart the control pattern, the rest of the chassis punching a hole through the floors of the airship.

The Blackspire began to list downward.

Then it crashed into the Dome City of Atlantis.

CHAPTER FORTY-TWO
DOME CITY

There, above the city—above their *heads*—a massive black blimp appeared. Sally knew it by its reputation and its design though she had never seen it before:

Mighty Khan's flagship dirigible.

The Blackspire.

"*He's* here," Professor Khan said, the distaste in his words never more apparent. Sally felt for the erudite ape—he was a creature without parentage, a half-clone forged from the genetic material of a primate dictator.

Edwin giggled. It seemed inappropriate, but she assumed it was just nerves. Edwin did not seem to be made of very hardy stuff. Besides, they were being paraded toward some Vizier—though now it wouldn't matter if the Conqueror Ape had arrived. She wasn't sure how long they could keep up the ruse. They needed to escape, needed to get away so they could learn more about what was *really* going on. If only some kind of distraction would—

The Professor gasped.

She looked up in time to see an all-too-familiar plane appear out of nowhere and crash head-on into the decks of the Blackspire.

Lucy.

Jet.

Mack.

No!

Sally screamed.

It's working! Mack thought, whooping and hollering inside his own mind even as he gripped the flight stick with a white-knuckled grip. All around Lucy the channel of space-time energy whipped and whirled and Mack's head reached out and he told the plane where he wanted her to go (*Blackspire, Blackspire, Blackspire*) but his heart told her another thing entirely (*Sally, Sally, Sally*)—

And suddenly, the plane banked left and cut clean through the continuum wall and appeared above Atlantis.

But all of Mack's vision was filled with the Blackspire.

Head-on. Dead-on.

No time to turn. No time to do anything.

He hoped Jet was buckled in. Because then at least one of them was going to make it out of this thing alive.

Lucy smashed into the Blackspire and all went black.

Atok had been ripped out of his old reality and thrown into a new one and for a moment he thought: *I have died and go to the hunting ground now to meet my forebears,* but when his ancestors scrawled their wisdom on the cave walls of the Hollow Earth's most sacred grottos, none of them said anything about a crystal dome, a lunatic city, or a giant airship.

His instincts kicked in—same instincts that told him he was about to be jumped by a slavering spider-cricket or gored by a mammoth told him he was about to crash into that giant black bladder filling the sky.

His mind told him one thing. But his body did another.

He let go of the iron bird.

Atok fell toward the alien city.

The Blackspire drifted downward, its buoyancy interrupted by the wing-slashed vent in its underside. The Atlantean people fled for their nooks and burrows and buildings as the dirigible's nose sank deeper and deeper until it plunged into the very heart of the Dome City.

Darkness, punctuated by plumes of fire.

Benjamin kicked open the pod, whose door had already been jarred loose, the hermetic seal broken. He spilled out only to find that the deck had collapsed, that fire was blooming from broken mains, and that everything was at a 45-degree angle.

As such, he started to slide. His hand shot out, and caught the base of Amelia's pod—he pulled himself up and peered in through the cracked Lucite.

Blood dripped on the underside of the window.

Oh, no, no, no.

He popped the door.

And felt hands grab his shirt while a knee came up into his gut.

Amelia hauled him up, nose cocked at a bad angle, eyes wild. She was screaming—"*Le Monstre! Le Monstre!*"—before sanity and clarity returned to her.

"Amelia," Ben said, feeling like most of his guts had gone up into his throat.

"Benjamin. I'm... I thought..."

No time for this. "We must've crashed. We need to get out of here while we still have our wits." He helped her out, and together they braced themselves against the walls. As the fire blossomed and lit the corridor, they could see how most of the pods were buried or smashed into one another. He could see some faces beneath, mostly undisturbed, but surely there were casualties—? Nothing could be done right now. They needed help to excise the heroes.

Amelia stared. Horror-struck.

"We have to go," Benjamin pulled on her.

"But..."

"Amelia! *We have to go.*"

"I think my nose is broken." She still looked dazed. Possibly a concussion.

"I know. Please."

She nodded, and together they let go and slid down the corridor.

Their ape guard went mad. The gibbon howled and Captain Chirrang made some mournful ululation. The orangutan bleated for Mighty Khan.

And then, chaos ensued. The apes bolted for the wreckage, leaving them alone.

Sally felt the strength leave her. Her knees buckled.

"Mack and Jet..." she said.

The Professor got his massive tree-trunk arms underneath her and lifted her up. "They may still be alive yet, Miss Slick, but not if we stand here feeling bad."

"Yes," she said. Swallowing hard. "Of course."

"We are heroes, are we not?"

She nodded. Her heart wasn't in it, not yet, but she heard herself answer, "We are."

"Then quickly, quickly, now."

As they ran, she looked back. "Where's Edwin?"

Neither of them knew.

Well, Methuselah-as-Spears thought, *that was unexpected.*

He exhaled a heavy sigh—he'd been holding his breath without even realizing it—and let go of the equation fragment he'd quickly conjured as the plane smashed through the Blackspire exactly where he'd been standing. The string of mathemagic extended an invisible but impermeable bubble around him—the wreckage of the Blackspire console and parts of the plane and other random scraps of the dirigible lay packed against that invisible barrier and suddenly dropped to the ground when he let go.

When he did, it revealed the tail of the Clipper plane (as well as one of its propellers) sitting there, still smoking, the metal inside making a cool-down *tink tink tink* sound.

Not-Spears poked his head inside a ragged tear alongside the plane and saw that Centurion—the one who was so fond of jet-packs—laying still under a collapsed set of lockers.

Perhaps his part of the sequence of events was over. Perhaps his place in the equation was *solved-for-X*. So be it. Spears gave a flip little wave and muttered, "Go forth with courage, you dippy corn-fed do-gooder, you."

Then Spears slid back to the console, kicked out the rest of the shattered glass, and hopped free as a bird onto the streets of Dome City.

Mack gasped and his head jerked upright.

He tasted blood. He couldn't see out of his right eye. Everything felt distant and disconnected. Where was he? Who was he? What had happened? It felt, quite seriously, the way he often felt after a long night drinking cheap Mai-Tais and waking up on a mat made of banana leaves with some local Hula girl whose name and—until she rolled over, anyhow—face could not be conjured from the depths of one's depraved memory.

He tried to move. Couldn't.

Everything was dark except for the occasional spark coming off the shattered console and dashboard. *Bzzt. Fzzt. Tzzt.*

Oh. Right.

Lucy.

Lucy.

"Lucy," he whispered. "I'm sorry, old girl."

The console answered with another sharp rain of sparks.

Mack tried to move again. Felt his arms respond this time. And one leg.

But not the other one.

Uh-oh.

Trying to move his left leg gave him a shooting pain lancing through his hip, but below that it was nothing—like his leg wasn't even there.

Uh-oh.

Already he started to tell himself, "Okay, Mackie-Boy, you don't need that leg. You fly planes. You've never run a marathon in your life—all right, yeah, sure, there was that time you had to run all the way across the island when that Samoan chief was chasing you, but you didn't know that broad was his daughter. Nothing wrong with hobbling along. Maybe earn a little sympathy. Maybe some kisses with that sympathy."

All of it felt like hollow bravado.

He hoped like hell that his leg was okay.

And then he realized: *Jet.*

Jet was in the plane when it crashed.

Wasn't he?

Oh, Jet, no, c'mon, tell me you got out of the plane before we hit.

For all their confrontation over... Sally, mostly, Mack couldn't stand it if Jet didn't make it. Being a Centurion had its risks, but to go out like this...

It was Mack's fault.

He said all those things to the Professor—oh, blah blah, we're heroes, we don't have to be smart, sometimes we just have to fly blindly into an alien gate and hope it doesn't throw our plane in the path of the enemy's very big and very pointy airship.

Good job, Silver Fox. You really saved the day this time.

Just then—behind him somewhere in the ruined bowels of the Clipper plane, he heard a sound. Like something was coming. Something big. Metal torn asunder. The ground rattling beneath him with every pulse. Like a T-Rex stomping forward, ripping parts of Lucy away, bite-by-bite, until exposing the sweet tender meat-treat within.

Mack was that meat-treat.

It was close, now. Just outside the cockpit door.

Mack fumbled around under his seat, looking for some kind of weapon, *any* kind of weapon, but every time he moved he found himself pinned and in pain and—

The door to the cockpit blasted off its hinges.

Two bright eyes stared inside, beams cutting through the space and blinding Mack. Mack yelled: "I'm armed! I've got a... Webley revolver... around here somewhere."

The lights—not eyes at all—turned downward.

"Mack, thank god," came Jet's voice. Jet set down his jet-wing on its base and the two head-lamps illuminated the bent and crumpled ceiling of the cockpit.

"How'd you get in here, kid?"

"I used the jet-wing. Pulsed the air-boosters. It's like having an invisible hammer. We better get out of here, c'mon."

"Listen," Mack said. "I gotta tell you something."

"Mack. We have to go."

"Hey! I said, *listen*. I'm trying to talk here."

Jet shifted uncomfortably. "Okay. Say your peace."

"She's yours."

"What?"

"Sally. I'm not right for her. I'm just some island-hopping palooka. I got nothing to offer her besides a big gift basket of heartbreak. You're the one she needs."

"Don't be hard on yourself. Besides, she doesn't want me. She thinks I'm... her brother or something."

Mack laughed. "I think you'll figure it out."

"Never mind all that. C'mon, let's get you out of—"

"My leg's done."

"What?"

"It's done for," Mack said. "Stuck under the console here. I can't even... sense it down there. It's like I don't have a leg at all."

In the already harsh light, Jet's face turned even grimmer. He hurried over and started feeling around, trying to lift the wreckage. But it was no use.

"I'm in there pretty good, kid."

"I'm not a kid. We're the same age. We're all the same age." Jet cracked his knuckles nervously. "The booster. I'm going to use the air booster."

He moved the jet-wing over toward Mack.

"Is that safe?" Mack asked.

"Yes. Maybe. Probably not. I think it's our only shot. I don't want you here alone. I already hear noises outside somewhere."

"Kid," Mack said.

"Yeah?"

"I miss my plane."

"I know, Mack."

Mack let out a breath. "Okay. How's this gonna work?"

"I'll fire the booster. It'll lift the console and... maybe your leg, too. Grab the chair behind you. Soon as that booster goes off, yank your leg out of there."

"I can't feel the damn leg."

"So pivot your hip. But if the leg is still there when the console crashes back down..." Jet didn't finish the statement but Mack picked up what his friend was laying down. *If your leg's not crushed already, it will be after that.*

Jet tilted the jet-wing.

"You ready?"

"Yes," Mack lied.

Jet counted down.

Three.

Two.

One.

Pulse.

The air booster blasted an unseen grapeshot of air at the console, lifting it up with a clamor and a clatter—Mack felt a sudden pressure release and he gripped the back and side of his cockpit chair and swung his body right (so as not to get the other leg trapped or crushed).

The console crashed back down.

And Mack's leg wasn't there when it did.

But he still couldn't feel his left leg. He tried to stand on it and the pain that shot through his hip felt like an arrow made of molten lead. Jet caught him.

In the light, they could see the leg looked pretty bad. Mack's leathers were torn ragged. Beyond the rips they could see pale flesh and a crust of blood.

"C'mon," Jet said, slinging the jet-wing over his one shoulder and giving Mack his other one. "Let's get out of here and see if we can't figure out what's going on."

Sally and Khan hid behind the corner of one of the Dome City's crystal buildings, this one the color of burnished topaz. Ahead they saw the wreckage of the Blackspire which itself contained glimpses of Lucy buried within her decks. The dirigible's massive air-bladder slowly deflated above, and once it did, it would cover the whole thing and make it a lot harder to get inside. "We have to move now," Khan said, again the one urging action.

"I'll take the front," Sally said. She did not say it, but the intent was clear to Khan: *That's where the plane crashed.* Part of him thought she shouldn't go, shouldn't see—

But it was her right. Those were her friends.

"I'll take the rear," Khan agreed.

Between them and the wreckage was a growing battalion of various apetypes, many of them standing around and hooting and ooking like excitable, agitated primates.

"How do we get clear?" Sally asked.

Khan smiled. "Let me take care of that."

Captain Chirrang was a loyal ape.

Loyal, not that bright.

But he was smart enough to know he wasn't that smart, and that's what helped him earn the role as captain of the guard here at the Atlantean Dome City.

Still, at the end of the day, Chirrang wanted one thing: to follow, not to lead. Mighty Khan—and his baboon Vizier—were excellent leaders, far smarter than Chirrang ever could be, and the good Captain was happy to accede to their authority.

So, when Khan's son came bounding up out of nowhere, waving his arms about and screaming about how *it's a trap!* and *it's going to explode!*, Chirrang was quite frankly glad to have the burden of leadership lifted from off his bony shoulders.

The good Captain inflated his neck bladder and hooted, demanding that his troops pull back to a safe location where they would await further orders.

The chaotic cavalcade of apes did as they were told. It was their way.

And as they all fled, none of them saw Sally Slick and Professor Khan duck inside the fresh ruins of the Blackspire airship.

The floor was caved in. It had a mean tilt to it. The Professor had to reach out with his prodigious arms and grab hold of the walls—bars, actually, for this appeared to be some kind of *prison level*—and for once he was thankful that he was ape, not human.

Is that what you are? he asked himself. *Is it time to admit you're something other than human? Something both lesser and greater in equal measure?*

Being an ape had served him well over the last several days.

That troubled him, but no time to nest over those broken eggs right now.

He hauled himself forward and upward, his palms slapping against the reverberating prison bars, until—

A hand fell upon his own from within.

The Professor jerked his hand back as if it had been burned.

Deep within the cell, he saw a pair of eyes gleaming back. Then came a brusque snort. Sniffing the air. The Professor answered with a snuffling sniff of his own, and he smelled the musk and wildness of—

The drums, the drums, those jungle drums—

—of another ape.

A familiar stink. Too familiar.

The Professor gasped.

"Son," came the voice of Mighty Khan from within. "I knew you would come to me."

At first, the Professor could find no response. The blood in his skull pounded and thrashed like the angry ocean surf, and he heard a sound in his ears like a thousand apes screaming and going to war against their enemies. When Mighty Khan called to him again—"Son?"—the erudite counterpart to the Ape-Lord found his voice.

"I am not your son," the Professor croaked.

"I had you created in my image. Like God with man." The Conqueror took a deep breath and thumped his chest. "We are ape. We are Khan."

"I am not you. I am nothing like you."

"You keep my name. And I can smell it on you—the jungle crawls from your pores. You hear it, don't you? The drumbeat of your heart. Let it loose. Free the beast within. Free *me* and I will show you how. I will teach you how to be ape."

"I don't want to be ape." Truth, lie, or something in between?

"We can rule together. We can rule as the Two Khans." Mighty Khan pressed his face against the bars. In the dark he seemed suddenly less the Mighty Ape-Lord and more the desperate zoo-kept creature unfairly caged. "Please."

"I cannot help you."

Professor Khan turned to go.

"I can help you," the Ape-Lord called after. "Don't you want to know who put me here? It's my maker. And yours. Doctor Methuselah. He is here. I can help you track him. I can show you the way and together we can defeat him. Just free me, son. Open my cell!"

Methuselah. A villain whose dossier made the Ape-Lord's look like a diner menu. If this was all his plan that meant far more was at work than they ever expected.

It made sense to free him. To free his... *not your father*, the Professor caught himself. *Your original template. The faulty one.*

But then he played it out. Were he to let the Conqueror Ape free he'd force all the ape soldiers to fall in line. The heroes would again be in danger.

It was just a ruse.

The so-called Mighty Khan had no interest in his son or helping the heroes.

"Goodbye," the Professor said.

Mighty Khan screamed after him until his hoarse voice could no longer be heard.

Sally clambered through the wreck, pulling the small palm-sized flashlight off her belt and shining its meager light to guide her way. The hallway ahead of her was torn and twisted, parts of the plane littering the ground. Here, a propeller. There, a swatch of scrap with the cursive letters meticulously painted on: LUC. The portion with the Y must've been somewhere else. Sally felt a well of sadness pulling at the space between her heart and her stomach, but she had to cap it and keep moving.

Nearby, she found a psychosaur pinned beneath a fallen duct. Head twisted at a bad angle, glassy eyes staring up and catching the light in glistening pools.

Dead.

What chance did Jet and Mack have?

It was then she saw: two figures at the end of the hall.

One of them—the smaller of the two—supporting the other.

Sally barely found her voice. "Jet. Mack."

She ran to them. Threw herself around them even through Mack grunted and mumbled, "Ow, ow, ow, ow, *ow.*" She kissed both of them on the cheek, not thinking about what that even meant, right now.

"I am so glad to see you two here."

"Hey, Sally," Jet said, smiling like a kid in a candy store.

Mack winked. "Hey, Slick."

Then she slapped both of them.

Leaving them both reeling and blinking.

"What was...?" Jet said, too stunned to finish the question.

Mack barked, "Hey! I'm hurt over here."

Sally thrust her finger up in both of their faces. "And you're going to be hurt a lot worse if either of you pull a numbskull move like that again. You'll have more to worry about than rebuilding Lucy. I'll knock both your brains out with my pipe wrench—which is a very big wrench, if you recall. Understood?"

The two men nodded. In tandem they said, "Yes, ma'am."

"Good. Now let's get you two out of here."

Sally and Jet helped Mack out of a peeled back strip of steel, easing him between two warped steel beams—out here, in the light, his leg looked pretty bad. His blood-slick skin now lay exposed to the air and the light. They just hoped it looked worse than it really was.

Outside the Blackspire, the apes were still gone—but a small crowd of Atlanteans had gathered. Their wan, wispy forms stood, craning their necks to see. Wide-eyed with faces wearing a mixture of fear and wonder.

"Are those Atlanteans?" Jet asked. "They're not quite human, are they?"

Mack pulled himself to standing, using the wreckage of the dirigible as support. "No wonder they got conquered. Docile like a herd of moo-cows."

A few of the Atlanteans spoke. To the ear it sounded like meaningless jabbering—a series of vowel sounds punctuated by the rare consonant. But in the Centurions' minds, symbols flared—flashes of light like sparklers or fireworks etching never-before-seen pictograms in their mind before fading away. They looked to one another.

"Anybody else get a mental light-show," Mack asked, "or am I having a stroke?"

Jet and Sally both said they got it, too.

"Jeez," Jet said. "It's too bad none of us can talk to them. They might know something."

"I can speak to them," came a voice from within the Blackspire.

Benjamin Hu stepped out. Followed by Amelia Stone and Professor Khan.

The erudite ape presented the two Centurions with a gesture. He said, "Look who I found wandering around in the dark."

Mack looked to Amelia and her broken nose. "You okay, Stone? You look like hell."

"Your way with the ladies really *is* legendary," Amelia said, smirking. "Besides, I look better than you with that busted up matchstick you call a leg."

The two smiled at one another.

Benjamin moved past the group and approached the Atlanteans. He said, in English, "I speak some Atlantean. It's really more of a written language, at least it was in terms of studying their artifacts. Worth a shot, anyway."

The mystic detective turned and faced the dozens of gathered Atlanteans. He bowed his head and spread his hands and then spoke.

He uttered the same string of mostly-vowels, a hard consonant popping up now and again—but he did so slowly, more clumsily than they did. In all their minds flashed symbols—but these were dimmer than those that came earlier, and some of the pictograms seemed broken or otherwise incomplete.

When Benjamin was done speaking, one of the Atlanteans—an old man with cavernous lines etched into his skin and a long bone-white beard forked at the end and bound to his wrists—pushed his way out of the crowd while hobbling on a knobby quartzite cane.

The old man from Atlantis spoke to Benjamin. And Benjamin spoke—or, at least, tried to speak—in return. Symbols danced between them. A strange mental light show.

Sally spoke to the others as an aside: "Maybe he can help us find that damn Ape-Lord."

Professor Khan shook his head and then, with an air of sadness hanging about his head, said, "Khan is inside the Blackspire as we speak. It turns out he is not the main malefactor behind all this, Miss Slick. It is Doctor Methuselah."

Sally tensed. Jet and Mack turned toward the erudite ape.

"Gosh. Not him," Jet said. "Anybody but him."

Mack sneered. "Makes sense why we haven't heard a peep out of that madman for years. He's been behind the curtain setting up a show."

"The *real* show," Amelia chimed in. "Professor, you should know something. Edwin Jasher is... he's not who you think."

Khan blinked. Stammered. "Wh... whatever do you mean? Young Edwin?"

"He's Methuselah." Amelia responded to the incredulous looks she suddenly received. "No, I know, it's hard to believe. But he fragmented his persona, his consciousness. One part of him lived inside Hu's nemesis, Gerard Spears. Another stayed with the old man's imprisoned body and the final piece went into Edwin Jasher."

"How..." Khan started, his brow darkening. "How much of Edwin is still in there?"

"I think the better question," Amelia said, "is how much of Edwin was *ever* there?"

That grim and unpleasant question hung in the air like a cloud of flies. Benjamin waved everyone over.

"This," he said, introducing the old man with the beard-bound wrists, "is—well, I don't know what his name *is*, but I think it means Speaker of Crystals? Or... Man Whose Wisdom Is Reflected in Crystals. Hard to translate without any of my inscription stones handy. He says that he has no idea where our quarry fled to, but he seems to indicate that below the city is a gateway—a portal like the others that's also a power source for the whole city. But, if I read him right, he's also saying that the power source has *changed*. Lashing out like solar flares—growing in power. Given the circumstances, even if Methuselah *isn't* down there, it seems like we certainly should be."

"Methuselah's crazy-powerful," Jet said. "He's got the playbook to the entire universe at his fingertips."

Sally withdrew her wrench, slapped it against her open palm. "We stopped him before, we can stop him again."

"This time you're doing it without me," Mack said. "My leg's like ground beef. I can barely walk."

Jet patted his jet-wing. "But you can fly."

"Oh, hell no," Mack said. "Did that. Still need to change my drawers. I'm staying here. With Lucy." He slid down to the ground. "Come pick me up when you save the world?"

Sally knelt by him. "You sure?"

"I'm sure, doll. Go. Besides, if Jet gets into another scrape, he needs someone there to catch him when he falls."

Jet shook his head, grinning. "I seem to recall pulling *your* bacon out of this fire."

"Time is wasting," Benjamin said. "The wise man said he'd send some of his men down with us to show us the way to the portal."

"Let's do this," Stone said, cracking her knuckles.

CHAPTER FORTY-THREE
ATLANTIS DOME CITY

The ape had gone mad. Mighty Khan's mental faculties were sinking slowly beneath the mire of the frustration, of the *madness*, of being caged. His own jungle drums beat to a furious rhythm inside his mind as he slammed again and again into the bars—first with his shoulders, then with his head, beating himself dizzy like a starving zoo beast.

Methuselah—

My son—

All my plans—

Gonga—

My son!

Suddenly, the wreckage of the Blackspire shifted. Just a bit—like an old house settling, but this was something far looser and held-together than an old house. The wreckage eased against other wreckage in a tectonic shift of metal groans and stuttering steel.

The ceiling above Khan's head shifted, too.

The cage bars buckled. They did not open, but the pressure sent cracks above Khan's head—he could not see them, not easily, but when he concentrated and pushed his consciousness above the wild drums, he could *hear* them. Like a spreading fracture across an icy lake.

It was then that Khan realized he did not need to go through the cage.

He began leaping up and down—again the mad ape, this time mad because he was *so close* to finding freedom. Khan ducked his head low and smashed his shoulder hard into the bars—the massive ape like a furry wrecking ball. The ceiling above cracked further.

Plaster fell away.

Revealing steel beams and rebar.

Solid as the cage on the outside. And impossible to get through.

Usually impossible.

These had bowed and buckled—spreading wide and leaving a gap to the floor above.

Khan snarled, and launched himself through the hole.

Atok dangled from a balcony—the brass and crystal cold beneath his leathery, callused grip. He'd been up here watching—watching the iron bird crash, watching the giant egg-shaped monstrosity come plunging into the center of the city, watching the apes and the strange citizens of this mad place go scurrying this way and that.

And it occurred to him: he was a very long way from home.

The battle for the Upland had only just begun and he fled the field of war to pursue a single combatant. His honor was important, yes, but it was the honorless dog who fled—Atok's honor was intact (though battered and bruised for letting his foe escape). And now his army was leaderless. *Headless.* They were trained, yes, but the war leader was not a role invented for no reason. It was a role of necessity. A firm hand and strong honor must guide the warriors. A pack of cave dogs worked because the pack yielded to the alpha. Without the alpha—

They'd find a new one.

The realization was crushing. After all that, he'd ruined his only chance to remain as war leader. Unless...

Unless he could return with the head of the honorless dog.

Surely the fool was dead. Unless dwelling inside the belly of that iron bird protected him, somehow? Couldn't be.

But then, what did Atok see beneath him?

A group of humans.

And one ape.

The ape. Khan.

If I brought back Khan's head...

He dropped suddenly, from balcony to balcony, then caught a golden wire and slid down it—the cable would've bitten into anybody else's hand, flaying the palm, but Atok's hands were hard like stone from years of training.

As they walked underneath a high trellis, Atok dropped atop it and peered down.

That was not the leader of the apes.

He wore the trappings of man. Spectacles to enhance the weakness of his eyesight. And a woman's skirt, by the looks of it.

But Atok saw something else: the one he fought inside the bowels of the Iron Bird. The one with his own set of wings.

If he made it out alive and unharmed, so could the other.

But the honorless dog was not here, was he? Not with this pack of humans.

Atok might find the weak-kneed "champion" yet.

Mack lay slumped against a nearby steel panel that had fallen off the Blackspire—at this point, the dirigible lay blanketed beneath the deflated bladder that once held it aloft, and so Mack chose to face another direction and gaze upon the magnificent—or, at least, magnificently *weird*—Dome City of Atlantis with all its gears and crystal architecture and brass artifice.

He decided to pretend like this was a little vacation.

Don't think about Lucy, he told himself again and again. Otherwise, he might've cried. *Your buddies will handle this. Sure, they're a little dim-witted without you—but they can handle this one tiny itty-bitty thing. Doctor Methuselah's not the world's worst criminal or anything.*

I should go.

He looked down at his busted leg.

What? And just be a burden?

A handsome burden, sure. But a burden no matter how you slice it, Silver.

Instead he just closed his eyes and listened to the hum and whirr of the city.

Then, he heard something else.

Footsteps. Bare feet.

He pried one eye open.

Oh, no.

"Honorless dog," Atok said, craning his neck so the joints popped.

Mack pressed his back up against the steel. "Great. It's you."

"Now we continue fight."

"Really? You know what you are? You're horrible. *Horrible*. You're ugly. You smell like a dirty horse. And you just won't leave that alone. So, that's what I'm calling you from now on. Atok the Horrible."

"Atok the Horrible crush you like bug."

Mack rubbed his eyes. "Hey, you big mook—I'm already crushed. See the leg? Leg-no-worky, pal. You really think I can fight you?"

Atok narrowed his eyes like this might be some kind of ruse. But then he smelled the air. "Wound sick."

"Yeah. Whatever. Go away."

Behind them: a sound.

The fabric of the Blackspire's balloon thudded from within, and then stretched out as if something big were pressing on it from inside. The fabric bulged at the seam and began tearing along that same line—and suddenly, the Blackspire birthed the Mighty Khan.

An undignified escape, but an escape just the same.

Atok and Mack both stared at the ape, who stood only twenty feet away.

"You," Atok seethed.

"Ain't this interesting," Mack said, leaning forward to see.

Khan sniffed the air.

"I... have to go find my son," he said.

And then the ape turned around and ran.

Mack was actually pretty surprised at how fast that monkey—sorry, sorry, *ape*—could run. Knuckles down, haunches up, zoom.

Atok pointed at Mack. "Later. You and me."

"Yeah, yeah, go catch yourself an Ape-Lord, Mister Horrible."

Atok snarled and bolted after Khan. One beast-man chasing the other.

They found a pair of squat thick-necked chimpanzees patrolling the crystal disc the old man claimed they'd need. Each holding an octagonal-mouthed sonic blaster.

Benjamin pointed to the chimps. "The old man says we're going to need one of those sonic devices."

"Let me," the Professor said.

He walked toward the chimpanzees. Holding up his hands and giving a faux-laugh. "Ho, ho, ho, gentlemen. It is I, Son-of-Khan. The... Vizier gives me permission to go... down into the... place. If you'll just step aside?"

The two chimps looked toward the erudite ape and then beyond, at the gaggle of humans and Atlanteans hanging back. As they each glanced past Khan, distracted, Khan punched both of them in the head. Both chimps dropped, unconscious.

Amelia applauded. "See, Professor. Knew you could throw a punch."

Khan's lips pulled back in a toothy smile.

The old man led them onto the crystal disc platform—smooth on the surface but beneath they could see the many facets and the darkness below. Above the disc was a brass funnel of sorts—it called to mind the mouth of a trumpet the way it flared out and gleamed golden.

"It's an elevator," Benjamin said, picking up one of the sonic blasters. He tossed it to Sally. "The old man says to point the blaster at the bell above our heads."

Sally looked up at the bell then down at the weapon.

"It's not a weapon," she said. "It's a tool." She smiled. "Fantastic."

She pointed the weapon at the funnel and fired.

The elevator beneath them dropped like a stone, taking them with it.

"They're coming," Edwin said.

Gerard nodded. He could feel the subspace vibration as pieces of the equation all drifted toward one another—symbols and numbers and variables in the great cosmic puzzle slowly finding out how they fit together.

Doctor Methuselah—the doddering body of the old villain—stood nearby, nodding and mumbling to himself. "I feel it," he said, but his heart just wasn't in it. Edwin rescued the frail old body from the prison here, from the dark hole where Khan left him to rot.

Gerard pondered keeping the three bodies separate. Certainly Edwin had a gawky likability, and the Spears-body was nearly ideal in physical ability and dripped with charm. And yet, he missed his old form—and upon returning to the original flesh it would dodder no more.

Down here, beneath the Dome City, beneath the ocean waters, lay a round cavern—epic, easily as big as the Blackspire was—with walls so smooth they looked sculpted, as if the walls were softened and dug out with a silver spoon.

The walls glittered with gems and crystals.

In the center of the space stood a crystalline platform held on by a spider's mesh of brass filaments, each fixed to a round tube-like structure running the circumference of the entire cavern—also brass, and ending in the middle in a great wide-mouthed funnel that emitted an eardrum-rumbling hum. Beneath that, a winding spiral walkway disappeared into the vortex.

But none of that added up to the most interesting thing about this place.

What was fascinating was what waited below.

Beneath the round crystalline platform on which Methuselah stood, a great portal expanded and contracted from a doorway into a sun-like sphere and back again, over and over, a great pulsing heart at the core of Atlantis. It was the eighth gate—or, more properly, the *first* of eight gates—and it was the most potent perforation into the space-time continuum this world had ever known. Khan had found it (or was led to it by Methuselah's ungentle hand) and used it to go back in time to what should've been the fall of the psycho-saur empire and the rise of Atlantis—but Khan of course rescued those foul saurian beings, bringing them here and starting in motion a chain of events that Methuselah could not have predicted but most certainly desired.

That was the trick: not to predict. It was the act of throwing a marble to see where it would land, what it might knock over, how it would roll. Place other objects—or, in this case, people and events—*just so* and the whole thing performed a dizzying mechanistic ballet that would've made Rube Goldberg pass out from the vapors.

Now, the gate was pulsing in a way it hadn't been before. The energy coming off it—energy others might not feel beyond a tickle in their throat or a raising of the hackles—was heady, intoxicating, full of such unlimited *potential.*

Nobody knew why it had suddenly gone mad, the portal.

Nobody but Methuselah.

He'd happily share. And would, in a few moments, when the Centurions arrived. Those thick-skulled, numb-headed wool-gatherers. Oh, the looks on their faces when they saw what they had wrought. They tried to save the world, but doomed it instead.

"Here it is," Edwin said, pointing up.

Descending from a hole in the ceiling came the elevator.

"Shall we?" Gerard asked.

Edwin nodded. Tottered over. The Methuselah body shuffled to where the other two stood—all three reached out, hands grasping for each other, forming a triangle of arms. The broken shards of consciousness began to unmoor from them, like psychic knives pulled suddenly from the cutting block of their minds.

It was time to again restore the mathemagic power to one body.

Glorious.

Sally was not the type to go off half-cocked.

But as the crystal disc lowered, she saw her chance—

There, ahead of them, stood the three bodies of Doctor Methuselah.

Linking hands. Beginning to glow.

Whatever that was, it wasn't good.

Before the platform dropped to the ground, Sally took a running leap off the edge—Jet called after her but it was too late—and she did a hard duck-and-roll, crashing down with her shoulder but coming up with the sonic weapon pointed.

She squinted one eye over the weapon, pulled the trigger.

The sonic charge—seen as a near-invisible projectile ring that had about it the air of *heat vapors* coming off a hot road—blasted forth.

Professor Khan yelled to her—

"No!"

The charge hit Edwin in the dead center of his chest. The triangle was broken as he staggered backward, reaching, reaching—

But then tumbling over the edge.

Edwin screamed all the way down. Disappearing into the portal—and his departure from this world was soundless but bright as the portal flared.

Gerard Spears whirled on her.

Both of his hands came together and his fingers danced as if he were maneuvering the beads of an unseen abacus.

And from both hands erupted a terrible red ray. It lanced out, struck Sally—her world lit up, her vision went from bright white to dead black, and everything bowled end over end until there was no more world to see.

Sally's body, limp like a rag doll, tumbled backward toward them just as the smaller crystal disc touched down upon the larger. Jet screamed as the red ray fired from Methuselah's fingers launched her backward at his feet.

Everything happened at once.

The heroes moved fast. Khan roared, launching himself off the platform. Amelia and Benjamin moved in tandem, fists cocked as they split up and moved along the edges of the platform. The Atlantean contingent merely cowered—soldiers, they were not.

Jet felt frantically for Sally's pulse and could not find it.

Not at first, at least. Suddenly his fingers felt a heartbeat fluttering in her neck.

He slung on his jet-wing.

The boosters kicked. A *foosh* of air from the pack launched him forward.

Sally, please be okay, please be okay—

Khan charged down the middle of the platform. Amelia and Benjamin came in from opposite ends. And Jet took to the air and planned to come down hard.

And then—

Methuselah snapped his fingers and everything—

—just—

—stopped.

Atok tackled the Ape-Lord. Together they rolled toward the lip of the elevator shaft where the crystal disc once sat and what was now just a great big hole carved into the earth. The Neanderthal smashed Khan's face into the ground and drove a hard fist into the back of the primate's head. Khan raged, got his legs beneath him and flung Atok off the way a bear might shake off a squirrel.

"I have no time for this," Khan snarled. "My son is down there."

"I care not," Atok said.

"You want this world?" Khan asked. "You can have it."

"I don't want it. I want *you*."

Atok charged. Leapt like a sabretooth.

Slammed bodily into Khan.

Together they fell over the edge.

Only Khan's hand darting out—massive fingers gripping the brass-ringed lip of the pit—stopped them from tumbling down, down, into darkness.

Methuselah spoke. His voice lifted Sally from her unconsciousness, but her awareness did not come without a price—awakening also awakened the pain that wracked through her, and she felt the burns that crawled up her side like dead ivy.

She looked toward the voice, and it was then she knew they were doomed.

Gerard Spears—Methusaleh, really—held out his hands, and all the Centurion attackers were frozen, held captive by invisible hands. Professor Khan stood poised to throw a fist that would never connect. Benjamin and Amelia both crept along the side, still as sculptures. Jet hung in mid-air, corkscrewing toward Spears but now paused there as if held by wires.

"Complexity yields complexity," Spears announced, his boastful voice booming through the massive chamber. Beneath him, the light show of the portal grew brighter. "What I sought was the most complex thing of all—the end of all time. Simple to say, but not so simple to achieve. I've long sought to unravel time, as you well know, so that I could be its master, but it never... quite worked out. As it turns out, I was a little too *handsy* with it all."

Methuselah wrinkled his nose. "Handsy. That's a Gerard Spears word. So sorry. His persona is like a mothballs smell I cannot quite eradicate. Regardless. What I mean is, I was far too controlling—trying to decide the equation when most of the equation had been written. I merely needed to fill in a few variables and let the rest write itself. Chaos and entropy—two powerful forces that breed like rabbits. Insert the right chaos into the system and the whole thing begins to break down as one desires it to do."

Sally tried to move. Tried to say something. Couldn't.

Methuselah continued: "I honestly didn't know how this was all going to play out but it's far more wonderful than I ever could've imagined. You know what did it? Your jury-rigged teleportation portal. Tapping into the ley lines was *genius*. Also: quite dangerous! Not dangerous for you, but for the *entire space-time continuum*."

Sally's heart sank. *My portal. I did that.* Could he be wrong?

"You see, it's like this. The Atlantean gates are both givers and receivers of temporal flux—they give off time energy and take it in. All in a big recursive loop, an infinite lemniscate of the snake biting his own tail. Oh, but you introduced a new wrinkle, a perforation of the ley lines that suddenly was another hole *greedily vacuuming* up whatever came near to it. It's eating time, don't you see? That's why this portal beneath us is growing stronger, brighter, more potent—it's *compensating*. More temporal flux leaks, and somewhere, on the beautiful island of Hawaii, more temporal flux is drawn into the Earth's mystical energy channels and chewed up like a baby bunny thrown under a lawnmower. How sad."

Sally felt hot tears crawl down her cheeks. *No, no, no. I did this. I have to fix this. That's what I do. I fix what's broken, and this time, the error is all mine.*

Buck up.

Chin up.

Do something.

Her hand felt around. Found something.

The sonic weapon.

Methuselah-as-Gerard tilted a playful ear toward the ape.

"What's that, Professor? Yes, I am taking questions. Yours is...? *Ah.* Yes. As the time vortex increases it feeds more and more time into your rigged-up teleportation gate and then—poof—time ceases to be. But what makes me the master of it, you ask? Excellent question. I am, as you have found, *incredibly* powerful. I am the keeper—the last keeper, if you must know—of the world's mathemagic equations. Furthermore, I'm foolishly old! Oldest creature walking the earth right now. The power I possess coupled with my age gives me a bit of seniority, I'm afraid. The governance of all the world's time will fall to me as its cosmic keeper. It's quite a job. Not far from god-hood. I hope I'm up to the task, don't you?"

Sally held her breath. Brought the weapon up with unsteady hand. The barrel wavered as she fixed Gerard Spears in her sights.

Her finger eased around the trigger.

No.

Wait.

What was it she said earlier?

It's not a weapon.

It's a tool.

Just taking out Spears or the old-man Methuselah-body wouldn't matter.

The portal would still give off time flux.

The teleporter she built would continue to leech it.

It's not a weapon.

It's a tool.

There. On the wall. Another funnel like the one that dropped the elevator.

Sally took aim as Not-Spears continued: "Thus I'd like to thank you all for your part in this great experiment. The results appear quite positive! But your time as variables in the equation is over—which is fine, really, as *all time* will be over soon enough. I thought it best to spare you the effects, though, in thanks for serving my needs oh-so-well."

Not-Spears tightened his hands into fists.

The Centurions began to choke.

Sally could hear their gags and coughs as they hung there, frozen in time and space, their breath cut off by invisible hands tightening around their throats.

Hang in there, Sally.

Hang in there.

It's not a weapon.

It's a tool.

She fired.

Atok reached for the lip of the hole. Tried to climb back up.

Khan grunted.

His fingers slipped.

"You fool," the ape hissed. "You've killed us both."

They fell.

The sonic pulse shot forward.

The rings connected with the funnel.

Sally had no idea what it did, but she could make a pretty good guess. The crystal disc on which she lay was an elevator.

And so was the larger platform, she believed.

Methuselah turned, heard the pulse punch into the funnel's mouth with a *whonnnng*, and then followed the sound with his gaze as it raced around the brass tube.

As it did, the filaments holding the larger platform up severed one by one, fast as lightning. Both of the Doctor's bodies cried out—

The Centurions unfroze.

The platform dropped toward the portal. Sally cried out for Jet—their only chance to rescue everyone before it hit—but being unfrozen must've knocked his balance out of whack. Jet rocketed forward, out of control, hitting the smooth sculpted side of the chamber—

And tumbling into the portal.

They all went into the portal.

The Professor. Benjamin. Amelia. Both the Methuselahs.

And Jet Black.

She thought—*Jump in there after them. Jump. Follow them.*

But she could barely move. The pain still wracked her body.

And beneath her, the portal began pulsing faster and faster like a heart about to explode—the bright light began turning red, then the red shot through the black as Methuselah's voice boomed through the chamber: "*NooooooOOOOOOOOO—*"

Out of the darkness above, two bodies fell and crashed into the elevator. One body—that of a Neanderthal who to Sally wasn't much more than a hairy blur—shattered the edge of the crystal disc and tumbled into the pulsing portal.

The other was Mighty Khan. Conqueror Ape.

He did not fall. He hung on the edge. Big feet dangling.

"You," she said, the platform tilting beneath her.

"My son," he said. "Where is my son?"

Sally shook her head. "He... fell. Into the portal."

Mighty Khan nodded, offering a chuff and a grunt.

"Thank you," he said.

Then he let go, and fell into the portal.

Then the whole thing flashed one last time—

And winked out of existence.

THE CENTURY CLUB
WILL RETURN

IN

BEYOND
DINOCALYPSE

BEYOND DINOCALYPSE

SNEAK PEEK

Jet Black fell.

He did not fall through open air. He did not plunge deep into water.

He tumbled through time and space. Everything was light and dark at the same time—bright flashes pulsing and long shadows stretching like cooling tar. Felt like he was falling through an endless tunnel, a pit-like perforation in the cosmic continuum.

All around him rose the voices and sounds of history: cannon-fire, erupting volcanoes, jackhammers breaking asphalt, the cheers and jeers of infinite crowds, the wailing of animals, the sobbing of children. All sounds warped, melting from one into another. A mad cacophony of noises kicking through his ear-drums and nesting deep in his mind.

It went on like this.

For a minute or a millennium, Jet could not say.

But for all the time, through all the space, one word formed crystalline in his mind, resonating like a fork tapping glass:

Sally.

When last he left her, Sally was crying his name. She reached out for him across the massive underground chamber, a sculpted space beneath Atlantis as he hung frozen and limp in the invisible grasp of not one but *two* Doctor Methuselahs.

She had fired a sonic blast through the funnel-tube that wound around the chamber like a golden snake, and then everything *unstuck* as the platform dropped suddenly toward the whirling portal below, the two Doctors going with it. Jet suddenly flew forward, slamming hard into the side of the chamber—seeing stars, his head tolling like a bell—before dropping down toward the portal with all the others.

All the others except Sally.

Sally, left behind on the elevator platform.

Reaching. Yelling. Her body damaged by Methuselah's cruel mathemagic attack.

Jet plunged into the portal.

He didn't fall to the ground so much as the ground fell upward to meet him. There came the vacuum *pop* of Jet exiting the continuum of time and space and—

There he was. Standing on wobbly legs.

A wall of humid air, hot as a bull's breath, hit him in the face. Colors and light resolved into shape and object, and as Jet's internal compass spun slower and slower, he saw that he stood in the middle of a wild, verdant jungle. Vines thick as his thigh hung between twisted jungle trees, trees whose roots lay exposed, whose trunks were bulbous and bottle-shaped. The ground lay spongy beneath his feet. Everything felt wet. The air, heavy. Thick like in a cloud of steam.

A dragonfly flitted before him, herkily-jerkily darting left, then right, then up, then up again. Its eyes were like golden marbles. Its body, a knitting needle of sapphires.

And it was easily as big as Jet's hand. Hell, it was easily as big as Professor Khan's massive primate mitt.

Huge trees. Leaves so big you could use one as a parachute. Dragonflies large enough to carry away a newborn kitten.

Jet had no idea where he was.

But he damn sure knew when:

I've gone back in time.

Perhaps to the very beginning.

A moment of panic washed over him like a cold rush of water, turning his sweat icy. Again her name drifted across the surface of his mind: *Sally.* But no. This was not the time to dwell on the hopelessness of the situation. Hope was part of who they were, part of what they did. Without hope, any attempts at heroism would be dead in the water.

The dragonfly darted off to heights unseen.

The dragonfly, he decided, had the right idea.

Time to fly, he thought. Get a view of the forest—er, jungle—for the trees.

Jet kicked the air-booster on his jet-wing, launched himself straight up.

He flew ten feet. The jet-wing's air booster stuttered. The wing tilted. Jet's body corkscrewed suddenly, and before he knew it, he flew sideways into a tree whose trunk seemed a braid of several smaller trees.

Jet Black fell.

Only about twenty feet or so.

Just the same, it was enough to horse-kick the air out of his lungs.

Gaaaaasp.

Then, a roar came, echoing across the jungle.

An all-too-familiar roar. The roar of a gorilla.

In the canopy above, big colorful birds took flight.

"Professor," Jet gasped, wincing as he hurried to his feet. His jet-wing may have been broken, but he was who he was, and one of his fellow Centurions was in danger.

Professor Khan struck out with a fist, but his fist froze in mid-air. He grunted, snarled, tried to pull away—but it was held fast by an invisible hand.

Their powers are different here, he thought. *Stronger. Not just telepathic, but telekinetic.*

The psychosaurs—no longer sporting the illusion of human faces—came sweeping out of the jungle riding ostrich-sized dinosaurs (leading Khan to believe they were some manner of Ornithomimus). The psychic saurians hissed and gnashed their flat razor teeth. Three psychosaurs to the front of Khan, then three to the rear.

They held reins of golden fungus, strung up around the necks of their dinosaur mounts.

One of the mounts darted a head toward him with an open mouth—that's when Khan took a swing, his fist trapped suddenly. Khan reached for his one fist with his other, but found *that* hand pinned by invisible forces, too. Both arms wrenched suddenly backward, his arms burning at the shoulders with twin lightning bolts of pain.

The psychosaur ahead of him reached out a clawed hand, palm down.

As the psychosaur raised its hand, so too did Khan raise off the ground. Like a puppet.

Khan thrashed, and roared.

The second psychosaur to the right reached down to the side of its mount and uncoiled a long lash—this, too, made of the thumb-thick glowing fungus. The psychosaur whipped the lash forward, and Khan felt the fungus snake around his neck. It tightened there, as if pulled taut by psychic hands. He felt his head pounding. Darkness bled at the edges of his vision.

His body weakened.

At first, he thought he was hallucinating. To his right, the air rippled like pondwater hit by a thrown stone, and then a body appeared out of nowhere—

Another gorilla.

Father, the Professor thought, the word a betrayal of his own mind. *No! He is not your father, you daft ape!* The Conqueror lay still on the jungle floor, a shaft of sunlight illuminating his nose—the Professor saw the gorilla's prodigious nostrils flaring, revealing that he was not dead but unconscious.

Then—

The sound of swift footsteps.

A shape darted out of the jungle.

The shape flew upward. Struck the psychosaur with the lash like a wrecking ball!

Both tumbled off the Ornithomimus, and the Professor saw a familiar flying suit: Jet Black had come to save him.

Just because his jet-wing wouldn't take him high didn't mean it couldn't still offer some advantage. Jet burst through the jungle into the clearing, and hit his air booster just as he took a running leap—the momentum carried him forward like a clumsy bullet tumbling end over end, and he crashed into the psychosaur holding the glowing whip.

The two of them thudded hard into the side of the next mount, causing that dinosaur to stagger suddenly, its rider tumbling over the side and on top of Jet.

Now Jet found himself beneath two hissing, writhing psychosaurs.

He brought a knee up, then lashed out with an elbow. Both found purchase and the two psychosaurs toppled off of him. "Offa me, you big palookas!"

Jet managed to stand. He hurried toward the Professor—

Then found his body jerked sharply backward. He lifted in the air. Blood rushing to his temples, thrumming in his ears.

The invisible hands threw him.

Hard. And far.

He hurtled sideways high in the air, flung like a child's raggedy doll. Through the trees. Crashing through vines.

Jet landed hard against something that broke against his body.

Dizzy, he tried yet again to stand—planting a hand on a curved concrete shape to his right. A shape which had a match to his left. Between them (and beneath Jet): shattered planks of wood, once painted green, the paint mostly flaked away.

Jet pulled his palm away, found a small hunk of black asphalt beneath it. *A road.*

A bench.

He pulled himself up, looked beyond it all—

Through the trees, he saw great canyons of stone pillars rising up. Pillars thick with moss. Choked by creeping green.

Except these were no stone pillars.

They were buildings.

A nearby street sign leaned crooked up against a tree, vines pulling it into a tangled embrace. The sign read: *6th Ave.*

"We're in New York," Jet said, breathless. *This isn't the past. This is the future.*

Behind him: a branch snap.

Jet wheeled. Two psychosaurs. Whether they were the ones he just knocked off their mounts or not, he couldn't know—they all looked the same. Suddenly, their faces flickered: human guises appeared and disappeared, and he felt their greasy unseen hands prying along the edges of his psyche. He felt at his temples, found the brass headband still in place—

But it no longer mattered.

Pressure closed around his throat. Invisible hands lifted him up. He felt the psychic barrier protecting his mind start to break apart like clods of desert-dry dirt between rubbing fingers. Fingers that then sunk deep into his consciousness—

The assault began anew.

You are weak.

YOU ARE WEAK.

YOU ARE WEAK!

Then, a sound—like something cutting air. A glinty flash caught a beam of sunlight and something whipped around in front of Jet, toward the psychosaurs. Both assailants shuddered.

Then the flashing shape was gone again.

Jet felt the psychic assault cease lickity-split. He fell to the ground on his tailbone.

The first psychosaur's head casually, as if pushed by the gentlest prod, fell off its shoulders and *fwud*ded against the soft jungle earth below. Then the other's chin dipped forward, and the head left its mooring, too. The second decapitated head rolled into the first.

Both saurian stumps burbled black blood over the scaled necks and shoulders. Then the bodies fell in opposite directions.

Jet blinked.

And about wet himself when a hand grabbed his shoulder.

"Get up," came a voice. A familiar voice.

Sally.

He leapt to his feet, his heart leaping right along with him—

Another chill. Another bath of icy sweat.

This was... Sally?

She was older. Not *old*, but... time had changed her, wore her down, drawn a few lines around her eyes and her mouth, framing there the scowl that sat plastered on her face. One eye lay hidden behind an octagonal black eyepatch. She wore a red jumpsuit whose material seemed as scaled and organic as the skin of the psychosaurs themselves.

In her hand, a bladed boomerang gleamed. She slid it into a holster hanging at her toolbelt, and there hung other implements of war, too: a cattleprod, a hooked knife, an Atlantean sonic blaster.

But no wrench.

Jet said as much: "Sally. Your wrench."

She sniffed. A momentary sadness crossed the dark of her eye like a ship traversing a black ocean. "I lost it years ago."

"When are we?" he asked.

"No time to talk," she said. "We have psychosaurs to hunt and heroes to save. Stay behind me. Follow my lead. *Don't* get us killed."

And then she was off. Striding forward into the jungle without him.

Jet felt far more unsettled than he had when he was plummeting through the time-space tunnel—this was more than just his body going topsy-turvy. His heart and soul felt suddenly like they were spinning end over end, faster and faster, refusing to return to kilter.

"It's... good to see you," he said quietly, and hurried after this time-worn Sally Slick.

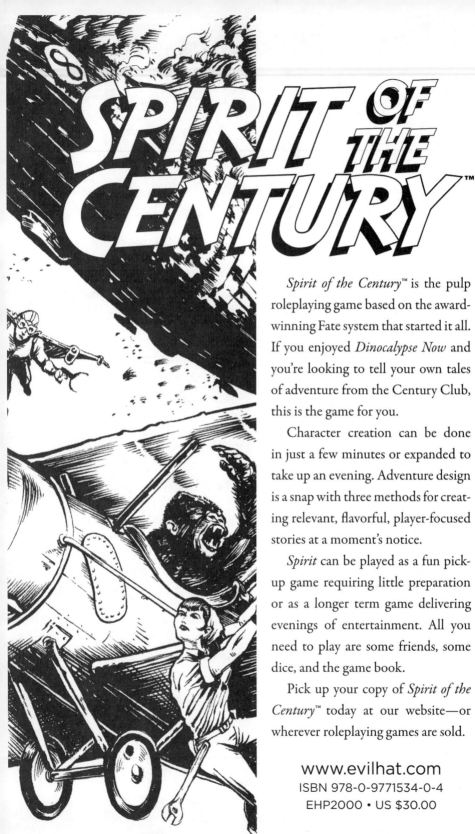

SPIRIT OF THE CENTURY™

Spirit of the Century™ is the pulp roleplaying game based on the award-winning Fate system that started it all. If you enjoyed *Dinocalypse Now* and you're looking to tell your own tales of adventure from the Century Club, this is the game for you.

Character creation can be done in just a few minutes or expanded to take up an evening. Adventure design is a snap with three methods for creating relevant, flavorful, player-focused stories at a moment's notice.

Spirit can be played as a fun pick-up game requiring little preparation or as a longer term game delivering evenings of entertainment. All you need to play are some friends, some dice, and the game book.

Pick up your copy of *Spirit of the Century*™ today at our website—or wherever roleplaying games are sold.

www.evilhat.com

ISBN 978-0-9771534-0-4

EHP2000 • US $30.00

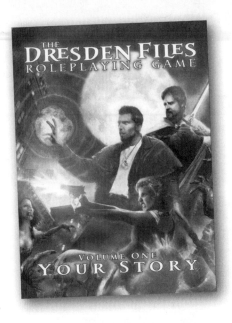

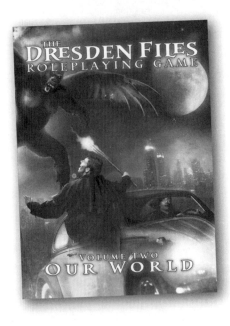

THE DRESDEN FILES ROLEPLAYING GAME

The award-winning *Dresden Files Roleplaying Game,* based on the New York Times best-selling series of novels by Jim Butcher, does everything you'd want a game based on your favorite books to do.

In this two-volume set, you'll find a game system that really "gets it"— whether it's producing the big scares and big laughs of the most exciting moments of the novels, or providing practically any kind of characters you'd want to play. They'll leap right off the page and into your game!

Wizards sling spells that feel every bit as real as Harry Dresden's magic— and just as dangerous. But if spell-slinging's not your bag, the full range of creatures from Jim Butcher's stories await you: werewolves, vampires, holy warriors, changelings, psychics—even ordinary people caught in the wrong place at the wrong time.

It's time you join Harry in fighting the good fight against the rising tide of darkness.

What's *your* story?

The Dresden Files RPG: Volume 1 – Your Story
ISBN 978-0-9771534-7-3
EHP3001 • US $49.99

The Dresden Files RPG: Volume 2 – Our World
ISBN 978-0-9771534-8-0
EHP3002 • US $39.99

www.evilhat.com • www.dresdenfilesrpg.com

ABOUT THE PUBLISHER

Evil Hat Productions believes that passion makes the best stuff—from games to novels and more. It's our passion that's made Evil Hat what it is today: an award-winning publisher of games and, now, fiction. We aim to give you the best of experiences—full of laughter, story-telling, and memorable moments—whether you're sitting down with a good book, rolling some dice, or playing a card.

We started, simply, as gamers, running games at small conventions under the Evil Hat banner, making face to face connections with some of the same people who've worked on these products. Player to player, gamer to gamer, we've passed our passion along to the gaming community that has already given us so many years of lasting entertainment.

Today, we are turning that passion into fiction based on the games we love. And, much like the games we make and play, we need and *want* you to be part of that process.

That's the Evil Hat mission, and we're happy to have you along on it.

You can find out more about us and the stuff we make at *www.evilhat.com*.

ABOUT THE AUTHOR

Chuck Wendig's novel *Double Dead* hit shelves in November, 2011. His second novel, *Blackbirds,* is already getting rave reviews prior to its publication in April of this year. Its sequel, *Mockingbird,* publishes at the end of 2012.

He, along with writing partner Lance Weiler, is an alum of the Sundance Film Festival Screenwriter's Lab (2010). Their short film, *Pandemic,* showed at the Sundance Film Festival 2011, and their feature film *HiM* is in development with producers Ted Hope and Anne Carey. Together they co-wrote the digital transmedia drama *Collapsus,* which was nominated for an International Digital Emmy and a Games 4 Change award.

Chuck has contributed over two million words to the game industry, and was the developer of the popular *Hunter: The Vigil* game line (White Wolf Game Studios / CCP). He is a frequent contributor to *The Escapist,* writing about games and pop culture.

He currently lives in Pennsylvania with wife, dog, and newborn son. You can find him at his website, *terribleminds.com,* where he is busy talking about storytelling and the art and craft of writing. You can find his writing advice collected in e-books such as *Confessions of a Freelance Penmonkey* and *500 Ways to be a Better Writer.*